Praise for *A*

An Audible Silence is a gift for the senses and good company for those who want to discover the light of truth beyond time. It's a book filled with useful tools for the seeker in all of us.

-Linda S., Phoenix Kriya Yoga Center Leader

J. A. invites the reader to a gentle yet focused awakening of one's body, mind, spirit, and heart. The 'aha' moments open the door to thoughtful reflections with real-life applications.

-JoAnn Del-Colle, LCSW, Clinical Social Worker

We all have those pesky voices inside our head that keep us from living a life of peace and love. What a beautiful way to address the noise – by taking us on a journey to northern Arizona. The insight and wisdom revealed in *An Audible Silence* will live on in us long after we part ways with these characters.

-Sherrie Dunlevy, speaker, host, and author of *How Can I Help?*

This gem of a book shines light on the process of self-awareness, self-reflection, and self-mastery required in the helping professions – and beyond. We are the vessel through which transformation flows to others! J. A. takes us on an insightful journey and teaches valuable lessons along the way that breathe real life into the adage, "Healer, heal thyself!"

-Dori DiPietro, LCSW, ACSW, President of the National Association of Social Workers (Arizona Chapter), social work professor, and program director

AN
AUDIBLE
SILENCE

a novel

J. A. Plosker

nobody
press

Published by Nobody Press, LLC
Contact us at: info@nobodypress.com
To find out more about this book, visit: www.anaudiblesilence.com.

Print ISBN: 978-0-9987283-2-2

For Mom and Dad, who sit with me in the silence

Chapter 1

Hopeless...

My last pill slipped from my fingers, bounced off the curb, and dove down into the sewer. Somewhere just under my feet, a roach would soon be munching on a snack with the power to lower its blood pressure and reduce anxiety. As for me? I was screwed.

I stepped away from the street, parked myself on the bus stop bench, and pulled a bright orange prescription bottle from my bag. I popped the cap off and slapped the tube hard against my palm, hoping another pill would materialize to help me catch this bus, get back to the office, and get somewhere safe. Anywhere safe. I knew the bottle was empty, but like a smoker desperate for another fix, the ritual smack and hollow pop of plastic on skin comforted me and bought me an extra few seconds to stave off the oncoming panic attack.

My panic attacks were growing in intensity. They were especially bad when I had client meetings downtown. A social worker by trade, it's my job to wade neck deep into others' discomfort and bring support and hope to people suffering in the worst conditions. Kind of like a superhero, but without any of the super and none of the hero – or, at least, that's how it felt. I loved my clients. Loved doing therapy with them. But the constant battles with probation officers, insurance carriers, lawyers, judges, and client demons and relapses took its toll. The client who spat at me in group and threatened to kill me wasn't quite my breaking point, but I was getting there – struggling to focus on my caseload's strengths while their battles brought out my weaknesses.

I pitched the bottle back in my bag and drummed my fingers on my knees with a delirious precision. "Where's that damn bus?" I muttered. A woman leaning against the shelter cast a suspicious glance my way, then shuffled nonchalantly to the curb, standing on tiptoe to search down the road for the bus.

I needed more air in my lungs. I needed a cloth to wipe the relentless beads of sweat from my brow. I needed that damn pill. My mind raced. My left thumb rubbed the dead space on my ring finger reserved for a wedding band. The image of a client who beat her partner, lost her kids, and needed me to make the phone calls to make it better flashed in my mind. I cringed at the thought of an empty apartment awaiting the sound of my key. I shoved a pinkie tip into my mouth and chewed the nail to the quick. I shot up in one smooth motion and paced the sidewalk away from the bus stop, trying to cleanse my mind with some kind of desperate meditation that only turned toxic as I resented the attempt.

"This is it," I said. "I can't. I can't. I'm done." My mind dropped behind a dark curtain like a wall switch flipped to off. The whine of an engine cut through the heat and caught my attention. A bus was hurtling down the street. I closed my eyes and said goodbye to my folks, my clients, and my friends. I had a few choice words for my lost loves and newfound devils and edged closer to the curb. The sound of indifferent traffic. The smell of exhaust. My foot dangled above the street, all my weight ready to release and propel me forward. As I stepped off, a hand grabbed my collar and yanked me hard. The bus shot by with a horn blare, and I stumbled backward into a shopping cart filled with cans and bottles. I got my bearings and found myself face to face with an older gentleman in a faded black t-shirt and ripped jeans. Teeth gone, face filthy, he smelled like sweaty days and hard nights.

"Mind yourself, son," he said. "The 4:15 express doesn't stop here. Just keeps on rollin'."

"Wh— what?" I shook the trance. My eyelids flitted to focus me. I wasn't sure whether to thank this stranger or punch him. He smoothed my shirt in a sure stroke and steadied me with one hand on each of my shoulders.

"You best make sure you're on the next one," he said. "Not cruising down First Street splattered on the front of it." He cackled. A wide grin oozed off his face as he knocked me between the eyes with an index finger. "Think, son. Think!"

I stood speechless. He patted me gently on the chest over my heart with a wrinkled right hand and took his place behind his cart. With a purposeful push, he rattled off, disappearing into the foot traffic and blazing heat of late afternoon in Phoenix. I shrugged off the encounter, ignoring the stares of strangers who knew nothing of my life. Desperate for the ironic, deafening silence of a head full of sound, I pulled my headphones from my backpack, untangled them, and stuffed them over my ears, turning my music up loud to drown out my embarrassment and confusion. I checked my watch, coolly gazed down the street for the next bus, and when it came, I got on and paid my fare as if nothing odd had happened.

Chapter 2

Old Problems, New Leather

"Where do you want me to start?" I asked.

"At the beginning, Jim."

"Again? We've known each other a month already, Doctor Eastman, but whatever. I was born in a small town in Ohio—"

"Wait."

"What?"

"Don't go that far back."

"Doc, don't drag this out. Just tell me what you want to know. No more tension."

"Tension frustrates you?"

"Only when I'm involved. Just spit it out."

"I want to know why you were about to step in front of a bus downtown, Jim. I think we're ready to approach that subject again. Wouldn't you agree?"

"I'd rather talk about Ohio."

"We can do that if you'd like."

"I didn't step in front of it."

"The bus?"

"No, Doc. Ohio. Of course, the bus!"

My jeans felt tight. I tugged at my neckline. I had to move. I shifted my weight, trying to find a comfortable position where my torso could fit for 55 minutes without too much distress. In an effort to mirror my body language and build rapport, Doctor Eastman shifted her weight and aimed her feet in the same direction as mine. She covered the move by rustling the crisp, yellow, neatly lined pages of the legal pad in her lap and flipping from one blank page to another. To maintain the ruse, she clicked the tip of her blue pen and scribbled what I can only assume was "Ohio," before meeting my gaze again.

The chairs in the office were as new to the place as I was, and I hadn't had a chance to make any of them mine yet. The result was that for my last four appointments – my only four appointments – I felt like a visitor. In reality, I was a visitor, but that doesn't mean I wanted to feel that way. The brown leather was stiff and unforgiving, and I couldn't find a comfortable place on it. The seats still had the showroom stench of optimism and opulence, fitting in perfectly with the plastic green plants and light gray walls. If it was a cage I was trapped in for the hour, at least it was a pleasant, if not comfortable, cage.

"I know you're not talking about Ohio, Jim. I want to know why you would even consider suicide."

"Who hasn't considered it?"

"I haven't." Our eyes locked. My brow furrowed. She didn't flinch.

"You're lying, Doctor Eastman."

"How do you know?" I uncrossed my legs and leaned forward. She uncrossed her legs and tilted her torso slightly towards me.

"Anyone who goes into therapy as a profession has considered it," I said. "I'm sure most have even tried it."

"Why do you do that, Jim?"

"Do what?"

"Deflect."

"I'm observing, not deflecting."

A grim silence grew between us – a standoff of therapists that had become our norm. Although, after recent events, I wasn't sure I should still call myself a therapist. I admit, I snapped. Or, I guess I could play the blame game and say my ex-fiancé snapped me. My loneliness snapped me. But let's narrow the lens further and say my clients snapped me. The file folders filled with soul crushing stories back in my office snapped me. I had been working hard as an addiction and mental health social worker, and one day, after a particularly rough meeting, I realized I was not only carrying my weights around, but the weight of my caseload as well – sociopaths who told grand lies in therapy sessions to shock me, depressed clients who cut through their arm muscles to self soothe, and folks who came in for their sessions so riddled with anxiety, it oozed from their pores and clung to me.

I loved my clients, but it was a fine line between loving the people and loathing the behaviors – not because I judged them, but because I was powerless against them. My clients weren't bad or damaged. They just wore the cloak of difficult lives. I realized over the years that being a licensed professional only gives a pretense to knowledge. What clients really wanted was solid wisdom to pull them through, and I was out of answers…and patience. I had slowly lost my filters and was taking everything from work back to my empty home, and it piled onto other things in my life I just couldn't handle. Clients appeared in my dreams. My mind drifted through my office, even when I wasn't there.

"Jim, we've discussed this before. Your job makes you sick."

"Does it? Or does it just bring out my sickness?"

"Clever."

"I try."

"Can we talk about Maya then?"

"Do we have to?"

Doctor Eastman knew about my ex, but I gave up those details with even greater reluctance than my foray at the bus stop. I wasn't even sure why the relationship crashed, so what could Doctor Eastman do about it?

"I'd like to see if there are issues there we need to work on, Jim."

I huffed and summoned a smile. "Let's save that if you don't mind."

"Did you hide from Maya like this?"

"Now who's clever," I snapped.

"Fine. Back to your work situation. Didn't you teach in the past? You have a degree in archaeology or something, right?"

"Comparative religion. Two degrees, actually. Undergrad and a master's."

"Right. Comparative religion. Have you thought about going back to teaching?"

"Every day." I reflected and tumbled into reverie. "I was good at that, Doc. Really good. I think that's the most confident I've ever felt…standing at the front of those classrooms."

"That's good, Jim. And ironic."

"How so?"

"Well, most people hate public speaking. A lot of them need some kind of prescription medication to get through a talk, then are relieved to get back to their regular lives."

"So?"

"So, Jim, you loved being in front of a group speaking, but needed medication to face the realities of life outside of the classroom. Don't you find that odd?"

"I've never really thought about it."

"Maybe you should."

"Why?"

"It's a strength, Jim. I'm no social worker, but you are. And I know finding strengths is something you probably excel at. Isn't that a cornerstone of your profession?"

"As long as it's other people, I'm on it," I said with a laugh.

"Consider turning that talent inward."

I sat in that truth. Before she gave up in frustration, Maya spent a lot of our relationship trying to build me up, pointing out things she thought I was good at. But for some reason, I deflected that stuff. Stomped it out. That tendency had labels now, like depression and low self-esteem, but even before that, it was simply a habit of mine from long ago.

"I wouldn't even know where to begin, Doctor Eastman. Honestly, it's been so long since I've...since I've felt..." I trailed off into a dead end, swallowing down a lump of emotion that tried each session to wriggle its way into my consciousness.

"Jim, my grandma used to say, 'There's no better time to remember the better days than right now.'"

"What does that mean?"

"Well, I'm going to do a little self-disclosure with you, therapist to therapist." Doctor Eastman leaned back in her chair and folded her hands on her lap. I sat back in my chair and cupped one hand in the other. "My grandmother was a very forward-thinking woman held back by terrible depression. She had a therapist way back when who taught her a technique that she practiced until her dying day. Something to keep her in the moment instead of in her fears or regrets – but through the power of memory."

"What was it?"

"Close your eyes, Jim. Now, think of yourself giving a lecture to a room filled with students. Can you picture that?"

"Yes."

"Good. Now, clothe that memory in the emotions, sights, and sounds of the best memories you have of lecturing from when you really were in the classroom. Can you feel that?"

"I can." I couldn't stop a faint smile from crossing my lips.

"What's it like?"

"Everyone's...present. The room's full. I'm focused. The students are focused. It's a lecture that really happened in one of my comparative religion classes, and everything clicked." I opened my eyes. Doctor Eastman was fixated on my expression.

"And? How do you feel?"

"Good," I said. "Really good."

"Jim, my grandma knew a simple secret – that all of our successes are here with us in this moment. Right now, right as you are, you carry with you all the good things that have happened to you. And, yes, you carry the crummy stuff as well. But remember – there's no time like the present to remember all the good things you are. That's where you can…I don't know…maybe find the strength to allow something new into your life. To let some light in so it can bring a little shine to the dull. You get what I'm saying?"

"I think so," I said. "But it's been a long time since I've been in the classroom. I'm not sure I could even get back in there."

"Maybe it's not the classroom you need to step back into, Jim."

"Well, then what is it?"

"Your life."

We spent the remainder of the session building out my long-term safety plan in case my suicidal thoughts returned. She didn't press me for details about the bus, and that gave me the permission I needed to share some of them with her. We put a few breathing techniques in my plan and collected a list of people I wasn't related to who could help in a crisis.

The beep-beep of her timer brought the session to an abrupt end. I rose from my seat, lighter than when I came in, and the leather crackled behind me, calling for the next patient. After scheduling another appointment with her assistant, I pushed the glass doors of the office wide and stepped out into the sweltering heat. I lingered on the sidewalk to take in the sun on this 110-degree day. I once read that getting more sun could help depression, so why not, right?

I hopped into my car and blasted the air conditioning. I thought about my conversation with Doctor Eastman and decided that one of the best things from my past that I could bring into the moment would be a good song. I called a favorite track up on my phone and turned up my car speakers. I took in the familiar melody and paired it with a sweet memory from high school as my body and mind cooled down. The regular beat and predictable poetry soothed me. My fingers mindlessly tapped the steering wheel in a rhythm that was now as familiar as the song. Quiet was an open invitation to my inner mess, so I found the reliable sounds of classic rock to be just the right tonic to take my mind off my troubles. When the song came to an end, the good feeling faded, and I was once again left alone in my head. Prickly memories needled me, and I did my best to hold them off. A touch of anxiety rose up, kickstarting my rapid heartbeat. I smiled at it.

"Grandma Eastman," I said, "You gave good advice to your granddaughter, but I think some of us may be too far gone!"

Chapter 3

Parties, Prom, and Life in the Side Pocket

J ake? You in here?" I entered the spacious foyer of the large, two-story home and searched the jumble of harried adults and hyper kids for my childhood friend.

"Over here, Jim!"

Jake's wife, Meg, waved me over to a table in the dining room piled high with gifts. I worked my way through the sea of humanity and put my offering onto the altar of their five-year-old's birthday. Meg smiled through gritted teeth as she swatted children away from cupcakes and punch.

"It's not time yet!" she yelled at one child who would not be denied. The vibrations of the crowd going about the normal business of herding kids sent waves like a gong through my body, triggering my nerves. When two screaming kids and their four yelling parents darted by, my face contorted. Meg came around from behind the table and yelled in my ear, "Jake's around somewhere! No idea where he's disappeared to!"

I knew exactly where he'd disappeared to. I gave Meg a thumbs up and jostled my way across the house to the grand staircase. I stepped over a gate separating the downstairs craziness from the upstairs solitude and hurried up to a massive room just off the landing. Jake was alone in his sanctuary, bent over a red felt pool table, taking aim at the cue ball with smooth strokes of his mother-of-pearl inlaid cue.

"The game's not as much fun when you beat yourself," I said. The shiny black eight ball slid into the side pocket with a thud.

"Yeah, well, rack 'em," he said. "It'd be my pleasure to beat you. Just like in high school. Just like in college. Just like five minutes from now."

"Shouldn't you be downstairs wrangling kids?" I asked. Jake slid the triangle down the table, and we pulled the balls from the pockets. "Or, at least, your kid? Meg looks a little frazzled down there."

"It's fine, Jim. I'll go down soon. Besides, I spent the entire day running around in the heat picking up food and setting up the house. And, I'll be on cleanup duty later while Meg's brushing chocolate gunk out of Hayden's teeth. She'll forgive me. How you been? You're looking good."

"Thanks." I hung the triangle on the hook on the wall and shot the cue ball to break. The one ball dribbled into a corner pocket. "I saw Eastman today, so I'm all cured! Three ball in the side pocket."

I took aim and missed. The three-ball banged around the cushions before knocking the ten ball, sending it into a pocket.

"Thanks, my friend! Beating you is easier when you help me."

"I'm good at sabotage, I guess."

"Hmm…" Jake was a pool-playing wolf sizing up his prey. He didn't strike right away. Instead, he took his attention away from the game and leaned against his cue to attack me. In a friendly way, of course. "What's your deal, Jim?"

"My deal?"

"I've known you forever, and you've always been a little…well… Jim-ish, but I don't know, man. Something's really changed in you." He shifted back to the table. "Nine ball in the corner pocket." He took easy aim and slung the cue ball dead against the nine. It cracked into the corner pocket and wound its way to the bottom. "What's really up? This is me, remember. Not your mom. Not Eastman. Me."

"Jake, you remember senior year when we both wanted to ask Ashlyn from biology class to prom?"

"How could I forget? That was almost the end of our friendship."

Jake took in the scene on the table and set his sights on the twelve ball. He prowled with pure focus, setting up the best angle.

"Well, remember how you finally let me ask her?"

"I do."

"Do you remember what happened next?"

"I do!" Jake stood up from taking aim and bounced the answer hard off of me. "You had a crappy time at the dance, and my date is downstairs chasing our kid around. So?"

"Well, that's kind of the story of my life."

"Twelve ball. Side pocket." Jake knocked the ball dead center and true to target. "The story of your life? Jim, that was…how many decades ago? And besides, you found Maya."

"I did."

"And you got engaged."

"I did."

"And…well…yeah."

"Yeah. Didn't work out so great, huh?"

"I'm sorry you two broke up, Jim. But I donno. Maybe it was a good thing that it turned out that way."

"A good thing?"

"Yeah. Admit it. You always knew, somewhere deep down, that you two weren't really right for each other, didn't you?"

"Well—"

"You and Maya even had a conversation about that. You told me all about it. You said that the two of you were toying around with the idea of a break. You guys wanted to explore a…what the hell did you call it?"

"An attentive separation."

"Yeah."

"For the record, I didn't pick that name. She read it in some magazine."

"Whatever. Anyway, what does any of this have to do with prom?"

"I don't know, Jake. Nothing, I guess."

"Eleven in the side. Damn!" The eleven careened around the table. I watched it bounce and bang into the other balls until it came to rest against the rail. "Hang on a sec."

Jake went to the bar in the corner of the room and pulled two tall glasses off a cherry wood rack on the wall. They were clean as whistles, emblazoned with the emblem of his law school. He had done well for himself, and his successful career had earned him the respect of the community. He was a proud father, a prolific volunteer, and a fantastic attorney. He filled both glasses perfectly to the rim with a rich, dark draught and handed me one. We toasted to my health. The bitter brew slid easily down my throat, and I savored the flavor.

"Jake, do you know what the name 'Maya' means?"

"No, but I think I'm about to get a religious studies lecture."

"Well, in Sanskrit, it refers to 'illusion.'"

"Uh huh."

"In Eastern tradition, the ancient meaning of it referred to the great power of the gods – the power of creation. But that changed along the way and it came to mean getting so invested in the material world, that we lose sight of what's truly real – the great self. The creator. The thing that lasts."

"And this relates to prom and the unfolding of your life how?"

"Jake, I don't know what's real anymore and what's an illusion."

"This is real, isn't it?" He banged the flawless wooden top of the bar with a fist, then flipped his hand and tapped the top evenly with his solid gold wedding band.

"Yes. And no. It appears real, but it's really just mostly empty space being held together by…well…who knows what. I'm not a scientist."

"This was some expensive empty space when those dudes came to install it."

"Jake, the point is, when I go through my day, the only thing that feels real to me is my emptiness. My anxiety."

"What about your clients? You help them, right? Isn't that real?"

"Is it? I went into social work because I believe in the goodness of people. I believe my clients can recover and build on their setbacks to really make it in this life. But what is this life?"

"I think you've had enough." Jake slid my beer down the bar.

"Jake, be serious for a second. I lost Maya because she and I never could get it together. And I know she got sick of my mental…whatever. She gave me every reason to change, and I gave her every reason to leave."

"That's harsh, man. Go easy on yourself. You didn't fail. You're human. Relationships break up because of two people. Not one."

"Well, maybe she was right to leave. I'm drifting out here, Jake. I have a good job and I pay my bills, but I don't have anything solid to hold on to. I couldn't even hold on to an engagement. I want to help the world be a better place, but I'm scared that I can't even get myself together. How can I bring anything good to a world that I don't feel comfortable in? How can I guide others when I always seem to make the wrong decisions? What the hell am I even doing?"

The sound of feet scrambling up the stairs drew our attention to the door. Hayden burst into the room, mouth and hands full of chocolate ice cream. He hugged me around the waist.

"Uncle Jim!" I scooped him into my arms and allowed his grimy hands to work their way into my hair. "We're going to sing happy birthday soon!"

"You are?" I asked, rubbing my forehead against his. "Well, I wouldn't want to miss that."

"What are you doing up here, sport?" Jake asked. "Daddy will be down soon."

"Well…" Hayden looked at Jake with eyes filled with the gleam and vinegar of a newly minted five-year-old. "Mommy says that if you don't come down now, you won't live to see *your* next birthday."

Jake and I burst out laughing. He took Hayden from my arms and squeezed him with a tenderness I rarely saw him exude, before setting him on the ground.

"You go tell your mommy that I'll be downstairs before the candles on your cake are lit, okay?"

"Okay, daddy."

Hayden ran from the room, his button-up shirt untucked and pants hanging low. He reappeared seconds later and yelled, "You too, Uncle Jim. You have to help me blow out the candles like last time."

"I will," I yelled as he whisked away.

"Look, Jim. I know things are a little messed up for you right now. I'm not a therapist, and I'm certainly the wrong person to ask when it comes to religion and all that stuff. But I do have an idea. Hold on."

Jake hurried out of the room. I glanced around at the decorations that adorned his man cave, and marveled at the sports paraphernalia, autographed jerseys, and the large TV on the wall. So much stuff. So many memories. It was neat and organized, of course. Jake and his family took a lot of pride in their possessions and kept them tidy. I found myself wishing I had more, just so I could have something to care for. Before I could venture too far down that road, Jake returned, swinging a key on a chain around his index finger.

"Here you go!" He offered me the key with a satisfied look on his face.

"What's this?"

"A key."

"Yeah. I see that. For what?"

"To the place up in Mormon Lake."

I took it and worked it through my fingers. Deep in its silver grooves were years of memories. When I moved to Arizona from Ohio, Jake became my best friend. His family put their toys at my disposal and took me on all sorts of high-country adventures, including vacations to their Mormon Lake home. I wasn't much of a mountain man, but I got nature's message loud and clear. To this day, I'm never more at peace than when I'm adventuring up there. I hadn't seen the Davis family cabin in years.

"Jake, I'm confused. Is this in case you get locked in up there and need me to let you out?"

"Funny, Jim. But no. It's for you."

"Why?"

"I'm taking the family on an RV trip to California this year. My folks are tagging along, so the place will be empty for a large chunk of the summer. Take the key. Go up there. Spend some time away. Get some fresh air. Be in nature. I can't say I know what's wrong with you, but if anything can cure it, this can."

I swung the key around my finger and pondered the possibilities. And the realities. The cabin was quiet, but was it too quiet? I did a quick mental count of my vacation days and all the logistics of taking a trip to northern Arizona. Was my car up for it? Was I up for it? Who would take over my caseload? I felt like Jake had handed me anxiety on a keychain, and now, I wasn't sure how to handle it.

"Jim?" Jake snapped me back from my head. "You want to go up there or not?"

"Sure," I said. "Thanks." I stuffed the key in my pocket and picked up my cue. "Eight ball in the side pocket, banked off the rail." I hit the cue ball square and executed the perfect shot. The black ball fell, securing my fate.

"Jim, That's the best shot you've ever made. And you wasted it on a loss?"

"It's more of a thank you for the key. My perfect losing record remains intact."

Chapter 4

Burning Party

I returned to my apartment later than I expected. After Jake's, I stopped to see my parents. A recent heart attack had sidelined my dad, and under his doctor's orders, he was spending most of his days resting. Although, I could tell his recovery was harder on my mom than him. Now that he had retired from his surgery practice, he was spending his days cutting into mom's life. When I saw them these days, it was usually to help her change an air filter or lift something onto or off of a shelf. But I also enjoyed spending time with Dad. Talking sports helped keep his blood pressure low, and also helped to calm and center me.

I ran the cabin idea past them, and they both thought it was a good idea, as long as I promised to stick to my suicide safety plan with Doctor Eastman. I assured them I was fine and that those feelings were nothing more than fleeting moments in a busy life. That helped ease their minds a little.

Back at home, I cracked open a beer and relaxed into my night. I flipped through the stations and settled on a show about two people from Montana searching for a second home in Mexico where they could escape in the winter. Apparently, gorgeous snow-capped mountains, breathtaking scenery, and crisp, clean air was something they couldn't wait to get away from. The dog-groomer husband was desperate for a Mediterranean-style home, but his computer science wife wanted something a little more modern. The show was edited to make him look like an unreasonable jerk and to make her look like an unyielding ogre. But one thing they agreed on, and the thing that probably kept their marriage together, was that they wanted a four-bedroom home for all the family and friends that would come to visit.

"No one's coming to visit you in Mexico!" I yelled.

By the second argument and their third margarita, I turned the TV off and tossed the remote onto the coffee table. It slid into the journal that Doctor Eastman wanted me to keep. I picked it up and opened it to the first page, still blank, and thought about her question to me earlier in the day. Why had I almost stepped in front of that bus? I revisited the moment in my mind. What was so awful that I had to escape my own life? Was it my breakup with Maya? Was that enough to drive me to suicide? Was it frustration with my job and the mad world of addictions, mental health, and a broken system? And what was up with that homeless guy? Had he been watching me the whole time? Was it that obvious I wanted to die? As I pondered my life and my situation, it scared me that I couldn't remember why, exactly, I looked down the street and became infatuated with the bus rolling down the road. I remember thinking how quick my death would be and how my pain would soon end, but what was the real pain?

My mind drifted again to Maya. Not the woman who left me, but the illusion of life. I tried to think of something solid that I could hold on to – to anchor me in reality – but nothing came to mind. Money gets spent. Possessions don't follow us to the grave. Relationships come and go. Even our own body's cells die and regenerate. Hair gets cut and regrows. Fingernails and toenails, too. Beliefs shift, politicians change, countries rise to dominance and fall into dust. What was permanent? What lasted? What mattered?

I closed the journal and tossed it back on the table. I pulled the key from my pocket and worked it through my fingers. If a vacation was going to happen, it couldn't happen soon enough. I downed the rest of my beer and headed into my room where I logged in to my work portal to block a few weeks off. I grabbed a suitcase from the closet and packed like I was on a mission of dire importance. I tossed in sweaters, jeans, and hiking boots – a list of items that sounded ridiculous in a city where the current temperature was over one hundred degrees. I also grabbed some religion textbooks that I had been wanting to re-read, as well as some boxes of my favorite protein bars and some trail mix with the generic, neon-colored chocolate pieces Mom gave me for the road, whenever I got on it. Finally, I tossed toiletries in.

The high-pitched tune of the zipper whizzing around the bag sealed my plan. The trip north wasn't theoretical any longer. It was a commitment. I promised myself I'd leave quietly, without a lot of fanfare. I wanted to forget. To be forgotten. I wanted to see how quietly I could be myself. How well I could avoid questions about my failed love life and my broken dreams. I wanted to be left alone. I wanted my anger. I wanted my fear. I wanted to wear the masks I wanted to wear, and I didn't want to say a damn thing about it to anyone.

I gazed into the mirror over the dresser and stepped toward my reflection. I made childish faces, craning my neck and sticking my tongue out. With the characteristic "ahh" of a doctor's exam, I licked the air and examined my tongue. I bared my teeth and wrinkled my nose. I clicked my teeth together and shot an exhale through them. I relaxed the tension in my jaw and edged back a step to take in my full form. My face. I ran my fingers into my receding hairline, scratching at the salt and pepper streaks in my hair. I dragged them down over the grizzly stubble on my cheeks, flicking fingernails at the tiny gray hairs poking through the fading black of my youth. Tugging down on my cheeks, I smoothed the wrinkles radiating from the corners of my eyes, then watched them snap dutifully back into place as I released the tension on my skin. There was a matching pair of those wrinkles settling in around my mouth. When did I get these grooves? Where did they come from? They formed in the line of my smile and right by my eyes, but I never saw them coming. My mom called them laugh lines, but I couldn't remember the last time I'd laughed hard enough to affect my mood, much less alter the landscape of my face. I let out a long sigh through pursed lips and poked at my stomach and hips. There was more of me there than I remembered. Recently, I was struggling to walk even short distances without getting winded. Maya wanted me to see someone about it. I wanted to try a different way. I thought about the gym membership card in my wallet collecting dust, and frowned. When did I stop using it? Why did I stop using it? Maya used hers all the time. I told Jake that I was part of the reason Maya and I fell apart. But was I the only reason I was falling apart?

My jaw clenched as my thoughts raced. My breathing quickened to mirror my rising heart rate. A panic attack was building, faster and faster, and I was defenseless to stop it. No one was around to soothe me. No one was around to help me. I paced the room like an animal, unable to calm myself. I settled my attention at my desk where I still had pictures of Maya and me – images that taunted and judged. I still had the candle with the glass base she bought me on her trip to Europe. It was "to light your way," she'd said. A stack of receipts for the dinners we'd had together around town sat in a neat and delicate tower on the foundation of a car rental brochure from our vacation to California. A collection of dusty memories and a lifetime of dreams in a corner of a bedroom that couldn't even bring rest to the life it held.

I felt the venom of this collection work its way under my skin and into my blood. I sensed the imaginary injustices of our relationship well up within. A primal urge overtook me, and I let loose a flurry of acid and nastiness. With one swoop, I cleared the desk with my arm. Everything went flying. Glass broke against the nightstand. I wanted Maya to suffer for no good reason. I wanted to suffer. I wanted my neighbors to suffer. And then, silence. Only the pounding of my heart in my ears and the echo of my torment.

I slumped down into the desk chair and rested my head in my hands. Strands of hair rained down on the white desktop. I brushed them away and laughed at myself and my insanity, realizing the great truth of every therapy session I'd ever held with an angry client: My desire for others to suffer was only causing me to suffer. When I got mad at Maya, my hair fell out. When I destroyed my possessions, I had to pay for it. When I got my blood pressure up, it was my heart that paid the price. I got onto my knees with a groan of protest from my back and legs and picked up the glass pieces and assorted papers. I placed them into a recycle bin and retrieved the vacuum. I sucked the lingering shards from the carpet and ran my hand carefully along the floor to make sure I collected every last piece.

After the cleaning session, I laid down in bed and searched for shapes in the plaster ceiling. I found a puppy, a cloud, and a clown making a scary face. It was amazing what I could see when I actually paid attention to what looked like random patterns. After resolving to plaster over the clown face, a thought drifted through my mind. I remembered Meg once holding a "burning party." She invited friends and family to her and Jake's backyard, and started a bonfire. One by one, people stepped forward and burned things from their past they didn't want anymore. Things that didn't serve them, as one particularly eager guest put it. Someone tossed in love letters from a high school boyfriend. Another threw in pictures of a parent who had abused them through childhood. I thought the whole thing was weird, so I just took off my socks and tossed them in. I said they reminded me how sweaty my feet were. Everyone laughed, but now, alone in my apartment, the purpose of that night hit me square in the chest.

I took the candle Maya had bought me onto my patio and set it down on the concrete floor. I lit it and was immediately hit by the smell of burning, synthetic vanilla. I went back inside and got a metal garbage can from the bathroom. I also grabbed the letter Maya sent me a few weeks after our breakup. I read it in a fog when it first arrived, but hadn't had the desire to look at it again until tonight. I opened it and smirked at the tan card with the silver flowers painted on it. I wondered where she had found such an ugly card. Did she say "Hello" in a cheery voice to the clerk who rang it up for her? Did she listen to a happy song on the way back to her apartment with the card on the seat next to her? Did she stop for a relaxing lunch with friends and run other errands? Was our breakup just another check on her to-do list? I brushed those thoughts away and read it.

Dear Jim,

I don't know where to begin. So many words have come to me since we separated, and I hope you know it's only because I love you that I'm writing them down and sending them to you. I wasn't sure how to say all of this in the moment, but I want to try in this card. When we first met, I started to believe in fate. We would talk for hours and hours about everything and nothing. We would dive into world religion and then dive into life and then dive into everything else we could think of. Whether it was miles of highway or a quick trip to the store, it was always an adventure with us. But I don't know where you went. I don't know where you are. I tried everything I could think of to get you back on track…to get us back on track. But there are only so many times I can make your favorite foods, watch your favorite movies, or take your face in my hands and tell you it will be alright. Jim, I love you so much. But I can't take the silence anymore. What can come out of silence? Please don't be mad at me that we didn't work out. Don't be mad at you. We both knew near the end that it was the end, and now we have a chance to find something lasting. Something to build our lives on. That's why I left. For both of us. I hope and pray that someday you find peace out in the world, because we both deserve something happy. If I believed in fate when we met, then I have to believe in it as we part.

Fondly, Maya

As the words passed in front of my consciousness, I saw them in a new light. I discovered in them a person just as afraid and uncertain as I was. I felt my blood pressure rising again as sympathy turned to anger. Why couldn't two broken people make it together? Why can't two lost souls find each other? I turned the letter over and over again, then dangled it over the flame. The orange fire danced around the edge of the card as if it, too, was unsure how to handle it. But soon, it found its way, engulfing the last vestiges of Maya's departure. Of our ending. I dropped the card in the can, tamped the flames with the bottom of the candle, and headed inside to bed.

Chapter 5

The Long and Winding Road

I left before the sun was at its fiery peak. To make the most of my precious vacation, I decided that an early start would buy me some extra time away. The previous night, I phoned one of my old philosophy professors – a mentor from college who had retired to Arizona. We agreed to meet for lunch at an Indian restaurant in Sedona. I now had a schedule to keep.

The road to Flagstaff is brutal in summer. The scenery is pleasant enough, but there are mountains to climb in the desert heat. Just before a major series of steep switchbacks, I turned off the air conditioning to avoid stressing out my car. I wasn't sure if that piece of automotive air conditioning advice from my dad was a myth, but it had become habit to switch it off to spare me the nightmare of overheating in the blazing sun. My car turned into an oven, but I felt safer.

Familiar songs, each with their own special memory, kept me company, painting beautiful scenes in my head. I tapped my fingers in the familiar rhythms that I knew as clearly as the lyrics. Outside stretched the lunar landscape of the desert. High mountains that Maya called "mounds of brown" rose into the sky. Towering saguaro cacti, arms reaching upward, supplicated rain gods to quench the parched desert. Their prayers would fall on deaf ears. Even the gods escaped this part of Arizona in summer.

The car strained on the climb, but I sweet talked it all the way. I trailed behind others heading for their own parts unknown. I wondered to myself if they were going somewhere or, like me, escaping to somewhere. Stalled campers with drivers whose fathers didn't give them car advice littered the shoulder. It made no difference whether they were shiny and new or old and worn. Their depleted bodies were strewn everywhere. As traffic ground to a halt on the hill, I watched a guy with a flannel shirt tied around his head working under the hood of a Jeep. A rather large dog wearing a green bandana stuck its head out the window with a sloppy tongue dangling. I laughed as I imagined the dog saying, "C'mon! When are we gonna get going?" The dog's owner looked calm and collected as he wiped his hands on an old rag. Our eyes met just as the traffic started flowing again. I considered pulling off to help him, but it took an eternity to get my car up to speed on these hills. This, coupled with the fact that I knew as much about car maintenance as space travel, convinced me to continue.

Clearing the hill, I stopped at Sunset Rest Point to use the bathroom and get a snack to ease my sugar craving. I wandered around the building taking in the colorful graffiti left by anonymous traveling poets who had been here before me. From what I could piece together from the scribbled verses, a man named Tony was gifted in his manhood, and a gracious woman named Anita would do certain unmentionable things for free. What a saint. In this economy, it was hard to find something for nothing. I found myself wondering if the lucky Tony and the selfless Anita would ever hook up. It would be a shame if their paths never crossed. The short stroll tired me out, so I wandered to the side of the building and sat on a roasting metal bench to take in the impressive view.

"Who the hell puts a metal bench at an Arizona rest stop?" I asked myself. Then again, who was dumb enough to sit on one in the summer heat? The area faced a large mountain range, and if you timed a trip just right, the sunsets were spectacular. Unfortunately for me, it was not quite noon, and the sun was blazing overhead.

"Not a bad view from behind the can, huh?"

I turned to the voice as a German shepherd with a green bandana dove its front paws into my lap. I instantly recognized the man from the Jeep. The flannel had moved from his head to a tight tie around his waist. Before I could say anything, such as apologize for not being a Good Samaritan on the hill about a half hour ago, the man tugged his companion away to a place on the dirt for a moment in the sun. They didn't acknowledge me as they walked back to their Jeep. I left the rest stop before them and continued north, air conditioning blasting.

I knew Interstate 17's gentle curves and rapidly changing scenery like the back of my hand. I had come this way so many times before. Sprawling seas of brown grass joined craggy, crumbly foothills, and the two rolled together into endless horizons of cloudless, blazing blue sky. The cement snake of road wends through the landscape to landmarks and towns that don't leave much of an impression on a map, but have a way of sticking in memory. Mesmerized by the monotony, my mind melted into a replay of a conversation I'd had with Maya when we made this same drive a year ago.

"It's so lonely out here, Jim." A fight at the start of our trip had turned to a standoff of silences for the last hour. She'd been staring out the window since.

"Was that a not-so-subtle message to me, Maya?"

"What are you talking about?"

"The 'lonely' remark. I'm in the car with you. I'm right here. Are you saying you feel alone even when we're together?"

"Jim, what the heck? I can't say anything to you anymore without you getting all…all…"

"Say it, Maya. Just say it!"

"Crazy."

My grip tightened around the steering wheel. An overwhelming urge to punch the dashboard overtook me, but I held it back. I remembered a breathing exercise for calming down that I learned while watching a kiddie show with Hayden at Jake's house, and I decided to try it. It worked.

"You're right, Maya."

"I am?" She could barely hide her shock.

"You are." I looked over to her with a smile. "I do get crazy." She smiled back. I winked at her and then turned my attention back to the road. "And I cannot begin to tell you how sorry I am about that. It's not meant to hurt you."

"It's okay, Jim. I know."

"Do you want to know why I get crazy?"

"Of course! I love a good explanation."

"I think about things, Maya. All the time."

"That's a good thing, isn't it?"

"Maybe, Maya. Maybe. I'll tell you what I think about and you tell me if you think it's a good thing."

"Okay."

"I think about things I've said and how those words affected people. Then, I worry I've offended them, and I feel bad about myself. Then I feel regret that I may have hurt someone. Then I get scared they won't like me anymore, so I start to beat myself up for it. Once that starts, I get all full of anxiety and guilt and paranoia that I can't get rid of, and I carry it all for days…weeks…or more. I think there's some stuff from kindergarten floating around in there. To fight that, I try to guess what other people might be thinking so I can create a roadmap of how to react to them to avoid conflicts, but of course, the things I think they're thinking often make me upset, so I lash out at them for things they probably weren't thinking at all. Then, I think about the things I've said and how those words affect people. And the cycle continues."

"Wow, Jim."

"Yeah, wow."

"How do you get out of bed in the morning?" She laughed. I laughed. She went back to staring out the window, but my smile faded. I wasn't actually joking around. I was scared. My mind scared me. My emotions scared me. I hated myself for my constant circles of anxiety and sadness, and I didn't know how to talk about it and, much like the landscape outside, felt incredibly lonely. I wanted Maya…anyone…to really hear me. But when I tried to open up, there was silence. Only silence.

Brake lights yanked my attention from musings on Maya and back into the present. As I passed familiar signs and land formations, making my way through the Verde Valley, it struck me this was the first time I'd been this way alone. A feeling of independence and isolation welled up within me – a dark shadow of creeping anxiety that tightened its grip for no apparent reason. I remembered my first night at college, when my new roomie left me on my birthday while he went off to do drugs that some guy had stashed under his bed. I felt utterly alone. The feeling remained as I exited the highway at a sign marked 'Sedona.' My lunch date was in thirty minutes, and I was running late. I could hear the professor's voice in my head from the night before, "Remember, Jim, left at the fork in the road," even though I'd been there a hundred times.

Chapter 6

Spicy Indian Food for Thought

I drove through the heart of this paradoxical town in the middle of Arizona, its bright red rocks playing host to both those seeking enlightenment and kitsch – sometimes both for sale in the same shop. Yes, people also lived in Sedona who were doctors, lawyers, and every other stripe of the human condition, but this spiritual hamlet was also the premier worldwide destination for people who wanted to find inexpensive crystals, have their auras cleansed, and go on mystical journeys with guides who had "found" themselves when a publisher signed them to a book contract. This town was a joy. A delight for the senses. A microcosm of the collisions of commercialism and spirituality that torment all who believe they have both a soul and a job that has to pay the bills. The dichotomy was as beautiful as the scenery, and it drew seekers like moths to flame. It was one of Maya's favorite places on earth, and we'd spent a lot of time here.

I pulled into the parking lot of the best Indian restaurant in town which, of course, abutted a dentist's office and a metaphysical bookstore. Reluctantly, I stepped out of my cooled car into the heat. The sun showed little mercy even on these higher elevations. Through the window, I saw Professor Arjun Singh already seated in the restaurant. As I slammed my door, our eyes met. He smiled his broad, toothy grin, and stood from the table. His tall, gangly frame, paired with the genial expression, changed something about my energy. My anxiety dropped away and a lightness appeared in my step as I opened the door. The smell of curry hit me like the blasts of hot wind in the parking lot. I found the table as the busboy trailed behind, filling my water glass as I embraced the professor.

"So good to see you, Jim!" Professor Singh had a pleasingly lyrical accent – somewhere between British and Indian. He gestured with long, bony fingers to the empty chair across from him and flashed another large grin. "Tell me, tell me. How is my protégé?"

"I'm fine, Professor." I returned his smile and basked in the glow of his much-missed company.

I was so happy to again be sitting across from this humble and unassuming man – my advisor in college, for whom I had written an honors thesis comparing ideas of the afterlife in Eastern and Western religious traditions. It was the hardest assignment of my life. He was an authority on Asian philosophy and world religions and his book, *A Path East*, was the cornerstone of Eastern religion courses worldwide. He had also been an advisor to the U.S. government on India's Hindu-Muslim relations. No one was quite sure how or why, but the consensus of his students was that he also worked for the CIA. The man was myth and legend. His stories from his time in the Indian army were like gold – rare autobiographical tidbits of insight into a person of great stature and low profile. Through our time together, I had learned a lot more about him than most, although so much was still a mystery.

His teaching career started as a struggling, part-time faculty member at a community college in California before receiving a tenured university position. His maternal uncle was a *sannyasin* – a religious ascetic who renounced worldly possessions to focus on the spiritual world within. His uncle had parted ways with his family in the last stage of his life, and wandered through India, meditating and visiting shrines. Professor Singh, whose father was Sikh and whose mother was Hindu, once told me that he admired the renunciant's way of life. I think he thought of me like his uncle – a renouncer of sorts, giving up monetary luxuries to serve humanity through my social work pursuits. Although that sounded too grand for me, I think he really believed it. He moved to Sedona with his wife after retirement from the college about six years ago, perhaps to try his hand at seclusion in a spiritual place. She died a year after the move. That was probably more solitude than he expected. No matter how much he admired his uncle, I always felt the professor was happiest in the company of his wife. However, he was a tough man with a tough spirit. He was a survivor.

"I've told you a hundred times to call me Arjun, Jim. Why do you refuse this request?"

"Don't know. It's a hard habit to break. I guess your first name has been 'Professor' since my time in your intro to religion class freshman year, and it just stuck."

The truth was, it's just plain difficult to call a man of his stature by his first name. It just doesn't seem right, though I am never one to stand on ceremony with many others. Nevertheless, I felt guilty. He had honored my request to call me Jim, instead of James, since our very first classroom roll call.

"Well, consider breaking this habit. However, if 'Arjun' makes you uncomfortable, call me what you will. That which is lasting in me does not depend on labels. But remember, we are the same. And, we are peers now."

It was hard to believe that a man such as Arjun Singh considered us similar, or even peers. We stood to roughly the same height, and we both had brown hair and brown eyes, but in my mind, that's where the similarities stopped. I could only dream of his clarity and fitness from my current state of confusion and exhaustion. I kept the material arguments to myself and focused on our academic pursuits.

"Professor, I taught a few classes ten years ago," I mumbled. "I'd hardly call us peers."

"Tsk tsk." Professor Singh pointed one of his long, bony fingers at me, just as he had pointed to places on the map of India in his classroom. "You taught," he said, now jabbing the table rhythmically with each word. "And you still teach through your counseling and social work. You bring knowledge to people. You are like their lover, except you come to them from the head and spirit, not the loins. You offer them something… knowledge and support…in a way no one else does."

"I guess." He sometimes had an awkward way of shedding light on a subject, but it was always strangely poetic.

"How are your parents, Jim?"

"Fine now."

"Now?"

"Dad had a heart attack a while back. He's committed his life to healthy eating and making my mom's life miserable, so I guess things are almost back to normal."

Professor Singh's eyes drew to the window and focused on the distance. His wife had died after a massive and completely unexpected heart attack. This was obviously a tough subject for him. I decided to attribute the water in his eyes to the spicy appetizers that had just arrived.

"I'm sorry to hear that, Jim."

"Oh, Professor, he's not suffering or anything like that. All's well now with a good prognosis."

"Then I change my prior observation. I'm glad to hear that!"

"Yeah. I saw him the other night and I feel a little guilty taking my vacation away from them, but he told me to make the most of my summer. I feel like things are crumbling around me, and I'm really struggling with my anxiety and depression. Dad said that I should recharge myself instead of sitting around with him all day getting more depressed while he reads the newspaper. I don't know, Professor…" I concentrated hard on the wrapper from my straw, twisting it into a tight snake and twirling it between my fingers. "I guess my life isn't exactly what I'd hoped at this point."

"I know you're struggling right now in your life, Jim, and it sounds like your mind is not where you would like it to be. I know how hard it can be when we want to be released from the past and to avoid the future. But your father is wise."

"How do you mean?"

Our server interrupted, silently placing two cold drinks on the table. Our heads nodded a thank you, and we reset.

"Jim, you cannot spend your life waiting for the shoe to drop. Sometimes you must put the shoe on and walk, especially when you feel stuck in your life. More is the better when you see your father and can share memories of this time." He lifted his frothy mango lassi and tipped it slightly towards me. "Then you create sweet nectar from bitter waters."

As our conversation progressed, the waiter brought insane amounts of food to the table. Professor Singh, who ordered in fluent Hindi, was a vegetarian and ate curried vegetable dishes with beans and greens. I savored the rich tomato gravy accompanying the chicken tikka masala. It always makes my taste buds tingle with delight. The professor kept plenty on hand for students when they came to his house.

"So, what are your plans for after vacation?" He delicately tore an imperfect oval of warm, garlic naan in half and offered me the bigger piece. As if on cue, we both ripped off pieces to soak up our respective sauces.

"What, you mean if I can get it together and manage to re-enter society?" I smirked.

"Of course!"

"Well, if fate and non-profit funding smile on me, then I'll be starting up a few addiction groups I've been wanting to do. My clients found out a little about my background and are now demanding more and more education on things like world religion and philosophy and how these things can help in their recovery."

"It sounds exciting, Jim."

"I guess. My boss told me to go ahead and prepare some things, and when I get back, she said she'd love to take a look at what I've got."

"Very good, very good. I know you will inspire!"

"It's funny how we place things in separate categories and departments in college, yet when we get into the real world, they all work together. My clients don't seem to care about the artificial boundaries between religions or philosophies. They're just interested in how some of those things can help them stay off drugs or get them through another day without a panic attack. It all just kind of works together, you know? It's not bookish. It's stuff that helps people...I donno...survive out here."

"Indeed, Jim. Indeed."

His face dissolved into a dreamy expression. With his right hand, he grasped a tiny key hanging around his neck on a string of beads and began to rub it. The key was tarnished, especially on its ornate top, which he rolled between his thumb and index finger. The beads were worn smooth, their fading finish betraying a once intricate design that had since given way to years of his slowly moving fingers. I remembered seeing this progression of events back in college during his office hours. He was preparing his mind to talk deep philosophy.

"The dramas of life continually blend and interact, Jim. And, they are sewn together with the wisdom from the ages. This is what I was telling you in class years ago. The age we are now in, with internet and television...everyone is getting closer. Ideas are spreading. This was the magic of the Axis Age. Do you remember from lectures?"

Professor Singh had a habit of asking me to recall information from his lectures, though they were far in my past. I'd sometimes tear through boxes to find my notes before calling him or answering his occasional emails, not wanting it to appear that I had forgotten anything. I crammed for our conversations like I'd crammed for his tests. If you asked me for it, I'd have trouble locating my undergraduate diploma. But I could easily produce a colorful hodgepodge of notebooks and stuffed folders labeled, "Singh."

"Yes, I remember the Axis Age." A twinge of relief swept through me that I'd paid attention that day.

"It was the dawn of something new and wonderful," he continued, key in hand. "A time of progress." He accentuated the last word, waving naan bread around illustratively with his left hand. We used to say that if you tied Professor Singh's hands behind his back, he would be unable to lecture. "It's the kind of progress only fully palpable from a distance, upon reflection over the centuries. Spiritual progress is that way. New leaders often call it reaction or revolution. However, it is also progress and evolution."

"I know. I often wish I could have lived somewhere in those hundreds of years before Christ."

"What a time it must have been, Jim. Just imagine it! Eastern figures questioned the prevailing ancient Vedic religion of the Indian subcontinent."

"Let's hear it for the Buddha!" I cheered.

"Indeed. He took the traditional Hindu pathways and caste systems of his day head on. Quiet challenge. Quiet strength."

"I always picture him wandering along the Ganges looking for a guru. Starving himself. Twisting himself into knots, trying to find the truth. Sometimes I think that if I could go on a search like that, maybe I could find the release valve for all this pent-up crap I feel inside of me. But it must have been a rough road. I can't believe he left a palace to do that!"

"But he did, Jim. Buddha paid a princely sum for that spiritual freedom in the most literal sense. He shed his kingdom and wandered the wilderness looking for another way to enlightenment, and under that famous tree he decided on a Middle Way of ethics and meditation. His was a compromise between the self-denying austerities of the ascetics and the luxuries of the nobility."

"Everything in moderation, right?" I heaped tangy chicken onto a mound of steaming white rice.

"Exactly, Jim! And remember, he truly lived his teaching. He gave up riches. He tried the greatest austerities. When he spoke after his enlightenment, people listened, because he had a truly authentic journey."

"He was a warrior. I'll say that for him."

"The Buddha led a peaceful protest against the idea that spiritual paths could only be trod by a privileged few." I could tell the professor was entering his zone, as he twirled the key. "But his was not the only hat in the ring, if you recall."

"I do recall." This time I was prepared, even without my trusty notebooks. "In China, Confucius and Lao Tzu were doing their thing."

"Their thing? Very elegant, Jim."

"Okay, fine. They were spreading their philosophies. Confucius wanted a more prosperous society through rules and relationships and Lao Tzu advocated for a more hands-off approach to life. But both wanted the same thing. Both wanted harmony. Better?"

"Yes." A gleam pierced Professor Singh's eye. "They were busy unraveling and reworking the mysteries of the Tao. They explored Yin and Yang – the proverbial swirling fish of light and dark in Chinese tradition. They recognized that each side of these intertwined teardrops contains within it a hint of the other, reminding us we need not advocate for one side of life, so much as appreciate its inherent qualities in light of the other." He dipped a pinkie in his lassi and placed it gingerly into his water glass. A bright, smoky lassi swirl descended through the ice before disappearing like a fading apparition into the water. "So you see, traditions from Asia inquired into the nature of the self, as well as broader questions about persons and ideal societies."

"But let's not forget the inroads made in the West, Professor."

"So true! So true! Walk us West now, Jim."

"One of my favorite Greek figures is that guy Thales who asked, 'What is the stuff other stuff is made of?'"

"And what was his brilliant answer, Jim?"

"Water." I tapped my fingernail twice against my glass, making a dull chime that perked our waiter up from his repose by the kitchen. "I loved teaching around this. It always got a laugh in class. But I try to remind students how important this is. That investigation, thousands of years ago, divorced Thales from religious explanations of our origins. It quite possibly helped to birth modern science."

"Absolutely. But there were those who knew that we would have to supplement Thales' search for physical, scientific knowledge and focus on the world within."

"Socrates," I said. "The ol' Greek gadfly."

"Indeed. The brilliant and irreverent Socrates emerged from the shadows of the Athenian marketplace, standing toe to toe with the city elite, challenging their pretenses to knowledge and asking all of us, 'What is the good life?' and 'How ought we to live?'" Professor Singh placed his palms firmly together under his chin as if in prayer, key tucked in between, and rocked his fingertips towards my chest. "These questions reverberate through the ages like an endless echo in the bottomless canyons of the mind."

"The unexamined life is not worth living. Right, Professor?"

"That's right. Socrates cut right to the core of all of us."

"Yeah. It's just...I don't know. Examining life. It really hurts sometimes, you know? It's hard. I know my clients don't always love examining their stuff. I sure as heck don't. There are things in the past I don't want to look at. There are things in the future that scare me. Something about the modern world seems so distant from those ghosts of the past, Professor. Examination is...well...lonely." I looked down at my plate and swallowed hard.

"You know, Jim," his words rushed in to save me, "we are once again in that time."

"What time? The time of Socrates?"

"Something like that."

"I don't know, Professor. It's pretty wild out there right now. Everything's so extreme."

"Was the time of Socrates any different, Jim? Is any time any different?"

"I guess not. But so many people I know today are in survival mode all the time and the people at the top don't seem to care. It's like they thrive on our pain."

"There is a great deal of polarization out there, no doubt. And people are struggling, Jim, as you say. You are struggling. Your clients struggle. People in offices across the globe sit and do their jobs with a solemn face, but inside, they struggle. Things seem out of kilter. And there doesn't seem to be any time or any way to work on ourselves when we're so busy working for others and working to survive."

"Yeah. So what's the plan?"

"Well, new figures seeking balance will come to urge us in new directions and to help us see and think in new ways. This is unavoidable. Fanaticism breeds compromise in the world. Otherwise?" In a pause, he let the key fall against his chest. "Destruction."

I pondered his point. Could people still come together around new ideas? Ideas these days seemed to be used more as weapons than building blocks. The United States, a country built on principles of dissent and change, had, within a matter of a few hundred years, polarized into a for-me-or-against-me way of thinking that frightened many of my friends and family on both sides of the political spectrum. New ideas were coming to be seen as threats instead of natural outgrowths of freedom. But it wasn't just America. This was global. When fledgling movements of any kind become strong, they bully their contemporaries. People shut down and suffer in silence.

"You're a lot more optimistic than I could ever be, Professor." I couldn't stomp down the creeping weeds of pessimism any longer. "I mean, things are falling apart. A lot of people in my generation are flopping around like fish in a boat, and no one seems to care."

"Maybe so, Jim. Maybe so. But you must never give up hope. Keep searching for new perspectives. I have seen and studied the blood that's shed in the dark shadows of religious and political intolerance. I have to believe a better day is coming, or maybe that it is here, behind the clouds. Even the most overcast day has warmth hidden behind it.

Gandhi, may he rest in peace, knew that goodness must underlie the human condition. He tried to see it in everyone – even in his persecutors. This is the key, Jim. We must strive to see others as ourselves. Behind the dark façade of difference lies common expression. As you suffer, never forget that the person in front of you is suffering as well. That is the first inroad to healing. And in that realization comes a chance for redemption. For all of us."

As our talk lingered on, I realized how much I missed his company. He had a way of teaching like it was a pep talk. Before I knew it, it was two in the afternoon. He was giving his credit card to the waiter. I reached for my wallet and he shot daggers at me.

"No protégé of mine will pay for lunch with me at this restaurant," he said, after sharing a few Hindi phrases with the bus boy. I thanked him and put my wallet away with a respectful nod.

"So, what else are you doing this summer, Professor?"

"Oh, nothing special. I was maybe going to hike and do yoga. I don't know. I am free and uncommitted."

Without thinking, I blurted, "Why don't you come up north with me for a while? I'm heading to my friend's cabin near Flagstaff. Get away for a bit. I can give you directions if you'd like. You can meet me there tonight." Before I considered what I'd done, Professor Singh replied.

"What a lovely invitation, Jim! I could use the conversation. My friends here are wonderful at talking cricket and bridge, but not much for philosophy and religious traditions. I'm so used to camping up there, I've never been in one of those cabins. Let me get a pen for the directions."

Arjun Singh called out what I assume was "pen," in Hindi, to the waiter, who brought him one, straight away.

Chapter 7

The Beautiful Tension of Thought

I called Jake when I was back on the road to let him know I had just invited one of the world's preeminent philosophers and religious scholars to his cabin.

"Jake, I'm sorry. I asked before I realized what I was doing."

"No problem, Jim." His demeanor never lost its characteristic nonchalance – a powerful tool that served him well in the lower courts where he dominated. "It doesn't matter to me. Just do what you can to keep the place clean. I'm assuming this Singh guy is an upstanding human, so I think we're on safe ground here."

"Doesn't get much safer."

"Whatever. What's mine is yours. And besides, you're doing my family a favor by keeping an eye on the place."

"I appreciate that," I said.

"How are you feeling?"

"I'm okay. Trying to focus on the cool air and the good memories. My anxiety attacks never seem to last as long up here."

"I'm glad to hear—"

The call dropped as the road curved behind a mountain. I fixed my attention completely on the narrow, two-lane road winding through Oak Creek Canyon outside of Sedona. To one side, the boulder-studded creek wended around rustic cabins and small bed-and-breakfasts where Maya and I had spent more than a few nights. On the other, giant red walls of stone rose like citadels. This stretch of road is a ready canvas for all seasons. No matter what time of year I come through, it's always a picturesque scene.

I had just entered that strange driver's trance where miles pass despite one's consciousness, when a clopping sound jarred me back into the realities of the road. I snapped to the moment, suddenly mindful, and gathered myself. I pulled over onto a narrow patch of dirt by a steep drop-off.

"Great," I sighed. "I'll bet it's a flat." Before exiting the car, I tried a breathing technique Doctor Eastman had shown me. I focused on my beating heart and took in a deep breath to the count of three. I held my breath for another four seconds before letting it out to a count of five. I did this cycle five times, and when I finished, I didn't feel any better and had to assess the damage with a new feeling of lightheadedness. Sure enough, my passenger rear tire had blown. On closer inspection on my hands and knees, I noticed a huge nail glaring at me from deep in the tread. I was still about a half hour outside Flagstaff in an area with almost no cell signal. "So much for the scenic route," I muttered, kicking the rim. I was pondering my options when someone pulled up behind me.

"Need a hand, kid?"

I turned to see the gray-haired man rolling to a stop behind me. His dog was still hanging out of the open-sided Jeep.

"I…I sure could use some help," I stammered, trying to overcome frustration and shock in the same breath. "Thanks."

The man strode over. He looked well over six feet, much bigger than he did at the rest stop. Perhaps this was because he was now poised to render assistance. He had broad shoulders and sported worn and muddied black hiking boots and even more worn jeans. The red flannel shirt had now moved onto his body for the trip through the higher elevations in the late afternoon when the temperature drops quickly, especially in the shade of the mountains. He had the striking appearance of a man who had left the world to cut logs in Alaska with his faithful dog at his side. I was self-conscious, standing just under six feet, wearing my newer jeans and t-shirt. I had the look of someone whose roughest encounters result in paper cuts from the office copy machine.

"Name's Silas." He extended a strong hand that felt in my grasp like it had seen hard times. "Dog's Casey." He nodded towards the German Shepherd with the green bandana tied around his neck.

"I'm Jim. Nice to meet you both."

"Nice to meet you, kid. Or should I say, nice to meet you again."

I felt ill-at-ease, wondering if "again" referred to our chance meeting on the bench at the rest stop, or the missed meeting at the side of the hill six hours and thirty degrees ago when Silas was the one in distress.

"Let's get this thing going," he said.

Between the two of us – but mostly Silas – the wheel was changed in no time. We both stepped back to admire our handiwork.

"Where're you off to?" he asked.

"Flagstaff. My friend has a place near there. You?"

"Eh," he grunted. "Here and there."

I let his response drop like a lugnut. Instead, we concluded with a bit of small talk about the freedom of road trips and the thrill of owning a Jeep, before he pulled away.

"Drive careful, kid!" he called as he drove around me in a cloud of mystery and good karma.

I waved and glanced inside his car, packed to the brim with stuff. He had a tent with a few sleeping bags, and what looked like a camera case and tripod. The Jeep, with the dog's happy head inside, disappeared on its way to "here and there." I was struck by the coincidence of encountering this man for the third time in one day, but I dismissed it as I tentatively sat behind the wheel. Driving on a spare is the closest you can come to walking across a lake that someone else assures you is frozen. It's all about faith.

I arrived in Flagstaff just after the tire store at the south end of town had closed for the day. Luckily, my spare was like new. Spewing a few choice expletives about modern customer service, I turned off the main highway to follow the Lake Mary Road to Mormon Lake. There's a lake there, for sure, but in all the times I'd been there, I'd never seen a lot of water in it. The Davis refrigerator sported a photo of a very young Jake holding up a very small fish, captioned, "Jake's Big Take! '78!" I couldn't help but think that a lake where Jake last caught a fish during the Carter administration should consider changing its name.

I drove through the heart of town where there stood a general store, restaurant, and saloon with one pool table that had seen more than one roll of Davis quarters disappear into its depths. I mused about the simple joys of small-town life – that half-baked, romantic reflection common in those who vacation in quiet places, but secretly crave regular activity in the city. I decided to pull over at the store to get a few light snacks. I stepped into the small shop and caught the eye of a man behind the register. We nodded a greeting before he went back to his task. A box filled with fishhooks and feathers, and wide mouth mason jars filled with finished flies, sat on the table in front of him.

I was examining a can of beans and franks when the store's rickety screen door creaked open. The man behind the counter and I looked to see a stuffed bear's head peering inside the shop. It was attached to the hand of a boy around six years old. Our gazes met through the screen, and the boy closed the door quietly, remaining outside. He seemed unsure what to do next.

"You alright, Mo?" the man asked. The little boy nodded yes. "Is Beary alright?" Mo made the bear nod yes. "You two lose your momma?" Again, the boy nodded and made the bear nod along with him. "Why don't you both come on in here and help me?" Mo pushed the door open with a gentle caution and stepped inside. He eyed me warily, then headed behind the counter to join the man at the register. The man tussled Mo's hair.

"Can you do something for me, Mo?" Mo nodded. "Step on that box there and get yourself nice and tall." After the boy was situated, the man slid the box of feathers to him. "I need you to go through this box here and take out all the blue feathers and put 'em in a pile on the table. Beary can supervise. Is that something you can do?"

Mo beamed. With great care, he picked through the box and placed blue feathers in a perfect pile. He and the man at the register didn't exchange another word until a woman wandered into the shop. She looked harried, with her dirty blond hair pulled back under a faded headscarf. A large quartz crystal dangled from a silver chain around her neck. Her sunken eyes met mine, and she flashed a fleeting smile before her eyes found Mo behind the counter.

"Sorry, Hiram. Is he bothering you again?" The woman extended an open hand from her side. Mo immediately stepped down from the box and took it.

"Mo is the best helper I could ask for, Liv. No bothering here. Your mom good?"

"As good as can be expected, Hiram. Volunteer work and card games are keeping her going. Thanks for asking."

"Well, you tell her Hiram says hello, and not to be a stranger."

"I'll let her know. Thanks again. Say goodbye, Mo." Mo simply smiled, and made Beary wave to Hiram.

I put the can back on the shelf and left the store in time to see Liv and Mo make it to the other side of the street. They wandered up a small incline and disappeared into an old, red house on the hill. Something about Liv seemed familiar. Maybe it was a memory from all the times I'd been up this way with Jake and his family. Maybe the whole town seemed familiar to me by now. I'd seen Hiram many times, although I didn't know his name. Perhaps Liv and I had crossed paths before.

I jumped back in the car and headed to Jake's place, crossing a cattle guard in the road. The grate vibrated rhythmically under my tires, signaling the official boundary between my problems and my newfound freedom. I found number 122, with its weathered, hand-carved sign swinging on rusty hooks that read, "Relaxing Ranch – A

Davis Place," and took a left up the hill. About fifty yards into the pines stood the most beautiful cabin in the area. It wasn't ostentatious by any stretch of the imagination, but something about it felt grand, even in such humble surroundings. It was two stories, painted a rustic blue with white window trim. Lace curtains in an upstairs bedroom sat lilywhite and silent in the fading afternoon light. Mrs. Davis's touch.

I parked on the dirt driveway and got out, shutting the door with a thud before taking in the immediate peace. The cool air, combined with the fresh scent of pine needles, snagged my senses and I was immediately drawn into that area of the mind reserved for good feelings and pleasant memories. Honoring a meaningless tradition of mine, I bent down to pick up a pinecone before walking around the back of the cabin and up a small incline to where an ancient ponderosa pine was precariously perched. In its upward journey, it had somehow sprouted a strange branch to the side while the rest of it continued to the sky. I took the key from my pocket and swung it on the chain as I drifted to the back door to let myself in.

The house, handed down through generations of Davis heirs, smelled like apple and cinnamon potpourri. Always. I couldn't help but think that every Davis family kept it smelling this way, as if mandated in the original deed. The odor permeated everything. It was part of this place – part of its long history. I always returned to Phoenix smelling like pie. I walked through the kitchen to the sitting room at the front of the house, drawing my hand along the lime green couch and over the hand-knitted quilts that populated its back. I tapped the pillows with the inspirational sayings knitted into them and lingered on my secret favorite – the one Mrs. Davis told me she knitted the summer Jake was born: "Two Plus One Equals Everything." Jake certainly was their one, I mused. I gently parted the delicate drapes to admire the view through the tress back toward the road, reflecting on the many nights I sat here with Jake, a game of gin rummy and a plate of Mrs. Davis's fresh-baked sugar cookies between us – the sweet tastes of memory so light on the tongue. It was hard to be depressed back then. Back when it was all so simple.

A thought blazed through me. It hadn't occurred to me when I asked Professor Singh to join me that I would be a guest entertaining a guest. I bolted up the stairs, two at a time, and rummaged in the linen closets. They had a pleasingly damp smell that hinted at everything good about a home in the mountains. Even on the warmest days here, the scent was reliable at night and recalled cooling rains and the fresh aftermath of storms. I made up the bed in my room, then went to the master bedroom to put sheets on the professor's bed. I hung fresh towels in his bathroom, checked the toilet paper situation, and paused to gaze longingly at the dual showerheads. As much as I desired them, I considered this room switch a small sacrifice for his company. I was digging around for extra blankets when I heard a car approach. I ran to the window at the end of the hall and saw a new Hybrid SUV coming up the driveway. When I remarked on it in the parking lot in Sedona, Professor Singh told me he wanted to do his part for the environment but didn't want to give up his occasional off-road expeditions. He called his new vehicle, "A beautiful tension."

I trotted down the stairs and greeted him at the door. He was balancing a pile of grocery bags in one arm and a suitcase in the other.

"Moving in?" I teased.

"Hello, hello!" Professor Singh was in full spirits. "I brought some things with me."

"Thanks!" I motioned for him to enter and took over the handle of his suitcase. I then relieved him of the groceries, closed the door with my foot, and led him into the kitchen. In my angst over the tire and my distraction at the general store, I forgot about dinner. I hadn't noticed how hungry I was.

"I was planning on an energy bar," I said, half-apologetically, admiring the food he'd brought. "But this sure beats that!"

"Indeed," he smiled. "Simply a small token for your invitation."

"Well, you'll have to come to Phoenix with these same groceries so you can thank my friend Jake. He's the real hero."

"I should like that very much, Jim!"

I unpacked fresh vegetables and chicken from the sacks while he stacked packages of curry powder on the counter. I could tell these were from his personal stores, and I knew they would be the most flavorful.

"I'm glad you found the place alright. I wasn't sure if you'd be able to find the driveway in the twilight. I hope you like it."

"Jim, my mother came from a small village. She lived in a one-room hut housing a family of five. It was six hours by oxcart from the largest town, which was probably the size of Mormon Lake. Trust me, lad. I'll manage in this two-story castle."

"Okay, okay," I said. "I just thought——"

"Jim," he interrupted, "that's your whole trouble."

Chapter 8

Timing, Expectations, and Invisible Friends

Professor Singh worked the antique stove like an orchestra conductor. Pots and pans simmered on all burners, bubbling in perfect tune. Soon, the familiar odor of cinnamon apples was ruthlessly colonized by the exotic scent of curry – the sort of smell one's senses initially protest, then crave. Before college, I had no taste for Indian cooking. But since sampling Mrs. Singh's recipes years ago, I was in love. I couldn't remember the last time I had Indian food twice in one month, much less one day. I could only imagine what the Davis family would say when they walked back into their cabin and were smacked with the smell of Indian curry. I loved them dearly, but their idea of foreign dining is french fries and Belgian waffles. I resolved to unleash an entire bottle of apple-and-cinnamon-scented odor remover before I left for home.

It was half-past eight. He'd been cooking for over two hours. The meal in Sedona was now a faint grumble in our stomachs, and we were both famished. Professor Singh placed dishes of piping hot vegetables and chicken on the table. He baked fresh naan, saturating it with garlic. The professor could cook dishes from all regions of his homeland, and his students used to joke about an unspoken kitchen competition between he and his wife.

We settled happily into the feast.

"Jim, please. A good meal is so much better with good conversation. Tell me more of your life."

"Are you sure you want to know? It's not exactly Hollywood entertainment."

"It's better, Jim, because it's real. How are things with you and your lady friend? I seem to recall you mentioning her to me in an email exchange a while back. What is she like?"

I laughed inside but didn't dare do it aloud. My grandmother and Professor Singh were the only two people I knew who used the phrase 'lady friend' without a trace of a blush.

"Maya? Well, right now, she's invisible."

"Invisible?"

"Yeah…" I savored a mouthful of curried spinach and chicken a moment longer than usual. "We were engaged."

"I had no idea."

"And now we're not."

"Ah."

"And she's gone."

"Oh."

"And I'm still here."

"Yes. Hmm. I see. Although, as you say, she is still invisible."

"Just rotten timing, I guess. In the end, I just couldn't live up to her expectations. I'd show you the last letter she wrote to me that kinda sums all of this up, but it's currently in ashes at the bottom of a metal trash can on my porch under a synthetic vanilla candle."

"Timing and expectations." The professor sang this phrase under his breath as he rummaged in the cupboards looking for another dish on which to place the gulab jamun and rice pudding he'd brought for dessert.

"Huh?"

"Oh, nothing." He returned to the table and cleared a space for sweets. Leaning back in his chair, the picture of relaxation, he tugged at the key around his neck with his right hand. "It's just this idea about timing and wanting things. Young people."

"Hey, I'm not that young."

"You're young enough, Jim. You have all the time in the world, and a world of opportunity, yet you only pay attention when you think your expectations aren't being met."

"What are you talking about?"

"Jim, what is it like for you when you think things are going your way? Say, for example, when you and Maya were together and having a good time. How did that feel?"

"Oh, man. Do we really have to do this?"

"Do you have something else to do?"

"We could find Mrs. Davis's knitting basket and make scarves. How does that sound?"

"You're right, Jim. This really isn't my business. I'm sorry."

"No. You know what, Professor? I'm sorry." I sat up straighter in my chair. "I need to break my habit of deflecting like that. It was rude. I actually think this is a conversation I need to have. It's long overdue."

"Okay, then. Can you answer the question?"

"I guess it felt great! I remember our first date. Our first kiss. Things felt easy. Actually, now that you mention it, I didn't really think about it at all. I was just…in it."

"How did you feel when the two of you disagreed? Say, if you had a disagreement about your so-called expectations?"

"Hmm." Professor Singh had a way of leading people to great illumination just by lighting a single match. Unfortunately, the wick on my candle was a bit short at times. "I guess it felt wrong. I got frustrated. We didn't call it expectations, though. It was more like we were just tired. Bored."

"Did you use phrases like, 'if only' or 'I wish' when things weren't going well?"

"Sure. I wish Maya and I could have been on the same page. I wish things had worked out differently. I wish I could have been the man that she needed or expected me to be. It never feels good to be out of sync. It's horrible sometimes. It dials up the anxiety to a crazy place."

Professor Singh stirred the remaining lentils on his plate with the fork in his left hand. I sensed he was waiting for me to finish my thought, but it felt concluded. My head was abuzz with curry and abstractions. Food and flies.

"Jim, life has a way of giving us what we need. There are things..." he paused and appeared to be studying my face for a sign of something, unsure how to proceed. He took a breath, as if ready to take a plunge. "There are things we see, and things we don't. There is knowledge we learn and knowledge we've earned. Both are there to help us. When the two of you argued and you wanted to throw in the proverbial towel in the relationship – perhaps because you blamed her for something – was it really because of something *she* did, or is it that *your* expectations were thwarted?"

"Good question, Professor." I thought about this while chewing on an impossibly sweet piece of gulab jamun – capping off a very heavy meal. This conversation foreshadowed a bout of heartburn. "Are you saying that most of the issues and problems in my relationship stemmed from me?"

"Well, not exactly. I would have no way of knowing that, as I wasn't there while you were in it. And although I'm sure Maya is a very nice person—"

"She is."

"A relationship is two people. So no, all problems don't stem from you. I'm just speaking from one vantage point. I know you are punishing yourself for things going awry, but maybe you can release yourself from that prison."

"Done! How do I do that?"

"By understanding that your job was not to fix the situation with Maya, but to accept it for what it was. Instead of cursing the path you wandered down from among your choices, or wishing things were other than they are, understand that you are being given an opportunity."

"But how?" I waved my fork around like a banner to rally my

troops. "My relationships always seem to go bust. You say my job isn't to fix the situation, and I get that, but c'mon. Something must need fixing, right? I know love and relationships are important, but sometimes I want to chuck it all!" The dessert flung from the fork into his lap. He picked it up and put it on the table. "Sorry."

"No bother," he said, without a trace of irritation. "I'll consider it an offering on the altars of knowledge. Anyway, that is the point, is it not? What you want to 'chuck,' as you so dramatically illustrated, is not relationships."

"It isn't? Well then what is it?"

"Your thwarted expectations. If you could accept Maya's situation, and your role in it, it would alleviate much pain. The ego is a powerful and jealous mistress that does not suffer peace gladly."

"The ego," I repeated. "You're pulling out the Freud on me now? I have a shrink for that, thank you."

"I don't think Freud and I are in the same context, Jim."

"Probably not. Actually, Maya bought some books on personal growth when we were together, and she used to talk about ego and stuff like that. I think she really wanted me to read them."

"Tell me a little about what you've learned."

"Not a whole lot. I never opened them while we were together. But Maya left them behind when she left, and I got curious. I picked one up the other day and flipped through it. It was pretty interesting, actually. I kinda laughed it off when she'd talk about it – you know how all those personal growth gurus can be."

"I do."

"But maybe there's...I donno...something to all of that. Ego comes up in therapy practice, and it's definitely something we stumble across in religious studies. But I don't know. How is it relevant here? If I know my ego is screwing me up, what can I do about it going forward?"

"Well, let's proceed by way of reverse. Instead of leaping forward to the next phase of life, go back a step with me and let's take a good look at ego."

"Okay."

"If we reflect on our lives, we find that many of the disappointments and struggles we face don't depend so much on what others are doing to us, but how we react to others' actions. The ego, as we're speaking of it now, is that part of you that has you disconnected from the 'growth' in personal growth or the 'spirit' in spirituality if that is the angle you choose. Ego is the mesh of desires and expectations that filters your experiences."

"How do you mean?"

"Well, instead of watching things happen in the world and letting it all pass before you undisturbed, the ego gets you involved in them. It invests your energy in passing matters to the point where you believe they are permanent. Rather than watching the movie, you become an actor in it. A full participant. Ego nature is reactionary, acting out in the world and seeking control. It is an inner voice that tells you to do something other than what you are doing now."

"Yes!" I said, a bit too loudly. "I decided to try a meditation I found in one of the books to quiet that voice, but I gave up. My mind wandered too much. I had a hard time focusing. I would think about all kinds of crazy things. Is that what you mean? Is that the ego?"

"To an extent, yes. I cannot point to an exact definition, but let's try to clarify what it is." He relaxed again against the back of his chair, working the beads around his neck through his fingers. "An untamed ego does not allow you to create your life spontaneously, as you do in dreams. There is a part of you that soars on eagles' wings, Jim, even if you are not aware of it. That piece of who you are is not reactionary. It's visionary. The ego, however, wants credit for everything that happens. It distracts you with the illusion of disappointment – a tool it uses to keep you from discovering grander possibilities that lie within you. Possibilities that could sever the tether between your everyday life of reactions and the limitless worlds that lie beyond."

"Now you sound like one of those books, Professor." I placed my fork down next to my last bite of gulab jamun, trading food for argument. "If ego is so distracting…so limiting, why do we have it? Why is it there?"

"We created it, in a way. It's a tool for guidance. Think of the ego as a little self that developed to guide the bigger self – I'll call it the spiritual self – through a complex, material world. The problem is that ego gets out of control. It began as a way of filtering, sorting, and mediating experience, but grew to monstrous proportions. It's a part-time personality assistant that totally consumes the person. Think of it as a pretty dandelion that eventually spreads and crowds out the garden. Or a puppy that grew bigger than its owner and took over the house."

"Why can't we reign ego in? What lets it get so out of hand?"

"We become dependent on ego because we come to believe it's our entire identity. We are intoxicated with the myth that the world was created for us to control, and that it revolves around us. We run experiences through the filters of ego to see if they meet an expectation or preserve our status quo."

"So how does it work? Are you saying I'm disappointed with my relationship with Maya because of my ego?" I got dressed in my defensive armor, resisting the urge to surrender to the conversation. He was questioning the entire foundation of my relationship, but in a way no one else ever had. Even Doctor Eastman hadn't begun to dig this far down.

"Well, ego is the origin of expectations, and expectations are the cause and fuel of disappointments."

"Thanks, Buddha."

"Aha! A compliment of the highest order."

"You're welcome."

"Nothing is ever good enough for ego, Jim. There is always more to gain, more for which to take credit. Ego is the invisible figure that gets offended and impatient or makes us feel we're being treated unfairly in a relationship, even though there is another person involved who has their own outlook and potential. We may, indeed, be suffering in our relationships. Sometimes in terrible ways. Unfortunately, most of the time, we've become so engrossed in ego, it gets hard to separate true suffering and injustice from our own disappointments. We may even feel like we want a relationship – or even our life – to die, because we're so consumed with our wants and struggles. But really, what we crave is a death of a different kind. A death of the ego. Or, at least, to tame it."

"I still don't understand. What does this have to do with Maya and me?"

"Everything! If we look at it from the vantage point of a relationship, we see that if you could check your ego and expectations at the door, accepting a woman you are with for who she is in the moment – where she is, how she is – while at the same time accepting your role in relation to her, you could move away mountains of disappointment instead of being imprisoned by them. A true relationship exists in spite of your ego and expectations, Jim, not because of them. The sooner you understand this, the sooner you will see the sun behind the clouds."

"I guess," I offered with a sigh.

"Well," he said, releasing both me and the beads around his neck, "we'd better get these plates cleaned up."

The night slipped once again into light discussion of what had consumed our time since college. The professor methodically washed a pile of dishes, and I dried them. Later on, we picked up threads of conversation from lunch and dinner and tied them off in tight knots on the sitting room couch. Just before midnight, he excused himself for bed.

"Mindfulness morning and mindfulness night, you know the middle will be alright," he sang, as he ascended the stairs. "I will see you tomorrow, Jim. Thank you again for this wonderful invitation."

"Good night, Professor." I thanked him for a meal that doubled as food for thought.

Chapter 9

Audible Silence

The darkness of the sitting room enveloped me. My breath came in easy streams, but as soon as I noticed it, I felt a tinge of anxiety creep in, although I had no idea what could possibly be generating it. I closed my eyes against that mystery and imagined myself as a tiny dot of light that could melt into the blackness. If that happened, I thought, what would remain? What would my contribution be? A stain on the Davis sofa? A memory in Jake's yearbooks? A difficult obstacle on Maya's continuing journey? Or would there be, as some of Maya's books say, a new life waiting on the other side of my disappearance? What would that be like? The silent backdrop of these ideas was potent. Filled with potential. My eyes grew heavy under the weight of my thoughts. I didn't fight them, allowing myself to give in to the blackout and to dreams.

"You hurt me, Maya." She stared at me, lips pursed. Quivering. "You took my things when you left, and you broke me."

"Jim, I left you everything. I left you with everything you need to heal."

"Sometimes when we leave…"

My voice trailed into the void. Maya put a soft hand on the side of my face and broke into a smile of pure love.

"We learn, Jim. We learn."

She held out her hand and a book appeared. I leaned over to see the cover, and saw my reflection looking back at me. The book flew open and a flash of light knocked me backwards. When I roused from the dream and checked the time, I was shocked to see it was well past midnight. Relieved to be back in the real world, and buoyed by the knowledge that I had no commitments the next day, I sat on the sofa and gazed out the sitting room window at the moon and stars glimmering through the still pines. I pondered the ego. Pondered the idea that I crowded my waking state with the endless noise of the material world, unable to weave my lines of logic into the spirals of spirit and the other mysteries of life. I remembered the time Doctor Eastman asked me what would make me peaceful in life. I wasn't kind in my response, telling her that I gave up looking for deeper peace in life – instead, wishing for a deep pool where I could drown out the pain of my world. When she asked if I meant suicide, I told her that would only be a bonus.

After three of the biggest yawns I could remember in years, I headed for the staircase. Upstairs, Professor Singh's door was closed, and no light spilled into the darkened hallway. I crept down the creaky corridor to my room, wincing every time a board made a noise under the carpet, and almost banged into an antique table supporting a gaudy pink vase stuffed with plastic flowers. I thought about the generations that had wandered this hall at all hours of the night. Jake and I had done our share, trying to figure out the quiet places on the floor that would get us down to the kitchen for late night snacks without waking his parents.

I entered my room where a dim bedside light was already on, casting a pale glow into the surrounding darkness. The light reflected off a cream-colored wallpaper decorated with green leaves and red berries, giving the room an eerily festive look – Christmas in purgatory. A pile of old journals with brown leather covers on my bed caught my attention. I picked them up to examine them and saw they were numbered and labeled, "Audible Silence." There were six in all – five filled, and one empty.

A note sat atop them:

Jim, these might contain a bit of what you are looking for. -Arjun

I leafed through their delicate, yellowing pages, smooth between my fingers. An initial inspection revealed essays with titles such as "One," "Forgiveness," and "Relationships." I opened the first, and oldest, journal, assuming it would be filled with the professor's thoughts on philosophy and religion, or maybe be a compilation of his lecture notes from class. However, as I read the poetic prose, I noticed that although the tone reflected his lectures, the content was very different. The first entry, dated March 13, 1958, read:

Imagine an eternal vibration that generates all appearances. Mystics of the ages have called it "om." As om vibrates through the universe, it creates. It sustains. It pulses. It is what it is for as long as it is, then it is again, whatever it will be. Pluck a string. See the pattern it generates. Watch it vibrate. Energy, energy, energy, until the energy fades into rest, awaiting the next vibration. Perhaps the greatest reward of plucking the string of creation is hearing the beautiful sound. But to clearly hear the sound of the creative string, we must reveal the pure artifact of silence that lies behind it. The tool to uncover it is meditation. When we sit with intention, layers of distraction emerge. When we remain seated with patience, they melt away. Once revealed, the silence stays with us. The deafening roar of audible silence is the ever-present companion to the sound of creation. Clear the cacophony. Find the silence. In that space, create.

This sounded like the professor, but I'd never heard him lecture like this before. I'd read some of his textbooks, and they all had the unmistakable approval of the academy, carrying the imprints of reputable publishing companies such as Oxford and Cambridge. What were these journals? Was this something he wanted to publish? Were they notes from a class he taught that I never registered for? I read and re-read the entry but found it hard to access. It frustrated me. It was as if he'd presented me with a riddle to steal my sleep, and what was left of my sanity.

I knew the professor to be a man of deep wisdom. Although he didn't make a show of it, it was hard to ignore the mystical sparks that occasionally burst from his electric lectures. When he talked to students about the wisdom of the ancients, there was always something that animated the discussion and made it spring alive from the stale stages of history. His students couldn't help but sense a side to him not bound by bland ritual or dogma, but energized by soulful exploration. Our dinner conversation was a powerful reminder of that. Still, I wasn't sure what to make of this. What was "audible silence"? How the hell could silence be audible? I wanted to run down the hall and argue; to rouse him from the sleep he was now denying me. But I knew better.

I gently piled the journals on the nightstand next to my bed and laid down. Staring at the wall, I watched the rhythmic revolutions of the second hand on an antique clock. I allowed the motion to hypnotize me as I listened for something in the silence of the night. All I could hear was the sound of my ears throbbing in the quiet, and the occasional mysterious noise in the wilderness outside – those detached sounds that seem to belong to nothing in particular.

"No silence is speaking to me," I mused, before drifting off to sleep.

Chapter 10

The Stain of Realization

The next morning, I awoke later than I'd expected. Stretching mightily, I attributed my well-rested feeling to the fresh air. These are the sleeps we wish would never end. Throwing back the curtains, I was greeted by the familiar view. Pines. My window looked out into a stand of trees about a hundred feet from the cabin where a path twisted into the forest. Jake and I had played many games of hide-and-seek in there, and it's where we became blood brothers. Nostalgia rained down, mixing with ideas still warm from the previous night, leaving me in a fog.

Out of the corner of my eye, I noticed Professor Singh disappearing down the path. I pulled on a pair of sweatpants and a sweater and bolted from my room. I wanted to run him down and barrage him with questions. I wanted to know about those journals. What was I supposed to do with them? How could he just leave a pile of ancient code on my bed with no method to crack it? I shot down the stairs like a cat and tore out the door toward the trees, tracking him like a wild animal.

"Good morning, Jim." He sat still on an old stump, eyes closed, in a small clearing encircled with pines – a theater that had hosted many of my life dramas. He was once again spinning the key through the fingers of his right hand.

"Good morning." I made a mighty effort to hold my breath steady. I hadn't moved that fast in years, and the pain of the sprint scared through every muscle. I feigned the carefree demeanor of a jogger out for a warm-up and pulled up a patch of dirt in front of him.

"A bit of a chill in the air today, is there not?"

"Yeah," I said absentmindedly. "But it sure beats the heat back in Phoenix."

"This is true. Orange?"

He left the key to dangle around his neck and pulled an assortment of fruit out of a sack.

"Thanks." I took the gift and tore into the rubbery-soft skin.

"Morning is one of the most powerful times of the day," he said, peeling a grapefruit in one continuous, spiraling rind. The motion was rehearsed and refined, and each finger knew its assigned task. "One should awaken each morning, greet the day with a blessing, and become mindful of the moment."

I popped a piece of fruit into my mouth. The flavor, tangy yet sweet, caught my tongue by surprise. I pulled a seed from my mouth and placed it on the ground, wondering if someday a tree might spring from the spot.

"I'm not really a morning person."

He laughed. "It's more about intention, Jim."

"But, you just said—"

"I know what I said. Extend your mind. You have to open up to the possibility of possibilities, even in language."

"Morning is morning," I mumbled.

"Perhaps, but must morning be mourning? The morning greeting – heartfelt recognition of a new day – doesn't have to go undone because you wake up late."

"Hey, I've never been late for work!"

"But have you been late for life, Jim?"

"What?"

"Time is not a reality, but an idea. Even if you arise at noon, you can wake up with the same glorious intention to greet life in joy – ever new. Morning is a concept, like good or bad. It only has the reality we ascribe to it. The moment your eyes first open is the proper time for blessings. Focus yourself on making the most of the time you have, and not on the time you've slept away." The smell of citrus enveloped us as we looked out through the thin stand of trees to a pasture beyond. A light breeze blew a renewed chill into us. "Let's walk a bit, Jim."

We munched and meandered further down the path. Professor Singh had never walked this trail, but his state of quiet contemplation and his nimble, sure-footed pace cast the illusion he'd passed this way before. He didn't fail to notice the birds or butterflies along the way. He even stopped occasionally and grabbed a handful of pine needles, rubbing them in his hand before smelling them. This is what a morning person is like, I thought.

"Professor?" He was poking his nose into the bark of a tree.

"Mmm…vanilla. The hidden secret of the pines. Yes?"

"What are those journals you left on my bed?"

"Ah, you finally asked!" He beamed like a schoolboy receiving praise from his teacher. "When you tore down the path like a leopard before, I figured that you would leap upon me with that very question in mind."

"You noticed that, huh?"

"Every bird that sailed skyward to escape the onslaught of your torrential footsteps noticed. Anyway, let's just say those journals are how I made the most of *my* time when I was a younger man."

"Professor, I—"

"Jim," he interrupted, clearly strolling the corridors of memory, "those volumes are the contents of a search over many, many years. However, they are not mine, but from the universal mind."

"The universal mind?"

"There are things seen and things unseen." He wandered a few steps away, as if he had said all he wanted to say. I was about to speak again when he grabbed the key tightly and continued. I knew better than to interject. "When I was a young student at boarding school in India, I got into much mischief. No longer confined to home, I was free to explore. One ferociously hot day I met some acquaintances by a market. Never minding the inconvenience of heat when it came to fun, we played soccer in the street. After we finished, we wandered down the sidewalk and spotted a man selling cold drinks from a pushcart.

"We were poor, our pittances spent on the necessities of education. Even the soccer ball was a found item from an obliging garbage dump. You don't truly appreciate the sport until you must inflate a ball every twenty kicks. We had precious little money for living, much less for diversions. My friends and I, ravenously thirsty, stole drinks from the man's cart. He yelled after us as we ran away, and we ducked into an alleyway. My friends escaped, but I…" He swallowed hard, as if a lump of burning coal was descending to his stomach. "I bumped into someone. Really bumped him. I fell to the ground. Though he looked like a twig that would blow over in a breeze, the man stood tall and still with a crop of white hair on his head. He merely looked at me. He was dressed in orange robes and donned a pair of well-worn sandals that I knew had seen many miles and many pilgrimages. A stout, wooden walking stick extended above his head, giving him the appearance of an oak tree supporting an orange leaf. His face was drawn in renunciation, and he looked very elderly."

"Did you hurt the guy?"

"No. That would not be possible."

"What does that mean?"

"Soon, you will see. I stared at him, not knowing what to do next. I noticed a red stain on his garments and realized it was my drink I had spilled on him. 'In a hurry, lad?' he asked. He put a withered, yet strong, hand on my collar and walked me out of the alley. An invisible force was drawing us back to the merchant. This ascetic somehow guided me to the pushcart. With a subtle motion of his head and a tweak of his bushy eyebrows, he urged me to confess to my victim. I sheepishly handed the empty cup back to the irate merchant. He was yelling at me, but the holy man put his hand up to silence him. 'Youth will thirst,' he said to the vendor. 'Let us quench it not with boiling lava to drive the pain, but with the cool, soothing elixirs of wisdom and forgiveness.' The holy man, possessing only his walking stick, offered the man a blessing in exchange for the drink I had taken. The man accepted graciously. I remember feeling embarrassed, especially because the merchant's daughter, who was my age, was standing next to him looking on with innocence and confusion."

"That must have been really hard. I'm sorry that all happened."

The professor smiled. "Don't judge the situation too quickly, Jim. The holy man led me away to a temple of the elephant god, Ganesha. We made an offering to this Lord of beginnings, remover of obstacles, and bringer of fortune and wisdom. The holy man sat in meditation while I looked on. Every time I stood to leave the temple to find my friends, the holy man pulled me back down, instructing me to sit quietly and focus on the image of this tremendous power, and to consider what Ganesha represents. This man was looking beyond the statues my friends and I ignored, fixing his gaze not on the cold stone, but the consciousness behind it. Within it. Around it. This was my first lesson in meditation. In mindful attention. Despite my attempts to escape him over the years, the elderly man became, and remained, my guru, instructing me a few days a week after school at his ashram in the city."

"I don't get it. If you didn't want him to teach you, why didn't you just stop going to see him?"

"Jim, escaping a guru isn't as easy as, say, dropping a college class if you don't like the instructor. It's not so simple to run from a living embodiment of holiness."

"I guess."

"It's true. If our soul is desperate to reach the shores of truth, it will bob a body along with the current until it washes up on its destination – no matter how much our flesh or ego resist. Truth is a force of nature. An invisible certainty. It reels us in with a relentless draw."

"Well, it sounds like he got you to where you wanted to be, Professor. You've helped a lot of students over the years."

"I appreciate that, Jim. My guru raised me up from the ashes of shame and showed me a way of wisdom. As the years progressed, I gained insight and knowledge through my meditations. Teachings came to me as a voice from somewhere in my being. A loud place with no sound. No throat. No tongue."

"The audible silence."

Professor Singh tipped his head with a broad smile. "My guru instructed me to record these teachings. I protested, telling him that was not the way I thought a person should grow and mature spiritually, and that I would rather seek stillness than a moving pen. However, he assured me that if my mental filter was strong and I found the teachings reliable, then I had a universal guru helping me from beyond this plane. And, I had an obligation to spread the messages...and live them."

"Wow! That's...I'm not sure what that is. It sounds unbelievable."

"It was. It is. But I'm sure many of the authors of those personal growth books you say you're exploring would tell you the same thing, as would some CEOs, inventors, and a host of other people out there walking their path."

"What would they tell me, exactly?"

"That we all receive guidance if we can quiet down enough to receive it. Call it a gut feeling, intuition, whatever you will. For some folks it's spiritual. For others, it isn't. We all receive sound guidance against a backdrop of still silence, whether or not we choose to hear it."

"We all have messages that come to us?"

"Exactly, Jim. Exactly."

"So, what happened with your teacher? Did he just disappear?"

"One day, my guru told me he could instruct me no more. He offered no explanation, but his word was law. I was devastated, but continued to faithfully record the knowledge, as he had instructed.

Those journals are the artifacts of that time, Jim. They record the teachings discovered in the audible silence."

A breeze blew through me, spreading goosebumps over my body. I pulled my arms in close for warmth, but the feeling did not stop. The chill warmed me, penetrating my skin and diving deep into my body. My spine prickled at the base, sending a rush of energy up to my head, and then through my extremities. I shook it off and snapped back to the moment. I didn't quite know what to say to Professor Singh. I was impressed by his honesty and willingness to share such personal memories with me. His criminal act had not led him to prison but freed him from bondage. His transgression became a method of instruction.

"What should I do with the journals?" I asked.

"Whatever you think is necessary. Read them. Ignore them. Cast them aside." He walked back to the trees and examined them again.

"There's a blank journal. What is that for?"

He pulled his nose from another vanilla-scented tree and looked directly into me. "That is for you."

Chapter 11

Beingness

Minutes passed. The sun rose higher. The trees swayed, then stilled. Professor Singh seemed lost in thought, and I was not sure how to process all of this. I felt like a new driver. There was a destination, I was sure, but I had no idea how to work the pedals to get there.

When we reached the end of the path, a wide meadow stretched out before us, running green and pristine into a stand of pines. Professor Singh took in a breath so big, I swore he could smell the other side. Instead of the beauty, I focused on my grumbling stomach. The orange and inspiration were wearing off, and I drifted into delicious thoughts of a hot breakfast.

"Forget about everything else for a minute," he said, reading my mind. "Take a look around. What do you see?"

"Well," I ventured, thinking more about the eggs in the refrigerator than the scenery, "I see grass and trees."

"Yes, yes. I see that, too. What else?"

"Dirt, birds…I donno. What am I supposed to see?"

"Life!" he bellowed. I got the feeling I'd lost him at dirt. "It's life being itself. It's one great expression. Nothing else exists here. It all springs forth anew, each moment."

"It springs anew each moment?" I still couldn't hop on board his train. "Professor, this scene has been here for years. I've had picnics up here with the Davis family. I've seen this before."

"Perhaps," he said. "But have you ever really seen it? Or has it just been the backdrop to something else you were doing?"

"What?"

"You heard me, Jim. Has there ever been a time when you've just gazed at a scene and appreciated it for what it is?"

"Sure. I used to come up here to clear my mind. To think."

"Thinking, thinking…" he muttered. "How can a person clear his mind and think at the same time? That would be quite impossible. Like peeling two oranges at once. It cannot be done, I say!" He gazed into the sea of grass, then set his eyes to the ground at our feet. He adjusted the chain of beads around his neck. I shifted the weight on my aching legs, fighting the urge to sit. "A person must be patient and allow the mind time to settle. Time to stop. Do you ever consider the concept of time, Jim?"

"Sometimes. After our conversation last night, I thought about my life and how I was living it. Or, more honestly, wasting it. I've been struggling with my future and trying to make a plan of some kind." I looked at him with a faint hope. "That's time, isn't it?"

"That way of seeing time is for the long stretches of daily life. However, I'm speaking about the beingness of time, not so much its usefulness for planning activities. Each second has a life of its own…a life waiting to be noticed and appreciated. Are you familiar with the concept of 'living in the moment,' Jim?"

"I've heard about it. It keeps showing up on social media and bumper stickers. That's the whole be in the now thing. Mindfulness, right? Been around since ancient times."

"Yes, this is the concept. The idea, as you say, has been around for ages. It didn't spring to life on a bookstore bestseller list, as much as people seem to think it did. The Sufi poet Mahmud Shabistari said, 'The past has flown away, and the coming month and year do not exist. Ours only is the present's tiny dot.' That tiny dot has also been translated as the pinprick of a moment. The pinprick, Jim. Do you realize that right now there are no problems?"

"Have you read the newspaper lately?"

"My nose isn't buried in a newspaper this morning. I'm talking about this moment right now. It is here, anew, and everything else only has existence in your mind. Life gives the appearance of a sequence of interrelated events to either regret or anticipate, but they all really boil down to this." He snapped his fingers at the right side of his face.

As I looked around, straining to see an effortless moment, I found this concept hard to believe. I had studied cognitive states and consciousness in my philosophy and psychology courses, but not like this. I knew about mindfulness from work, Doctor Eastman, and my comparative religion training, but only as part of larger systems of spiritual and religious dogma or as a clinical exercise on a treatment plan. But I couldn't really see how any of it applied to me. I had a broken relationship I was struggling to understand. I was a grown man trying to figure out what in God's name I was going to do with the rest of my life – or even if I wanted to keep the life I had – and the professor was telling me there were no problems in the moment. What did he know about it?

"I guess," I said. Projecting those other thoughts into the open somehow didn't seem appropriate.

A faint smile and delicate sigh softened his already gentle demeanor in what seemed a deeper acceptance of my ignorance. "Jim, there is a perception of life that makes us think we should be moving onward towards a goal."

"Shouldn't we?"

"Maybe. But goals are simply points in infinity beyond which we cannot see the horizon. We set up cycles of expectation and mark the calendar. Life passes us by while we're busy living. However, life is this moment, Jim. Thoughts of coming and going do not reflect reality. They are distractions. When we come upon a scene like this meadow here, or even when we are sitting in traffic, we must strive to be, as the Buddha would say, mindful. We must pay notice to our thoughts and emotions in the moment, without judging them, so that we can handle situations not for what they will become or what they were, but for what they are now. After all, a thing or a situation can only be what it is now. It cannot be the myriad other ways we want it to be or, for that matter, do not want it to be."

"So, we should ignore the issues and problems we have in life? My career stress and issues with Maya consume me. Crush me at times. I almost gave my life to them. My clients suffer. They're struggling. Folks on the news live in pain. Some in horror. Is all of that nothing?"

He shook his head, then regarded me with a smile. "Jim, I'm not saying life doesn't have problems. I'm simply saying regretting the past or fearing the future causes deep distress and distraction. It causes you to miss what's in front of you. If you gaze at the beauty here," he swept his hand across the entirety of the landscape, "but are consumed by the smoke of time and worry, you will see nothing."

"You're wearing a watch!" I pointed to his wrist like a five-year-old child relishing a victory over an adult. "You have commitments. Don't you worry about being on time?"

"Indeed. As a responsible human, we ought to conform to standards of decency, and punctuality is one of those standards."

"Well, then I guess I don't understand."

"Humans created time," he continued, unperturbed. "I know this shocks your ego, but it's true. There was most certainly a time when things happened as they happened, without the benefit of calendars and stopwatches. Eons of terra displacement and deposit did not rely upon measuring instruments. At one time, it was necessary to do things in daylight, and not during work hours – which now can stretch interminably. The necessity of timing things numerically on the wrist is quite recent, evolutionarily speaking. The planet itself revolves around cycles, Jim. Trees grow, flowers bloom, and life emerges and passes away according to the rhythms of nature. Long before geologists measured erosion, sands flew from the mountaintops. Imposing numbers and dates upon the seasons is comforting to the human mind, and often necessary in the business of human endeavors. Thus, calendars were created."

"But professor, cycles of seasons and flowers blooming are *time*. What else could they be?"

He bent low and plucked a delicate wildflower bud, taking care not to disturb more than he needed for illustration.

"They're *timing*, Jim."

"Clever wordplay, Professor."

"No. There's a difference. To see it, we must divorce ourselves from commonplace definitions. Time, with accompanying emotions, in terms of worry about something that has not happened yet or regret about things already in the past, does not seem to exist in the natural world, apart from humanity. I'm no biologist, but I'm probably safe to make that assumption." He twirled the wildflower with a delicate motion. "Timing means that when it is the moment for a blossom, it simply occurs. A bud sits patiently as a bud until it is gently coaxed into action by the rhythms of life. It does not consult a calendar or suffer performance anxiety. It meets its potential in its place, under the conditions it has. Humans alone feel the need to regret and anticipate. I have never known a carnivore to regret a meal. Prey grazes and pricks its ears at a sign of danger. Yes, some animals gather nuts, station lookouts, and such like that, but I don't see them pulling out day planners or entering lookout duty or nut gathering into a calendar. Nature progresses in natural rhythm, with tasks done when their moment arrives. Humans, on the other hand, adapt the environs to suit their needs on an imposed schedule, and this carries over to the part of us that should flow naturally."

"I think I need some toast before I can take this all in. I'm still stuck on flowers with performance anxiety."

He grinned and pushed on. "Forget the time of breakfast and consume this idea: Instead of blossoming naturally, people regret not blooming earlier, or, perhaps, they fear they may not bloom. In the meantime, the allotted moments in this world – the garden strolls of life – become journeys of peril and fear. Remember the locker rooms of your early school days?"

"Don't remind me."

"Some boys had a way of making other boys feel inadequate if their bodies were not on the same schedule. This leads to feelings of inadequacy instead of an appreciation of our potential right now. I don't think the girls' locker room fared much better for many."

"I suppose. I can't say I'd know for sure!"

"Let us return to the house." He handed me the flower. "Give this bud time to open."

Chapter 12

Live Blissfully in Both Worlds

I twirled the flower between my thumb and middle finger as we wandered homeward. The professor pointed out wildlife and plants along the trail, but I was lost in the maze of my mind and didn't feel much like talking. Despite my efforts to stay focused on the walk, my thoughts floated to Maya and the crumbled ruins of my engagement.

I started a conversation in my head about all the things she never understood about me and what I thought I deserved from her. In one of my darkest periods of depression, on a road trip to the Grand Canyon, I had a vulnerable and authentic moment with her and mentioned my thoughts of suicide. It scared her, and she shut down for the rest of the trip, seemingly indifferent to how much those thoughts scared me, too. She refused to discuss it and stonewalled the conversation. That sent a powerful message to me that I couldn't talk to her about things that really mattered; things I really struggled with. I felt she wasn't a safe person except when things were good between us. Now, on this trail, years separated from that moment, my blood still boiled as I convinced myself that she didn't care about me when I needed her most.

But then I practiced what Professor Singh had talked about. I brought the musing to the moment and shifted my thoughts. I tried to see the situation from Maya's point of view instead of indulging my own ego. How would I feel if someone I loved suddenly admitted to me that they were thinking of killing themselves? My eyes widened and a cloud lifted from my mind as I glided down the trail behind the professor. I realized that if someone I love had admitted that to me, I'd be afraid of losing them, and it might make me distant. Angry. Frustrated. All the things Maya must have felt. I'd be afraid of abandonment. I'd feel that I was somehow failing them in my support or that my love wasn't enough. It would probably bruise my ego.

Suddenly, it made sense. The truth hit me square. The strange goosebumps and spine tingle returned with vigor as my brain cracked open and a yolk of insight dropped out. Maybe the relationship didn't fail because I was wrong or broken. Maya wasn't wrong or broken, either. Maybe we failed as life partners because we both knew, deep down, that we couldn't truly be partners to one another. We both had toyed with that idea. Others saw it and mentioned it. It had come up in conversations and her letter, but now it had light behind it. Clarity. Maybe Maya wasn't being selfish on that trip, but totally, utterly, authentic. Maybe I needed to be the one to understand. Through that lens, I realized we were both absolutely where we needed to be in the moment.

Before I could formulate this to share with Professor Singh, the cabin appeared through the trees. I once again drew the veil across my consciousness and replaced the insight with thoughts of a proper breakfast. We headed straight for the kitchen and sorted through the remaining groceries, resolving to head back to the general store later in the day.

We cooked and ate breakfast in relative silence, letting our chewing speak for us. After finishing our eggs, curried potatoes, and toast, the professor disappeared into his room. I headed to mine and closed the door. I opened the window for some fresh air and laid down in bed. A silent breeze tickled the feathery curtains as it entered the room. I tried to nap, but my mind was once again consumed with thoughts and worries, even with nature's peace around me. Again, I had no idea where the unease was coming from, and it frustrated me. The inability to find peace in paradise had always been my nature. Dad once told me I could find a problem in Eden. I knew he was right about that. I always knew. I worried incessantly, and usually wound up with an upset stomach. Or worse. Again, Maya drifted into my mind, and I thanked her a thousand times for putting up with me for as long as she did. I chuckled and realized she had been my partner, but also my prisoner.

Between the morning walk, the conversation, and my inability to relax, I was exhausted. I needed an escape. I grabbed the stack of journals and leafed through them. I came across an entry entitled, 'Time.'

"No way," I whispered. I gave in to the coincidence and read the entry.

How long is life? Minutes? Years? No. It is infinite. But even infinity is limited by word and thought. To conceive of endless time, one must accept the irony of using words and thoughts with ends. A Buddhist or Hindu might refer to time in kalpas – long eons of existence. Earth, life, and the potential for earth and life have been here for the longest eons. Time before time. What is the nature of this ambiguous measuring stick called time? Some may say, "Surely, time exists and is encompassed by the clock on my wall or the watch on my wrist. Simple." But are these not man-made expressions of a human concept? Humanity, in the creation of minutes, hours, days, months, and years attempts to fence in the source of all things, as if the artificial creation of calendar days causes reality. Cycles of the seasons, crops, growth, and evolution are on a timetable set in motion by the universal source. Humanity, in its quest to quantify what cannot be quantified, seeks to measure feats in temporal increments. Clocks and calendars, however, are all empty vessels. Watch hands grasp nothing but human flesh. It is the creative source that measures. And this is beyond concept. All things that appear and fade away are the whim of the source. Things are to be appreciated in the moment they arise and witnessed as they fade away into the vast ocean of infinity.

My gaze drifted to the open window and I again considered the idea that we reduce the natural, unbreakable flow of life to discrete moments or definitions. But was time really of no essence? How could this be true? My inner skeptic pressed on with the questions from the meadow a few hours earlier.

"What about day-to-day living?" I asked the ceiling, as if the answers were above me. "I can't call in to work sick, telling my boss that time is unimportant. I'd get fired and lose my salary and benefits. Why pay attention to the moment if it could ruin the rest of my life? Doesn't time mean anything?" The next part of the entry provided the answer:

> In the course of practical living, humans need temporal pegs to pin down life. Children are born, school begins, and appointments come and go. Humans depend on conceptions of time to keep within imposed patterns of living. Unless one is an ascetic in a cave or isolated monastery, human time will be important. However, we must not forget we are also part of the infinite consciousness, and therefore, beyond measure. No clock can face us, and no calendar can mark us. Although bound to the apparent realities of time in one way, in another, we participate in unbound celestial clockwork. We will return again and again and again until we have accomplished ourselves. Therefore, in the eye of the creator, we have all the time in the universe – time to meet a partner, raise children, work, die, be reborn. Time to exist. We are in time and we transcend time. We are in the limited world of responsibility, yet part of unlimited consciousness. We existed then as we exist in this moment and will exist in the future. So, what is our hurry? Appreciate this moment simply for what it is, without judgment or evaluation, and live blissfully in both worlds, through your human and divine natures.

I stared into the dusty, ornate mirror above the antique dresser across from my bed and addressed my reflection. "Holy crap! We have no time, but all the time we want." My mind raced. I fell back on the pillows. "Problems don't come from the concepts of time others stick on me, but from the concept of time I've stuck on myself."

I turned these scattered thoughts over in my head. I felt like I was grasping the idea, but I wasn't sure. In a state of mild confusion, my unsettled ego and I creaked our way down the hall. I knocked on the closed door.

"Enter," came the soft voice. I pushed the door gently to discover Professor Singh sitting in the cross-legged lotus position on the bed, atop one of Mrs. Davis's clownishly colorful quilts. He looked like a tree growing through the hole in a painter's palette. This was his daily meditation.

"Professor? Sorry to bother you. I had a question."

"Only one?"

Chapter 13

The Chain of Time

I walked in, unsure of what I wanted to ask, but sure of my insecurity. My feet sometimes carry me further than my brain.

"Professor, I read the entry on time in your journal, and I think I understand what you're saying, but—"

"It's not really 'me' saying it," he said.

"Well, I just wanted to talk to you about it."

"Please." He extended his hand to the corner of the room where an old wicker rocking chair sat. It had a red, puffy cushion festooned with hens and roosters. "Why don't you sit down?"

I took a seat across from his bed but did not rock. The antique latticework creaked and stretched below my weight.

"Are you saying time is and is not real?" I asked.

"That's my protégé. Right to the heart of the matter!" Right on cue, he took up his necklace and rubbed the key. "As I suggested this morning, the idea of being present in the moment, or mindful, is not new. Authors, seers, and saints both ancient and recent have made that plain. The concept is quite simple to grasp intellectually, but it is one of the most difficult spiritual principles to put into practice. I think you can see how important the time paradox is from a narrow standpoint, but you are not seeing it from a larger viewpoint."

"How much larger can it get? Every time I try to wrap my mind around this stuff, the thought balloon gets bigger and bigger and I can't quite grasp it. My arms aren't long enough. It's like life chains me to my old ways of thinking. No matter how hard I try to focus on a moment in time, I feel like I'm being pulled in a thousand directions."

"That's an interesting metaphor you use."

"What...balloons?"

"No. The chain. This is intriguing...the thought of life being like chain." He pushed his lips to the side, cocked his head, and regarded the pause before squaring himself to the conversation again. "But I do not think that life is merely a cold, unfeeling iron chain binding us to the past or pulling us into the future. At least, not as we commonly think of it."

"Well, what is it?"

"Tell me yourself. Actually, before you do, let's honor our commitment to go to the general store. We resolved to go earlier, but never did. Let's again put on our walking shoes, stroll, and talk. Are you up for that?"

"Sure," I said. "A good breakfast was all I needed. But I'm not disturbing your meditation time, am I?"

"Jim, the time to meditate is when we meditate."

We went downstairs and got our shoes on, then exited the cabin and headed to the main road. We turned right at the bottom of the driveway and started our journey to the store.

"I interrupted us before, Jim. Let's continue our discussion. I suggested life was not simply a cold, iron chain pulling us around, and then you asked what life really is. Let's find the answer in yet another question: Can you describe the properties of a chain for me?"

I pondered the question but could only create a basic picture in my mind. I kicked a stone down the road and watched it tumble into the ditch.

"I'm not sure I can give you much detail, Professor. Isn't a chain just links of metal?"

"It can be."

"But you said not to see an iron chain."

"No, I didn't say that, exactly."

"But you—"

"What is the shape of the chain in your mind's eye? What else is happening? Be descriptive, Jim. Engage all of your senses to create an image. In that way, these concepts won't be idle. They will spring to life and dance in your mind."

"Okay. I'll try. I guess I feel hardness. Solidity."

"Yes, Jim. This is a good start. What else?"

"I see the silvery links interweaving."

"Good. Very good."

"I hear the strong clink of the pieces as they're tested by someone pulling on them. The oval pieces interlock like a team on a mission to resist the force. I can smell the iron on my fingers as I pull. Each part connects to the other."

"Fantastic, Jim! And what does that do?"

"The progression of pieces creates reinforcement. Strength."

"Anything else?"

"Not really. It's a chain. It's just simple and useful."

"Elegant, is it not?"

"I guess. But what else is there?"

"Space, Jim."

"Space?"

"The oval pieces surround open space."

"I guess I never thought about that before. But so what?"

"So what? So it's the answer to your question!"

"How?"

A truck came up from behind and we stepped to the side of the road. As it passed, we both waved at the driver who smiled and waved back. After it disappeared, the professor continued.

"This is what life is like, Jim. The hard, oval pieces of the chain-link are moments in everyday, solid time. This is much like our bodies in the material world. Naturally, solid links come to a person's mind when one is asked to describe a chain."

"Oh, good!" I said. "So, I'm batting the average with this stuff, then?"

"Yes. That's a good place to be. We all choose to describe solidity over space."

"Why?"

"It honors what we believe to be true about ourselves and our lives. When someone asks us about our day, they want to know about performance and production. Measurables. Deliverables. In other words, how we used our time, made our money, or completed our tasks. They want us to describe the events of the day that chained us to ordinary, solid consciousness. The round form of the link reminds us that we participate in these cycles of manifested, material life."

"So, what's the space?"

"The open space each oval piece surrounds is our fluid life-breath. Our spirit, so to speak. Solidity frames the open space, yes, but the air freely weaves in and out of the solid, material imposition. Stop." We froze, staring at each other.

"Professor—"

"Listen."

A swell of wind came from behind us and rushed through the pines lining the road. It sounded like a great, bellowing outbreath of a giant, and it struck us in waves of refreshing cool.

"It's like that, Jim. Trees and pine needles frame our solid view, but the wind that permeates the spaces creates the true joy. Do you feel it in this moment? Do you see it in your mind's eye?"

I closed my eyes and envisioned the wind as a wave wending through the trees above. "I can, Professor. Now that you mention it."

"And so it is with iron, Jim. And trees. And us! The frame of iron cannot bind air, as tree cannot bind wind, as body cannot bind spirit. Ordinary time, then, in its useful aspect, means that each solid moment of our day reinforces the others, creating strength in the whole enterprise, giving the appearance of living a solid, strong life. Time is a humble servant, helping us through the day – creating a space and placeholder to work, go to our child's school plays, take our beloved on dates, and travel to distant places for enjoyment and relaxation. Meanwhile, the energy of our true being plays and moves throughout the imposed structures on its eternal journey, unbounded. It transcends material time and does what it needs to do as well, according to its own schedule. It provides our sense of intuition and guides us as we move along through the daily rounds of life. Both are important."

"Okay." My brow crinkled, reducing my eyes to slits. I picked up a stick from the side of the road and traced a circle in the dirt with a dot in the middle. "But doesn't that put us back where we were? Isn't that like being in a prison cell and appreciating each bar that holds us in?"

"In a way, yes, but only in the very narrowest sense. Although we're not often concerned with it, life is as much about noticing the open spaces in the links as it is being aware of the links themselves." He took the stick from my hand and traced squiggly lines through the center of my circle. "But once we grasp both concepts, this can be magical. Liberating. The miracle of a material day is not contained only in its hard twists and turns, but also how we draw smooth breath each second in the midst of it. Spirit and breath are present in the material moment, but not bound to it. What cannot be chained cannot be contained. This is the un-witnessed miracle, Jim. We think we are bound, when part of us – a very important part – is quite free. We only know the joy of freedom through the appreciation of each metallic moment...the illusion of bondage."

"Illusion?" I laughed at his seemingly careless casting-aside of concrete realities. "Professor, it's a chain! Isn't that real? Isn't that binding? How can you dismiss the body so easily? Aren't we bound to it?"

"I'm not dismissing it. You're right. In one sense, we are bound to our bodies. Chained to them. But it is not a malevolent reality. You know stories about gurus or monks who appear to deny or denigrate the body, but that's not exactly accurate. What you're hearing are stories of people who have acknowledged the truest reality of the body and transcended it."

"Some of those stories creep me out. People putting swords through their skin or vowing to stand upright until they get a sign from their dead spiritual teachers. But what does that prove? If people abuse their bodies, what does that teach us?"

"You take the lesson from it that you need, Jim. Both the body and the spirit are real and necessary. Where they differ is their function."

"Their function?"

"Yes. The body is our transient vehicle, carrying us through sensory experience. We can paint it, change the tires, clean it when it gets dirty. Yet, we have a consciousness that can transcend the material enterprise. We have the unique ability to experience each material moment in its apparent reality, while also being aware of the vitality of the life force that exists despite the world's seemingly binding nature. The body moves us, but it cannot ever really contain us. Think about the truck that passed us a few minutes ago. It was free to stop or to drive – with a driver, of course. But the point is, humans are that way, too. We don't always have to be in motion. We can, if we so choose, pull over to the side of the road, get out, and take in the scenery in this moment. We can even steer the body where we want it to go when we get back in. We are surrounded by solidity, but journey with fluidity."

"I guess that makes sense. Like you said before, iron can't contain the air. And I guess Jake's cabin gets a cold draft in the winter, even though the walls and windows are solid. Although, that could just be because the place is so old."

"Maybe, Jim. Maybe. But you see? The solidity helps us appreciate the fluidity."

"Okay. So you're saying we are in the body, but not only of the body?" I pulled the skin up from my arm and let it snap back into place.

"Yes."

"And we can be in touch with both the body in ordinary time and the spirit or energy or whatever the heck it is, as it moves along according to a separate clock, right?"

"Right – a clock that marks ordinary time, but also transcends it."

"Simple metaphors get complicated quickly, don't they, Professor?"

He laughed. "Absolutely. Humans are masters at that."

"It's weird. As wild as this all is, it's also kind of familiar."

"That's no surprise, Jim. Many religions and spiritual teachers present this idea but paint it with different brushstrokes. But in our example from the material world, each oval has its own space that must be appreciated as it is. Of course, no metaphor is perfect, Jim, but I cannot stress the point enough. Stop walking. Look at me." We halted again, and I gave him my full attention. "When we spend our time only in the solid, limited picture, we may become depressed because we perceive that we are chained to a past we cannot change. Or, we may be overcome with anxiety because we feel a pull toward a future that has not arrived. From this perception, we miss this place. Right here. Right now. This link, if you will. We miss the moment as it is, and all the possibilities contained herein. Do you understand?"

"I do, Professor. I do."

"Good." We walked on. The tingling sensation from the base of my spine once again crept up through my body. I focused on it and kept my pace to a slow, methodical trudge. "Jim, how many times have we lost the feeling of noon because we were busy regretting 11:59 or anticipating 12:01?"

"How many times? All the time!" We shared a laugh.

"Exactly. It really does little good to be alive if we are busy looking back or craning our necks to see ahead, and not engaging in the business of being here. It is akin to sitting down to a piping hot holiday meal, concerning ourselves with the argument we had over the stove with a loved one or the leftovers we won't be able to fit into the refrigerator, before we've enjoyed the supper. Yearning for or regretting the past, or fearing the future, is as useless as attempting to bottle light for a dark day."

I knew he was right, but I needed a minute to process. I turned my attention again to the pines towering above. My gaze relaxed, and the solidity of the trees swaying carelessly in the breeze yielded to a soft wave. I thought about things and people that caused me worry. All the dates on the calendar I dreaded that passed without incident. All the things from the past that haunted me at night that I couldn't change. Was I too bound to all of this? Near the end of our relationship, Maya would ask, "Where are you, Jim? Why are you so distant?" Now I knew. And, I now knew where I wasn't. I wasn't present. At times, I felt I really enjoyed the life my vehicle took me through, but did I pay enough attention to what was going on in between the solidity?

◆ ◆ ◆

We wandered into town to the general store. We entered to find Hiram at his place behind the register, tying flies. He tipped his head in greeting, asked if we needed any help, then put his attention back to the task of tying. We picked out bread, vegetables, eggs, and fruit from the meager choices available. Hiram rang up the total and, after a brief but friendly argument with Professor Singh, I handed over the cash. After we had our change, Hiram returned to tying his flies and we exited the store. I swung the door open and then grabbed it with my free hand as it narrowly missed hitting Mo, who was standing on the sidewalk with Beary in front of his face.

"Hello, young man," I said. I looked around for Liv, wondering if Mo had wandered off. "Is your mommy around?" He shook his head yes. "Is she coming to get you?" Mo shrugged his shoulders. "Do you want us to wait with you?" Mo smiled and nodded yes. I looked back into the general store and caught Hiram's eye through the screen door. A faint smile crossed Hiram's lips, and he nodded to me before returning to tying flies. "It's Mo, right?" I asked. Mo beamed and held out Beary's hand for me to shake. "It's nice to meet you, Mo…and is this Beary?" Mo nodded again. "Well, Mo and Beary, I'm Jim and this is my friend Professor Singh."

The professor offered his hand to Beary. "It's nice to meet you both," he said. Mo motioned for me to follow him. I exchanged glances with Professor Singh, who took the bags. "Go on ahead, Jim. I'll catch up."

Mo led me down the wood-planked sidewalk to a picnic table where two toy cars sat. He picked one up and started moving it back and forth across the faded wood planks in the table. He made whooshing and zooming sounds to make the car race and crash. He pointed at the other car.

"Aha! You want to race, huh?" Mo nodded. "Well, I have to warn you, I was a pretty good racer in my day."

I picked up the car and rolled it across the table. Mo mimicked my actions, and soon, toy cars were screeching and careening all over the table. Mo squealed with laughter as I pretended that I was part of the crash, then he gave me a thumbs down when I beat him in a race and pretended to cheer for myself.

"I haven't heard that laugh in a while." Liv's voice caught my attention, and I turned to see her standing at my shoulder. The headscarf was tied tight on her head. The crystal hung from the chain around her neck.

"Oh! Hi! I...Mo and I were just...well...I'm sure you saw."

"I did." She smirked. "But I know better than to break up roughhousing. Ready, Mo?" Mo gathered the cars and took Liv's hand.

"I'm Jim, by the way. I heard you call him 'Mo' the other day, so..."

She sized me up before thrusting a hand at me. I took it and kept eye contact as we shook. Her hand was softer than I expected, and her cool touch complimented my warm hand.

"Olivia. Well, Liv. I saw you in the store that day, so it's all good."

"I'm staying at my friend's place up the way," I said. "122."

"The Davis place?"

"Yeah. How did you know?"

"Jim," she said with a roll of her eyes, "in this town you can say any set of numbers, and I can tell you who lives there. Just one of the joys of small-town life."

"Right." We shared a smile.

"Mrs. Davis here? I thought they weren't coming in this summer."

"They aren't. I mean, they might be. Jake might be. I'm just staying there for a few weeks. I'm actually here with——"

"Arjun Singh." The professor walked up behind me. "It's nice to meet you."

"Hi, Arjun. I'm Liv. Just collecting Mo here. We're up on the ridge back there. Taking care of my momma. Isn't that right, Mo?" Mo nodded and smiled. "She needs a man around, so Mo fits the bill just fine."

"Is it alright with you if he has this, Liv?" The professor held up a new toy car from the general store, and Mo's eyes got as big as saucers.

"Fine with me," she said. The Professor handed the car to Mo who took it with a smile. "But you better watch out, Arjun. You may have a friend for life."

"Friends and toy cars are things we can never have too many of," the professor said.

We exchanged our goodbyes, and Professor Singh and I watched them run across the street. Mo turned back and waved, and we headed for the cabin again.

"She seems nice," the professor said.

"Yeah," I said. "She does."

Chapter 14

Monsters, Ghosts, and Meditation

Afuter contemplating space versus solidity on the walk back to the cabin, we sorted the groceries on the counter and prepared a light lunch. As I ate, I pondered chain and space. The ideas were still fuzzy, and I began to feel like a train was leaving the station without me. I peeled a banana and decided to clarify some things.

"Professor?"

"Mmm?" He was working the sticker off a bright red apple with his index finger.

"This whole thing about time and moments."

"Yes?" He crossed his arms and bit into the apple.

"I want to be present in the moment. I do. I think that might really help me."

"I'm glad, Jim."

"Religious devotees have been trying to be present for centuries."

"The have."

"And, to be honest, a lot of what you're saying is stuff Doctor Eastman's mentioned and stuff we offer clients where I work – mindfulness-based therapies and things like that."

"That's good to hear."

"Yeah, and to experience both the link and the space – I think I'm sort of getting it. I've even tried to meditate a little bit back home. But when I sit down to do it, I can't stop my mind from drifting to other moments or distractions. I can't stop the pull. It's all too...solid."

"You have just identified the busy intersection between solidity and space on the road to peace."

"I sense a crash looming."

"Only if you are distracted."

"Well, see, that's the thing. I'm distracted a lot."

We worked on our fruit and stared into space. When I laid my banana peel on the table, he set his apple core in front of him – still and upright, in perfect balance.

"Let's go upstairs," he said. "I think the time to meditate is once more upon us."

We headed up to his room and settled in. He got back into his twisted position on the bed, and I took up my spot on the rickety wicker chair in the corner. The lattice again stretched and creaked in protest, reminding me it was as old as the house. Or older. After a tense negotiation between my rear end and the seat, I settled in.

"Before we begin, Jim, do you grasp that the root of much dissatisfaction is being out of touch with the present moment?"

"Yes."

"And are you sensing that the biggest obstacle to getting back into the present is thinking too much or planning too much?"

"I do. But how do you keep thoughts from disturbing you? I remember the videos you'd show in class of Buddhist monks in meditation, and I know meditation helps calm the mind, but how do you get distractions out of the moment? How can holy men sit so calmly for so long? How is it possible to accept limits and appreciate the limitless at the same time? How do you keep the links from tightening and pulling you away from right here?"

"Ah, you ask the toughest questions."

"Do I win a prize for that?"

"No."

"Darn."

"Letting links go limp instead of being drawn tight is one of the meditator's goals, Jim. Unfortunately, quieting the thinking mind seems to make about as much sense as keeping a mouse from cheese."

"Exactly!" I pounded my thigh with my fist. "Aren't we supposed to think with the mind?"

"Well, yes and no. A person may resist meditation because it seems to take him away from instinctual thinking. Most people spend their days lost in thought, so meditation seems counterintuitive. After all, the mind was made, in part, for thinking, as you say. Even when we're trying to avoid them, thoughts can be little ghosts that descend upon us, chasing us from our paths to peace. However, you were quiet of mind before you were full of ideas. The latter came later through conditioning and sense perception over the years. Our true resting state is silence and stillness."

"But we need our thoughts, chain or not!"

"We do need to think."

"It's how we make our living, isn't it?"

"Indeed. Much creativity and progress happen through the crowded, twisty avenues of thought. However, the thinking to which I refer is the more devilish side of mentation – the side that causes expectation, fear, regret, over-excitement, despair, panic."

"Watch it. Those are my friends you're talking about."

"Those phantoms have their roots in ordinary thought. The phantoms, in turn, frighten us from the moment, causing us to put our attention on things that have no reality."

"Doctor Eastman told me that about my anxiety…not in those words, exactly, but the same idea."

"I'm sure. You might find that as you meditate, these devils link a thought to you, and before you know it you are pulled down an aimless path."

"No kidding! That seems to be the only meditative experience I have."

"Jim, when you were young, did you think there were ghosts in your closet?"

"Sure. All kids do."

"How did you rid yourself of this fear?"

"Mom did. She looked in the closet for me."

"Really? It was through her efforts? She checked, gave the all-clear, and that solved the problem for you?"

"Not exactly."

"What did?"

"She made me get out of bed and look in the closet. There was nothing in there but clothes and stinky shoes. I guess when I saw that, I moved on to other problems, like what was hiding under my bed."

"So, you had a fear that seemed natural to you."

"Sure."

"'Of course I have ghosts in here,' young Jim said before his mini-enlightenment through investigation. Why? Because the darkness of your closet in the darkness of your room was the natural place for ghosts to be, or so you always thought. But once your own efforts proved the ghost-in-the-closet hypothesis false, you slept peacefully."

"I did."

"Jim, when you sit down to meditate, your aim is that resting state of peace. A guru can instruct you and tell you there is nothing of scary substance in the closets of the mind, but it is only through your own efforts and investigation that you can satisfy yourself of the truth. When a false thought disturbs you, and you begin to think it is reality, tell yourself it is a ghost, keeping you from your peaceful state and inducing fear. To remind yourself there are no phantoms in the closet, simply open the closet and see for yourself."

"How?"

"Gently redirect your perception to sitting peacefully in a room in this moment and remind yourself you're not truly experiencing the thing you are regretting or anticipating. Be mindful that the current distraction is a baseless overlay on an already peaceful moment, and bring your attention – your awareness – back to right now. Notice your thoughts and let them blow easily across your mind like feathers in the wind. Distracting thoughts are phantasms of no reality. What is real is what's here. This moment. Remember, you are both solid and beyond solidity."

"The trouble is remembering that. Staying centered in that."

"Maybe the trouble is believing there's something else you need to be doing, Jim."

"How do you mean?"

"Remember our trip to the general store before? Did you notice the man behind the counter as we walked in?"

"Hiram? Sure."

"What was he doing?"

"Tying flies. Every time I see him, he's doing that."

"Right. When we walked in, he stopped tying those flies, gave us his full attention, and greeted us. He asked us if we needed help. He was fully attentive to his job."

"I guess that's true."

"And when we politely declined his offer, what did he do?"

"Well, I guess he went back to tying flies."

"And when we approached the counter to pay for our groceries?"

"He gave us his full attention again."

Professor Singh sat stone still, save for a fleeting smile. As he waited, I pondered, then slowly came to another realization.

"And Mo," I said.

"What about him?"

"We were playing. He was absorbed in it. It was fun. We were happy. We didn't even notice Liv coming up behind us."

"Total immersion in a moment, correct?"

"Huh. I guess so, Professor. I guess so. But okay. How do I translate that mindfulness or immersion stuff into a meditation session? Grocery shopping and playing with toy cars is one thing. But meditating...isn't that something different?"

"Not really. The key to transferring mindfulness to meditation is the breath. You should be conscious of your breath when you meditate, Jim. Your breath is here, now. Breath is the basic building block of your continued existence in the body. It is the only thing you know for certain is happening, otherwise you would not be here."

"I can't argue with that."

"There is nothing hiding in the closet of the mind, Jim. There is nothing that can pull you away from the moment. There is only breath and peace."

Chapter 15

Lemons and Letting Go

I asked if he wanted a glass of water. I needed an excuse to move. To think. To give my thoughts time to rest. He declined.

I filled a paper cup in the bathroom with cold water and tried to focus on the splash of the liquid in the container. I drank it down and consciously traced the chill into my stomach. Unlike the dirt-tasting water back home, I had no fear of the tap water up here. It was clean and crisp, with no filters. I watched my hand slowly crinkle the cup, then I tossed it over the toilet to the metal trashcan. My aim was off, and instead, it careened off the wooden toilet paper holder sporting a hand-painted, lime green duck face. I bent low to pick up the trash and dropped it in the can where it bounced around with a hollow thud.

I groaned as I stood upright again and dug my hand into a sore spot in my lower back. I took in my reflection in the mirror, revisiting the wrinkles. The lines. The parts of me that had given in to age and a tinge of indifference. But unlike the scene in my apartment a few days earlier, this time I didn't feel anger or panic welling up. Instead, I simply took myself in. I imagined who I would be if I were peaceful. Present. Who I would be if I wasn't so convinced of who I was in moments of solidity.

Upon reflection, I couldn't say that I had ever felt sustained peace. I was a nervous kid. A sad college student. An anxious guy. In fact, I often shared the news with others when I felt good, as it was something so out of the ordinary. I wondered how others managed to get through their life difficulties without being totally consumed by them. Things that made me want to end my life were, to others, just another obstacle to overcome or a chance to say 'whatever.' How would my life be different if calm was my new normal and the uncomfortable stuff was just one part of my life in motion? Was it possible? Would Maya and I still be together? I smirked at the idea and my image in the mirror, now standing in the realization that so much about how I was dictated who I was and where I was in life, and that so much of my isolation wasn't because people left, but because maybe, just maybe, I drove them away.

When I returned to the bedroom, I was still bothered. Chains and ghosts? Every metaphor was uncomfortable. I stood at the side of the bed with my arms crossed, staring up at the ceiling.

"Okay," I huffed. "So, there's only peace?"

"Eventually." I looked directly at him.

"Professor, there isn't just peace." My inner child was back with a vengeance, throwing a tantrum. I couldn't let go of my everyday thinking. "There is still that knot in the stomach. Don't you ever feel that?"

"The effect of the emotions."

"Wait, emotions or thoughts?" I rolled my eyes back up to the ceiling, grabbing the back of my neck with fingers interlocked, stretching to a painful pull. My ribs spread and I felt a tug in my back, leg, and arm muscles. I noticed the full force of the tension residing in my body.

"Think back, Jim. We know that one of meditation's great goals is quiet presence in body, mind, and spirit, and not being pulled by the chain."

"Okay."

"But we have seen that thoughts distract us, disquieting the mind."

"Right, right. I'm with you on that…I think."

"And if we examine those thoughts, we see that they are of no substance. We are usually not living in the things we are fearing or regretting. We are only creating a thought pattern out of a perception, distraction, or habit."

"I'm sure I could find some exceptions if I tried, but for now, agreed."

"And, we know that breath is the basic building block of meditation, for it truly is the one real thing we know we are doing at any moment. It is the truth that keeps us living, to even be in a meditative state in the first place. It is the ineffable, invisible reality that weaves in and out of the progression of solid moments, unimpeded."

"Yes, I understand that."

"But now you have ventured further down the path – to the 'knot,' as you say, of emotions. You are curious about the feelings that accompany thought."

"Am I? I guess I am. Let me talk this through."

"Please do!"

I set myself carefully back on the rocking chair. It took issue with my return, but I again found the comfortable spot.

"Even if a disturbing thought goes away, I still feel nervous or anxious."

"Right, Jim. That's your emotional knot."

"Okay. So, it's sort of like a contrail that lags behind an airplane."

"How so?"

"I hear the plane. I see the plane. It disappears. All is quiet. But that line. That lingering line in the sky. It hangs there. A memory. It takes forever to fade. What do I do with that?"

"Are you talking about a general background feeling of discomfort or anxiety? Like white noise in your gut?"

"Yes! White noise. White contrail. It's white and it sucks." I finally felt like we were getting close to the same page. "Even though, like you said before, I know rationally that there's no ghost in the closet—"

"A white ghost?" He smirked. "I want us to be consistent."

"Sure…whatever. Even though I know there's no ghost in there, I still have the effect of fear of that ghost distracting me. That feeling's always there, lingering in the background. I remember once going to the doctor because I wasn't feeling well. I didn't know exactly what was bothering me, and neither did the doctor, so he put 'general malaise' in the chart and then we talked about generalized anxiety disorder or something like that. He wasn't sure what else to do for me, so I left. Hell, I'm not even sure what to do for me. Generalized anxiety is a thing, I know. Millions of people have it. But the problem for me is, it's reached a point where it's a lot more in the forefront than the background. It's at a place where…well…"

"You'd do anything to stop it."

"Right. Even if it means…"

"Stopping your life."

"Yeah." The room fell silent. I bit my thumbnail and stared into space. I drew in a deep breath and let it out in a rush. "But thankfully, it's a background anxiety most of the time. I usually only notice it when it's *not* there. How crazy is that?"

"Not as crazy as you might think, Jim. This is caused by the often-irrational part of our nature called emotion. It has been the silent backdrop of our recent conversations, but we have not examined it squarely. Before, we referred to emotions as generally associated with anticipation or regret, perhaps felt in the form of fear, guilt, or anxiety. But there is also anger, resentment, envy, sadness, jealousy, and so on. These are all varieties of the emotional experience. They are the fingers of thought, gripping us tightly. If the emotions didn't exist, thoughts would be powerless against us."

"Do we really need to dump emotions if we're on this path? I mean, we have emotions and they help us to figure out how we feel about things…where we stand in relation to people and experiences. They help us make decisions. And besides, isn't there also joy and happiness in that mix?"

"Indeed, Jim. It's not wrong to feel. Emotions serve us dutifully in love and life. But they can destroy us when they clash with the peaceful side of our nature."

"More clashing?"

"Collisions wake us up to change, Jim."

"I guess."

"To truly understand this concept, we have to descend again into the den of thoughts. We must examine how thoughts and emotions are tied together to see that they are both irrational when used in an irrational way. It's not a question of judging thought and emotion as good or bad, Jim. It's a matter of staying conscious of them and how they affect us."

"Okay." I shifted my weight in the rocking chair and again felt the pull in my back. The professor, on the other hand, had hardly moved anything except his lips since we began talking, only rubbing the key and sliding the beads effortlessly through his fingers.

"Thoughts are interesting things, Jim. One can feel fine about life in general and be present for tasks at hand. Suddenly, a random thought comes. About what?"

"I don't know…what?"

"Certainly not about the present. In a manner of speaking, there is really nothing continuously happening at any given moment." Raising his string of beads, he continued. "What we see as inextricably linked, critical commentaries on future and past are really just individual images or words, whole in themselves, that form what appear to be one long, engaging storyline. This is often where we create personalities to participate in those narratives. We identify so completely with this fully illustrated, emotional, storied timeline, that we lose all sense of our current image or word, because the illusions of story seem so logically linked together."

"Well, isn't it? My life is my life, Professor. It's a story. It has a beginning, a middle, and an end. It has drama and intrigue. It has love and loss. It has fight and feeling. That sounds like the formula for any good movie. Isn't it all linked?"

"Perhaps. But perhaps not. The problem is that we become

invested in the story's passing and outcomes, when really, there is only now. This meditation, if you will." He looked around the room, taking it all in, from the curtains to the bedcovers, before continuing. "Nevertheless, a thought comes. Past pain or future fear becomes attached to this moment, and there is an automatic, preprogrammed, emotional response, or pull, if you will, that creates a disturbance in our physical body and mind in the moment. It could be likened to plucking a guitar string at one end, creating a wave down the string until the vibration is felt at a distance."

"Right. I saw that in one of the journals."

"Thoughts create an immediate ripple in time. A disturbance that reverberates. Inevitably, upon their arrival, a response begins. It almost seems paradoxical to call it a 'response,' as the thing to which the body is responding biologically and psychologically is not even happening outside of us in the moment. The body might respond to difficult memories in the form of sadness, for example, or else it can respond to thoughts about the future in the form of nervous anticipation or fear."

"Depression and anxiety," I said.

"Those are certainly possibilities, Jim. The network of the brain and the reactions of the body exist, so it seems, independently of a peaceful spirit."

"I suppose." I knew he was right. Not from reason or logic, but from real-world experience. Because of my penchant for worry, I was voted 'most likely to die of a stress-related illness' in high school – an honor forever immortalized in my senior yearbook and almost sealed by a city bus. My friends still had a field day with that high school title. My habits of anxiety-based reactions had become an identity I'd learned to live with.

"Think of a lemon." His voice interrupted my thoughts.

"Excuse me?"

"Close your eyes and picture a juicy, yellow, sour lemon."

"Um. Alright."

"Peel it, Jim. Smell it. Taste it in your mind. What is happening to you as you sit here?"

"Well, I'm salivating a little. It's like I'm having a…lemon episode."

"Are you sitting here actually eating a lemon?"

"No, but it seems like it." I opened my eyes to get rid of the unpleasant sensation.

"There."

"There?"

"There it is, Jim!"

"There what is, Professor?"

"The truth."

"The answer to life's greatest mysteries is lemons?"

"In a way. The brain can often not distinguish between its own creations and the reality of the moment, and the lemon example illustrates it perfectly."

"Point taken."

"But? I sense a 'but,' Jim."

"Well, how do we stop it? Professor, I don't mean to sound impatient or rude, but we've spent hours discussing these concepts, and I don't really know if I'm any closer to understanding. I feel like I'm trying to climb out of a pit, but I keep falling back in."

"Well, you can truly say you are on the path now."

"What? Why?"

"Frustration is a sign that you are engaging the subject matter with your whole being, and that it is important to you."

"That's funny. But if I think about it, I suppose it's true."

I remembered how frustrated I would get in his classes. Concepts blended together, and it was often difficult to parse out the fine lines between histories and philosophies. Yet, in retrospect, I realized just how much I longed to attend them again and how much richer those classes made me.

"Jim, as we said, the issue is not that we have thoughts or emotions. You don't have to walk around like a blank slate all the time. It's okay to be frustrated or overwhelmed or anxious."

"That's a relief!"

"The problem is that we come to believe every thought and emotion is based in reality and requires our complete attention and response, while ignoring the more peaceful state we possess. Emotions are the remnants of thought. If we allow them to affect us too deeply, we will become so bound to the non-existent hobgoblins in our closet that the reality of peace in the moment is lost upon us, and we will never truly rest. Anyone can be laid low in their life path in this way."

"That's great," I said, barely able to shield my growing restlessness. "But how do we enter peace instead of going to pieces?"

"Meditation is a good start. My guru said it takes tremendous courage to even begin a session of meditation. It is a task of pure self-examination. It is when we sit to meditate that we become totally self-aware. Distracting thoughts come to conquer us. Emotions revisit us. A cunning warrior can easily slay any demon save those of his own creation. Memories and regrets of the past can destroy our current well-being, and anxiety about the future can dismantle our destiny. The same can be said of yearning for past glory or harboring unbridled expectations of eternal happiness. It is thoughts and their lingering emotions the ego uses to keep us distracted. They are the uneasiness in the darkness even after the closet gets the all clear. Discomfort is the visible scar after the knife of thought and emotion cuts clean. Meditation can help if we practice."

"Well, that sounds great, but I'm just sick of spiraling. I'm sick of being so out of control inside."

"To control thoughts and emotions – and it really is about control – you must learn to accept them."

"Why would I want to do that? Why would I accept the things that come to distract me? My emotions have nearly killed me, Professor. I don't really want to accept that."

"You should accept them because you created them, Jim. Hatched them. But you must let them fly away on their own. Acknowledge them passively and let them go, like a mother bird pushing her children from the nest when the time is right. When managed appropriately, emotions, like thoughts, help us to integrate our being – ensuring that we stay in touch with life and act virtuously. When misused, they become nothing more than perpetual egoistic distraction. The nest is only so big."

This was so hard for me to accept. Over the years, I'd collected a lot of well-meaning advice to calm my anxiety and tame my depression. I could hardly count the number of thought balloons of every color and size I'd made in my mind and sent floating away, or the streams of guided meditations I'd tried to get myself centered. People told me to eat more, eat less, or eat nothing, or to take up drinking water like it was a job. "Hydration is the key!" they'd say. But every time I tried something new, it was a struggle. I'd come to realize that when something works for a person – nutrition, exercise, breathing, or whatever – they assumed it would work for everyone. I stopped reaching out for help in order to avoid the advice.

"I've been battling this stuff for years, Professor. My thoughts. My emotions. I'm tired of fighting. Something is going on chemically in my brain, I know it…but…maybe I'm just not cut out for this life. I'm just so tired and frustrated."

"I know, Jim. I know. Some of it is, indeed, physical. Some of it may not be. Humanity lives and grows on a spectrum, and what is normal for one person is not for another. Whether we're talking about height, weight, or brain chemistry, that principle holds true."

"I tell my clients that all the time. That insight has been huge for me as I work through all of this."

"It is, indeed, a great relief sometimes to know that our biologies can differ. Body chemistries can vary. Modern medicine helps some people, but not others. It can be tiring. It can be frustrating. And what we're exploring here is meant to complement the steps you're taking to get your life back, Jim. Not replace it. You must do what you can – however you can – to reach a state where you feel settled. Peaceful.

Able to experience your life in a way that is fulfilling for you."

"I appreciate that, Professor. I know this is all meant to help me."

"It is, Jim. And here's some good news for you: This process we're speaking of now is peaceful enough if you allow it. Emotions and thoughts have a life of their own. When they enter your space, to fight them is to give them more power. Your only defense is patience, and it's something you can practice."

"That's not really a strength of mine."

"It's a skill worth building. My teacher used to say that patience is the greatest of the virtues, while impatience is the greatest vice. Patience breeds peace, and vice versa. One can certainly not achieve peace by fighting. Victories gained in this way are hollow. When thought and accompanying emotion arrive, do not fight them off, Jim. Simply allow them a happy trespass on your peaceful estate and permit them to move on."

"That's it?"

"That's it?" The professor raised his eyebrows halfway up his forehead. It was the first time his expression had measurably changed since we'd started. "My goodness, protégé. That's a lot! Nothing could be simpler in essence yet harder in practice."

"Sounds like golf." I rolled my eyes.

"There is no cure-all for these matters, Jim. The spiritual pharmacopeia, like the physical one, contains no magical potion or pill. Any healing or spiritual practice requires work and patience. Testing."

"Yeah. I guess I don't really know what I was expecting."

"Expect discipline, practice, and simplicity. The exercise of meditation is the end in itself. In fact, it is almost the prototype of simplicity."

"Simple and impossible."

"It's not impossible. You've already done a lot of the hard work. Consider this: You have arrived here, now, in this moment, not because of your fears, regrets, and anticipations, but as a simple fact of being. Try to get back in touch with that knowing. That flow. Fear does not get the work done and regret is not a tool for healing."

"I know, I know. But I still can't quite get my mind around the fact that I have to actually let go of what seems so natural. Emotions and thoughts are like childhood friends."

"Well, don't think of them as friends. Think of them more as relatives from overseas you like to see on occasion, but with whom you sometimes don't really get on with." We shared a laugh. I started to rock the chair slowly, ignoring its protests, pushing my toes into the floor. "Jim, in the practice of meditation, emotion and thought are not the overall goal, but they are there, like it or not. If they weren't, we'd have no reason to meditate."

"It sounds like they're there to help us practice, then. They're not bad, just…kinda there to give us a way to build the meditation muscle."

"Now you're getting the idea. Eventually, however, we can lessen their burden on us as we get stronger and stronger. If we don't, they can really slow us down."

"It's like training for a marathon, Professor."

"How so?"

"Well, if you want, you can train with weights in the gym to increase your strength and endurance. You can practice for the big day and build those muscles up. But if you show up at the starting line on race day with weights tied to you, you'd never finish."

"That's right, Jim. Eventually, you have to break free. In some ways, our phantom thoughts and lingering emotions are the very weights that keep us from performing at our best. They help us practice."

"But if we don't learn to control them, they'll kill our momentum." I smiled. "If I can learn to use this stuff in my head in the right way, I can win with its help. Otherwise, I'll lose because of it."

"Excellent, Jim. Excellent. Now, we can race forward another step."

Chapter 16

Our True Occupation

The professor took a few moments to relax. He closed his eyes and took in a deep breath. I wasn't sure what he was doing, but I decided not to disturb him. I pushed my body up from the chair to release blood to my legs. My foot was falling asleep, and I wasn't sure how much more ground we had to cover. My mind kept wandering downstairs to the refrigerator, but I urged it back into the room. Another part of me longed to be outside in the trees with my earbuds in listening to music, but I yanked my thoughts back indoors.

I was suddenly so aware of my thoughts and the emotions that accompanied them, I couldn't help but try to focus my consciousness. It was a new feeling, but it excited me. I couldn't remember the last time I'd had a discussion that was this intense for this long. Maybe this was a meditation in itself. Eventually, he came back to the conversation.

"Are you ready to continue, Jim?"

"How many more steps do we have?"

"It's infinite."

"Argh!" I offered.

"Do you have a pressing engagement?"

"Not that I can think of."

"Good! Then let us pay a visit to the sages of the past, whose voices call to us from the silence. Let's look at the Buddhist notion of *tathata*, or 'suchness.' Do you remember from lectures?"

"Uh." I regretted the absence of my class notes. "I think that had something to do with seeing things as they are…seeing the nature or essence of something in your own personal interpretation. It's like…well…it's like something is there in front of us, but we can't describe it."

"Yes. In one sense, that is true. There is a nature to things that precedes their name. Suchness is special, for it reminds us that things are as they are, as they are happening. No explanation necessary. If the essence of life is beyond thought or description, then right now, if we are truly present, we can appreciate the subtle, indescribable nature of things as they are – both their rigidity and their fluidity. The solid and the space. A moment is not stressful or scary, happy or terrible. Rather, the ego imbues the past and future with such beliefs and leaves our body no choice but to follow suit with its natural reactions of panic, fear, depression, grief, and expectation. The moment is actually natural and essential. It is only our response to it that creates problems."

I rocked backwards on my toes and clunked the back of the chair against the wall. I let my feet fall flat, allowing the chair to roll back to the resting position. I was growing restless again, and for some reason, the professor's calm demeanor triggered agitation.

"That's great in religious theory, but I'm not sure it translates to reality, Professor."

"Jim, please close your eyes and imagine the following…"

"Lemons again?"

"No lemons this time. Imagine you are hiking a path into the forest."

"Okay."

"Hear your feet crunching in the leaves and pine needles blanketing the ground. In the distance, fingers of wind create a current that tickles the tops of the trees, and the laughter of the pines grows louder as the breeze blows nearer. When it reaches you, it is cool and scented, mixed with a light mist. The mist's source is a waterfall, cascading gently from rocky outcroppings with mossy overhangs. The spray curls and twists in the atmosphere. A pinecone drops, scaring a sparrow, whose frantic chirps draw your attention. As you stand in the warm sun breathing in the crisp, clean air, you suddenly feel that yes, this is the way of things. This is the nature of nature, simple and beautiful. This natural scene was here before you, is what it is while you linger, and will remain when you depart. You enter for one brief moment. It will never look quite this way again. You will never perceive this scene the same way twice. Yesterday's disagreements and tomorrow's angst are present in the recessed networks of your brain, but not at the forefront. In this moment there is not yes and no, this and that, come and gone. There is only the experience of this place – forever remembered as one might remember an enchanting perfume. Leave your camera untouched. Pause your recordings. A photo cannot capture the essence of the scene. It reveals itself to you because you are present, and nothing more. Can you see and feel this?"

"Yes." The word passed my lips with only the barest movement. It was an effortless response coordinated by the slightest outbreath and lazy, focused movement of the back of my tongue. I had no desire to speak. For so long this feeling eluded me. But in this pinprick, I was not only here, but here now. As the moments moved in slow progression, my body instinctively melded into the crevices of the antique chair upon which I sat, now embracing my form instead of working against it. The seat settled perfectly into my frame as I allowed my struggle with it to end. I took a double inbreath into my relaxed lungs, and let the air out in an easy, calm stream. After many distracted and discarded attempts in a life filled with anxiety and darkness, I was meditating. I lost track of time. I had no experience outside of this moment. After who knows how long, his voice re-entered the flow.

"Being present makes sense in such a scene, Jim. We have all been in a natural setting we wish we could wrap and open when we need the gift of refreshment. Admiring the view atop the Rocky Mountains or watching waves break on the shores of the Pacific, one finds they are consumed by the splendor. A clock might as well not exist."

"It's almost like time would distract from the beauty," I muttered, still faintly enveloped in the serenity in my mind.

I was savoring the fleeting experience of one-pointed concentration now punctuating the vast expanses of distracted possibilities in the mind. At moments, while he had described the scene, it felt as if the description was all that existed.

"We must be present in everyday life. Sometimes, I am sure you remember, when you lectured to students – and Jim, let me assure you, I have had this feeling, too – they seemed unresponsive." I hoped he was not referring to me. Professor Singh's classes were usually offered in the early morning and I was often in a catatonic state at that time. "Yet, quite often, I would suddenly have a feeling that I will never give the same lecture the same way to these students again. Once that realization came over me, it was energizing. No matter what else may have happened or would happen, I realized I had the moment. Sometimes I found I could take the lecture to such a level that the energy of the room changed. I discovered the students who were paying attention and focused on them. And we all benefited."

"I know what you mean." My eyes opened wide, shifted, and brought their full focus again into the room. Onto Professor Singh. "Sometimes I have that feeling when I'm doing a group session with clients. I start out thinking everyone is judging me. Expecting something from me. Bored with me. But something happens as I just give in to the energy of the room…the circle. I strike a good chord and the group comes into harmony. It doesn't feel like me. The words seem to be coming from another place. I find clients open up more in that space."

"And now, Jim, your circle brings us full circle in the illusions of time. Our Sufi poet had the right idea. No matter what the past may be or what the future may hold – for we don't really know what fruits our actions will bear – we have a choice now. We have this tiny dot. This pinprick of time. Being in the moment is not about gaining magical abilities, plucking money from the trees, creating things we desire out of thin air, or concocting a magic potion to find love or reverse loss. The power of the moment is that you quiet the chattering voice in your head and ease the nervous energy in your body. You focus on the task at hand. Not for the sake of reward, but for the sake of its presence alone. It lifts you. It lifts the moment. It lifts those around you."

"I felt that in the scene you described before. I got focused. Lighter. I've sort of been drifting in and out of that place even while we've been talking. It's weird. I never thought I'd get around to feeling like this. I always thought it would be something I'd figure out someday down the road."

"Tell me this, Jim. How many times, when talking to friends or loved ones, do you hear, 'Someday, when I get more settled, I'll relax. It's just too much right now. I'm too stressed.'"

"That's my story." I grinned.

"Alright, so what you're telling me is that when you are less stressed, you'll take on a stress-reducing mentality?"

"I guess that doesn't make a whole heck of a lot of sense."

"This is the very point. You don't have to sit with a Himalayan guru for fifty years before you can handle a difficult student, long line, busy freeway, or work deadline. The pinprick is the perfect metaphor for the journey in the moment. A pinprick can be jarring, urging us back into the present. It can arouse us from apathy and return us to engaging the current flow. It can be quick and harmless, but just intense enough to do the job. Its motto is, 'If not now, when?'"

"We should try to find peace in every moment," I added.

"A perfect goal for our imperfect human existence, Jim. Whether we succeed or not, we should at least try."

"Sounds like something I should do."

"If you had a family member with a terminal illness, would you rather spend their last moments comforting them, or worrying about their funeral arrangements?"

"Yeah." The details of death intruded into my peace. My thoughts drifted to my grandfather's last days and how everyone in my family was scrambling to take care of the business of dying – coffin or cremation, trying to find a will with his last wishes – things someone should have taken care of, but never did. I thought about my father's current health issues and wondered if Mom was prepared for his departure. Death, or the specter of death, brings with it responsibility and obligation outside the moment and away from the dying person. It's easy to lose sight of impending loss when we're thinking about the arrangements we have to make. It's a cruel reality of life when the hard certainty of death arrives. I stopped this train of thought and steered my mind back to the room.

"None of us knows what is to be or how what has happened will affect our life going forward, Jim. We only know what we have now. There is only this task. This conversation. This breath. We have this seat in this quiet room, and the work of peace is before us. The pinprick of this moment is the wake-up call..."

I sensed he was waiting for me to take up the lead here, but I was unsure what to say. But somehow, I knew that at the right time, the right words would come. I snapped from the remnants of relaxation and stretched. I didn't know how much time had passed, but I didn't care. The conversation was intoxicating, and I decided I wanted to stay in the room, no matter how late the time or how hungry I was.

"Professor? Would you mind if I sat here with you and meditated for a while?"

"I would be very happy if you would join me."

◆ ◆ ◆

For the first time since I'd come into the room, he moved significantly, yet methodically. His legs slid from underneath his body in a smooth motion of uncoiling silk and he nimbly relocated to the floor with a quilt. Taking the care of an origami master, he folded it into a precise rectangular cushion. He set this masterpiece squarely against the foot of the bed frame, then plucked a decorative pillow from the bed and set it next to him. He motioned for me to join and once again pulled himself effortlessly into the classic lotus position – his right foot on his left thigh near his hip, and his left foot on his right thigh, near his other hip, relaxing his hands in his lap. He looked like an incredibly comfortable pretzel.

I could not detect a single cracking joint. I found no sign of strain written on his face. There was no resistance to the stretch. A steady breath accompanied each movement, with no hint of labor. I had seen this position in books and old photographs of some of the great gurus but could never achieve it. And I wasn't sure I wanted to. But I tried, painfully aware that my attempt was, in all ways, the complete opposite of his.

Likely inspired by the limits of my untrained body, he said, "Jim, if you cannot sit like this do not worry. You may meditate in any comfortable position. It is no good to attempt calm and quiet if we are thinking about the pain in our body. For now, simply pull yourself into the half-lotus."

Under his guidance, I pulled my right foot onto my left thigh, and kept my left foot tucked under my right thigh. I rested my hands in my lap.

"Much better," I said with a smile.

"Alright. I have put us on the floor because I want you to use the edge of the bed to support your back...like this." His body sprung bolt upright, forming a perfect parallel to the end of the bed. He humored me, using the frame to brace his body. I knew he didn't need it, but he knew I would. I sat as straight as I could, but felt bolts of tension and strain shooting through back muscles I wasn't aware I had.

"I know this can be a little uncomfortable at first, Jim, but as long as we are committing to the sitting posture, have your back as straight as you can without pain. There's a natural curve in your spine, so let it curve, but keep the idea of straightness in mind. Although you can be in any position, once you choose a posture, be mindful of it. Now, let your chin relax and allow your tongue to rest comfortably against the roof of your mouth. Allow the tension to drain away from the rest of your face. Again, back as straight as you can. This opens up your inner space, easing your breathing pattern."

"Okay." As my lungs filled with only the gentlest prodding, I had a flash of insight. "Professor, I just noticed that when I became aware of my breath, it's as if I didn't even notice it before. Like I wasn't really breathing until now."

"Yes. Breathing becomes routine – part of life's background – when, in fact, it is the centerpiece. Like so many things, we only notice it when it is difficult or irregular, such as when lifting a heavy box."

"Or choking."

"Exactly. When you breathe in a mindful way, you give breath your full attention. Meditation is about concentration, mindful awareness, and relaxation. That is why comfort is paramount. We should meditate with an easy flow of breath for self-reflection and a mindful pursuit. Not to prove we can endure pain."

My next question sounded odd in my head, but in the spirit of openness and exploration, I asked anyway. "So…how do I breathe, exactly?"

"In. Out. In. Out."

"Thank you. That's very helpful."

"I guess that doesn't really help you, does it, Jim."

"Technically, you answered my question."

"I'll demonstrate. Watch closely. And listen." His breathing was deep through his nose, but not labored. Like a cat tiptoeing through the house, I knew the breath was there, but there were only traces of movement. Hints of two lungs filling and emptying. Faint sounds alerting me to the process but not disturbing it. I realized he was merely freeing up a naturally simple process at the intersection of biological necessity and meditative focus. I tried to imitate him.

"Relax your shoulders," he whispered. "Then, your face and your neck will follow. Let the tension go."

My upper body was tight. But when I dropped the tension in my shoulders in a mindful way, the resistance in other areas melted away as if on command. My posture felt natural once I gave it permission to be itself. As its upper partner relaxed, the lower body followed. A specialized, conscious gravity pulled the body tension down into the earth, leaving the rest of me floating. I was simultaneously supple and firm, my buttocks planted in the ground and my torso sprouting naturally from them.

"Breathe from below, Jim."

In this one area of the meditative life, I had a head start. One thing that kept me sane through school was singing in choirs. I already knew that deep breathing is low breathing. Choral directors all over the world tell their singers to keep their shoulders down and breathe low. I inhaled deeply, keeping my shoulders still, while feeling my lungs fill. I exhaled fully and gently, allowing my bellybutton to contract towards my spine, before taking in another breath.

"Be aware of the mechanics of breath," he said. "Breathing is a sentence of two words – in, out."

"It's a rhythm."

"Yes, Jim. However, you will notice that the process of breathing is not constructed of two points on a line. Rather, it is an elliptical motion. The small pause before the next cycle is a position on a curve, returning the breath to its original point. It is not a sharp angle. Do you feel that?"

"I do." At the end of an exhalation, I felt the next breath waiting to slide seamlessly into the infinite loop.

"Mind the breathing pattern, Jim. It can save you. We become so ensconced in our daily dramas that we forget this life-giving force. We forget *how* to breathe. It is amazing how shallow and irregular breath becomes. As we said earlier, breath doesn't normally enter our consciousness unless we are acutely aware of it – panicking, running a race, or maybe having an asthma attack. The only time breathing receives attention is when we are in a crisis of sorts. This isn't healthy. What you are exploring right now is a genuine experience of breath in its purest state. You are filling yourself completely and consciously."

I filled and emptied, allowing the natural process to pursue its natural course. In less than the time it took to complete three cycles of breath, the process made sense. I became aware of the technique and how, night and day, it filled me with life. Where I once breathed to live, I now realized that I should live to breathe. After years of breathing by habit, I was finally breathing with purpose.

"In meditation, breathing is the natural point of departure and return, Jim. The Buddha was very much enamored with breath. He said that being mindful of one's breathing is essential. He asks us to picture a quiet man. Mindfully, he breathes in, and mindfully, he breathes out. Unconscious breathing is not enough. We must breathe mindfully to maximize the benefit of this inborn calming device."

We sat in silence, letting breath flow without interruption. Soon, however, the ghosts in the closet emerged – at first in a subtle interruption, then in a burst of force. My mind flew with these spirits on excursions of fantasy. I saw myself with Maya in an amorous embrace. It created a tingling sensation in my lower body. I allowed the thought and the accompanying emotions to pass, but in the next episode, she and I were fighting. This constricted my chest and restricted my breath.

I also detected levels of commentary in my consciousness. At one point, I was having a conversation with myself about which scene would be more likely if Maya and I met again – loving or fighting. Above that, another voice observed this dialogue, chastising me for thinking during meditation. Fumbling with my thoughts was like wrestling with smoke. I opened my eyes in frustration.

"Professor, I can't stop my mind from wandering."

"Jim," he said calmly, as if expecting my query, "you may never be able to stop that. It is part of the practice. Meditation is a journey without end in this lifetime. For if it does end, it means your lungs are no longer attached to a living, breathing being. There are many sights to see along the way, as well as memories of places we've been."

"It's driving me crazy," I said, swatting at the invisible specters of thought circling my head.

"Heed what we said before, Jim. Your thoughts and emotions are your own creation, and they are coming back for a visit – for tea and cake, or a game of chess. You don't need to entertain them. Simply let them flit through your consciousness like a butterfly before your gaze. You are unperturbed and happy to let them continue on their way. Keep yourself focused on your breathing. You are not a participant in these illusions, Jim. You are just a witness. Do you leave a movie theater believing that the characters are going to follow you home?"

"Well no, but—"

"There is no 'but.'"

I stopped my protest short. Never in all my years with Professor Singh had I heard him negate a questioner to present a definitive answer. However, he did this with such mind-boggling gentleness that I respected it without hesitation. I closed my eyes and focused again on my breath. Within seconds, a chain of thoughts led me away. The destination was insecurity over my job and working with my clients. I felt their pain. I wondered if I was the right person to help them heal. I let that chain drop and gently refocused on my breathing. A ghost of Maya emerged in my mind and tried to scare me – would I always be alone? Would I ever find true love? I smiled at the phantom and let it pass into the darkness.

Waves of thought rose and fell. Tides of emotion ebbed and flowed. I understood now – in a way that went so much beyond the intellectual. This was not a study in breath, but the process of breathing. This was not a struggle or competition, but an allowing. I was choosing to be taken away on clouds of thought. I was choosing to re-focus. Permitting distraction to appear and drift away disarmed the battle. It was live and let live. Meditation was simply a silent truce of consciousness.

"Breathing is your occupation, Jim. All else is a hobby."

Chapter 17

On to the Next Adventure

I awoke early the next day refreshed and invigorated. I leapt from bed and pulled on a sweatshirt and a pair of jeans. After tightening my belt to a previously unused hole, I paused to say a brief prayer of thanks for a new morning. Hours of conversation and meditation the day before renewed me and I felt like there were worlds of experience to explore.

The professor and I took a vigorous walk in the woods that left me feeling great. To my surprise, I was able to keep his brisk pace without getting winded. A simple breakfast of fruit and toast was relaxing, yet focused. We concentrated on our food, and nothing else – an exercise in mindful eating. By the time we finished, it wasn't much past nine. The mood in the house had been pleasantly subdued and light since we sat together yesterday in meditation. Professor Singh probably sensed that I needed some time to process all of these ideas, and he was happy to give me the space.

The previous night, I wrote awkwardly in my new journal – rethinking and revisiting concepts from the day and listening for the silence. But I was bothered by the fact that I could not accurately recreate the conversations with the professor on paper. I put that feeling aside and fell asleep, but today, as we sat in the parlor looking out at the trees, a frustration crept back into me that I hadn't grasped everything, and that maybe I never would. The machine of mind activated full speed, and instead of processing the experience, I felt like

I wanted to own it. I realized I was still very confused about how all of this fit in with my larger worldview. I shared this thought with the professor.

"A little confusion does not concern me," he said, before excusing himself for a nap. As he headed up to his room, he added, "I would suggest you continue pondering what we've spoken about over the last few days and integrate some of it before you make any new decisions in your life. You already know from your studies in philosophy that all points of view are merely perspectives. You may find you have a fresh perspective on things when you make a new teaching your own."

He was at the top of the stairs before I could ask him what he meant. Anyway, I didn't want to disturb his chorus of "mindfulness morning." After he disappeared, I relaxed into the sofa to think. I had been toying with the idea of contacting Maya again to clear the air, but I couldn't face an argument. The trigger to anxiety was just too great. I ran my hands through my hair and tried to figure out why our breakup was so difficult for me. People break up all the time. It's fine. It's healthy. It's normal. Why was I so bothered by it? Was I afraid of the possibility of new experiences? New places? I smiled at the notion that letting thoughts pass undisturbed was fine for sitting alone in meditation, but where Maya was concerned, I was sure they would not pass so easily.

Despite my fears, I had a deepening feeling that she and I should talk. Really talk. Or, at least what passed for talking in this day and age – a quick email. But I hesitated. Professor Singh's words echoed in my mind: "I would suggest you continue pondering what we've spoken about..." I decided he was right. I knew all this information would have a direct and palpable effect on my life and I needed time to sort through it before jumping into action. Any action. It would be hard to make small talk with Maya after so much time and I didn't want our first discussion to be a chaotic, angry mess. I decided to head upstairs to my room to try out my new meditation techniques.

The morning's exercise left me relaxed, drowsy, and a little sore.

Although it was easier, it was still difficult. I wasn't sure how true to the sitting meditation position I could be, so I laid on the floor with my back straight and my arms at my sides, palms touching the carpet. I stared up at the ceiling, acutely aware of my body in relation to the perceived solidity below it. However, as my breathing became conscious and steady, concepts of 'body' and 'solid' blurred. It was as if I were at times melting into the ground, and at times, floating above it. My mind wandered here and there in between my intentional breaths, and eventually, I entered a light sleep.

A dream settled upon me. I was sitting in a waiting room, half bathed in light, half in darkness. Unsure what I was waiting for, I decided to read. I pulled a large book out of nowhere and tried to read it, but I couldn't concentrate. I was fidgety. Restless. A vague sense of foreboding welled up within me. I let go of the book and it evaporated into a fizzy blur. I tried to meditate in a chair, but couldn't. My agitation grew, and I felt as if some terror was stalking me. I stood up and paced in the light. Breaking out in a sweat, my chest heaved. I turned to face the darkness and felt a hard knock between my eyebrows that sent me reeling to the floor in a blackout. In my dream, my eyes opened, and I was standing with my back to a precipice before a spiritual teacher whose face was shrouded in mist. "Where are we?" I asked. The mist lifted, and I realized the teacher was Maya. "Here!" was her reply, as she pushed her hands into my chest, sending me tumbling backward off the cliff toward the valley floor. I fell and fell until I crashed through the ceiling of the waiting area, but before I hit the ground, I awoke, back in the cabin.

As I lay there, disoriented and confused, heart pounding, I heard a loud gurgling that sounded like it was coming from the kitchen. I ignored it, as the professor had mentioned over dinner the previous night that, like thought and emotion, we should accept bodily feelings or outside sounds during meditation and simply let them pass. I figured this was the perfect time to practice that advice. As the sound grew louder, however, I couldn't ignore it. I got up, still a bit shaky, and went downstairs. As I walked into the kitchen, I stepped in the cold, wet disaster at my feet.

"Damn it!" I yelled, breaking the peaceful demeanor of the cabin. I was standing in a puddle of vegetable cuttings and curry-scented, brownish water.

The professor appeared and surveyed the scene. "Calm down," he said quietly.

"What am I going to do about this?" I was near hysterics. "Jake and Meg are going to kill me!"

"They will? Are they here? I'm embarrassed. I haven't greeted them."

"Professor, I—"

"Jim, go get me the phonebook by the telephone, please."

I turned my rant inward and did as I was told. I plucked a book from the shelf that read *Phone Listings: Flagstaff and Surrounding Areas* and handed it to him.

"Plumbing...plumbing. Ah! Here it is. Look. There's a listing circled. Sammy and Sons Plumbing. It must be someone they know. Probably the people who manage the water here each season. A call to them will be our best course of action."

It was. After my torrents of panic subsided, I remembered that I had been here before when Sammy, or one of his alleged sons, who, oddly, seemed much older than Sammy, answered a call. The plumbing in the house was archaic and there were often problems. I remembered a legendary incident involving Jake's dad and an upstairs toilet. The Davis family rarely made a practice of fixing the problems themselves, as they had been warned about the instability of the pipes.

"Hand me the phone, please." I handed the receiver to Professor Singh, and he calmly dialed the number. "Hello? Yes, my name is Arjun Singh, and I am at a cabin in Mormon Lake. It is owned by the Davis family...yes...we seem to be having a mishap in the kitchen."

"A mishap?" I mouthed in earnest agitation, motioning to the quagmire at our feet.

He ignored my mounting tension. I couldn't hear the conversation on the other end of the phone, so I paced the living room like an expectant father, except the sink had already given birth to a mess. I watched as the professor, phone in tow, went into a closet for a bottle of industrial strength drain opener, which I could only assume was left over from the last emergency. He poured it into the sink and chatted with the person on the other end of the line about their family and the weather. In a few minutes, the drain belched a sigh of relief, releasing a few bubbles. The water level dropped. After a few more exchanges with Sammy or 'son,' the professor hung up.

"Well, that should do it," I said, relieved.

"Not exactly." He tossed a roll of paper towels in my direction, then found a mop in the pantry. "The plumber knows this house from previous calls."

"I'll bet."

"Sammy's people left the drain opener here, thank goodness. They have the Davis file earmarked."

"I figured."

"He told me this might be a sign of a bigger problem, and suggested we refrain from using the plumbing, if possible. He said we could risk it if we had enough drain opener on hand. Since we are in Mormon Lake and he is short-staffed, he had to schedule us two days from now. I said that would be fine, as I think we should use people the Davis family uses. The plumber has a key to the house in his office and has written permission from Jake to come in and fix things."

"Dang it, Jake," I muttered, my hands clutching a clump of soggy, brown paper towel.

"And how, exactly, is this his fault? Was he supposed to suggest you not come here in case there is a plumbing problem that may never happen?"

"I guess you're right, Professor. It's not like we're tearing the place apart."

"These things happen, Jim. They test our mind. They test our patience. Will you pass or fail?"

I stopped scrubbing and sat back to blow a bead of sweat from my brow. "Fine. But what are we supposed to do now? I guess we can just pack up and go. I really don't want to use the bathroom and chance a catastrophe."

"That is great wisdom and good counsel, Jim."

"I'm sorry about this, Professor."

"You know, this does not have to end the adventure. It can be a new phase!"

"The phase where we use the toilet at the lodge restaurant and bathe in their bathroom sink?"

"No." He brushed away my sarcasm with a flick of his hand. "I have another idea."

Chapter 18

Gathering Wood

Around noon, Professor Singh's SUV was packed. He suggested we head for a campsite outside of Mormon Lake. We had camping gear, clothing, two folding chairs, and assorted sundries and fruit. We heaved in a cooler filled with water, vegetables, nutrition bars, and Mom's neon trail mix. I ran back inside for toilet paper and matches. I had already taken the liberty of packing the journals in a backpack.

"I think that's it," I said, shuffling bags around in the back seat. "Good ol' Jake. I knew he'd have his camping gear up here. I just didn't expect to use it."

"I always keep mine in my car."

"Well, aren't you just Professor Prepared!"

"One never knows when plumbing will fail, Jim. Anyway, if we need anything, we can come back for it. I'll just make one more pass through the house to make sure everything is closed up. Don't worry. I won't use the bathroom!"

While he was inside, I caught my toes pushing into the ground, elevating my heels. I was bouncing. I was happy. Giddy. I couldn't remember the last time I felt like this. Renewed with eagerness and courage, I turned on my cell phone to find a weak signal. There were two messages waiting for me. My lightness gave way to a pounding heart. Was it Jake? Was something wrong with Dad? I took in a conscious breath, stopped the barreling thoughts triggered by absolutely nothing in particular, and checked the messages. One was from my parents, wanting to know how I was doing. I relaxed a bit. The second call was from Meg, checking in on me. Hayden was yelling, "Hi, Uncle Jim!" in the background and I could hear him telling Jake that he missed me. A smile crossed my lips, and I decided to call Jake on the spot and tell him about the situation. The call went right to voicemail, so I gave a brief rundown of what was happening and let him know all was well.

After I hung up, I noticed the lack of anxiety in my body. I was just a guy relaying information to another guy in a moment in time. It felt good. Next, I dialed my parents to fill them in and to check on things at home. Mom wasn't keen on the camping adventure, but I convinced her that Professor Singh was not an axe murderer and had been quite the soldier in the Indian army. I also let her know her trail mix was making an appearance, and that gave her a laugh. "Have fun!" was Dad's offering.

"All set, Jim?" The professor reappeared and opened the driver's side door.

"Yup!" I turned off my cell to conserve battery and got in. Professor Singh fumbled with some of the gizmos on the dashboard. I got the sense that this was the first real gadgety thing he'd owned. In class, he never used modern technology except word processing functions to type up tests, and I suspected he did that on a typewriter. The SUV still smelled like the showroom floor. He pulled up a map on the touchscreen.

"Uh, Professor? I don't think we need the navigation system. We're going to a local campsite, not Alaska."

"Yes, yes, Jim, you are quite right. But listen. It talks to you!"

"So does the turn-by-turn direction app on my cell—"

"*Turn…right…proceed…approximately…one…quarter…mile.*"

It was giving us directions to the Mormon Lake Lodge, just up the road.

"Isn't that wonderful?" He was clearly pleased with this purchase and I was happy for him. "Just a minute," he said, as his car announced our arrival twenty-seven seconds later. "I need to stop in the general store."

"Give Hiram and his flies my best!"

He left the car running and disappeared inside. In a lovely small-town cliché, the bug-admitting screen door slammed behind him on its restless hinges. Inside, I could see Hiram look up from his fly tying exercises to acknowledge Professor Singh. I glanced in the side view mirror and saw Mo riding his bike across the road. I turned around in my seat and watched him pedal back and forth. He steered in a way that suggested this was a new experience for him. Suddenly, the bike swerved, and he fell. I pushed the car door open to run to him, but Liv appeared on the scene with a mother's consolation. She saw me standing by the car and waved.

"Hi, Jim! He's fine. Really. He'll get it! Isn't that right, Mo?" Mo shook his head, smiling. "He's going to be the first kid from Mormon Lake to be a Hollywood stuntman."

"Well, he certainly has a supportive mother," I said. "That's what'll make him really successful."

"Kids. You gotta let 'em follow their dreams, right?" She helped Mo back on his bike and they headed back up the hill. Liv turned one more time to wave, and I sent a wave and smile back.

Just then, Professor Singh emerged, juggling two overflowing grocery bags like a circus act.

"Something for later!" he said, as I jumped to rescue a toppling sack from his arms.

"Professor, I could have bought these groceries! Why didn't you tell me you were buying all of…well…whatever this is?"

"My treat, Jim! And, my pleasure."

We continued on our way without the benefit of the computerized woman in the dashboard. Clearly, she had no idea where we were going, either. I stole one last glance up the hill, but Mo and Liv had disappeared. The professor's voice brought me back to the car.

"So, where do you like to camp?" he asked as we bumbled into the bumpy terrain that marked the end of the paved road and indoor plumbing. Sammy and his alleged sons would certainly get no calls out here. I had been to this area often and had tried a number of spots.

"Well, these places at the base of the hills are usually pretty loud from dirt bikes and stuff like that. And they can smell like crap because people ride horses here. Let's head up higher and see if there are any sites there."

He obliged. It was an excuse to test out the SUV's four-wheel drive. We toured, bouncing over small boulders and driving the mobile sofa up steep inclines until we came to a plateau with pullouts scattered among the imposing pines. There were groups camping on the turnouts all the way up, but the top of the hill was empty territory, as most people were accustomed to taking the first site that caught their eye. We broke to the left, down a series of rutted paths that couldn't support two-wheel-drive sedans. To the right, at the end of a dirt trail, was a campsite with an incredible view. There was a neatly ringed fire pit and large pines growing close together. It would be cooler during the day and sheltered at night. A unanimous choice.

We stepped out into the dust and dirt of paradise. Neither of us spoke, rooted to the place. The silence was overwhelming, and my eyes watered under the sting of a quiet punctuated only by the occasional crunching of dried pine needles under our shifting weight and the tick-ticking of tree bark as squirrels scampered about, investigating the new visitors. A light breeze made the occasional whooshing sound through the treetops. I approached one of the pines and sniffed it, as I had seen the professor do days before. There was the vanilla. The small reward for those willing to scratch just a tad below the surface. I thought back to a time when I went to buy Maya a gift basket brimming with body washes and creams. All the odors that now greeted my nose for free had been bottled for a hefty price and carried names like 'pine paradise' and 'vanilla luxury.' The idea was both sad and humorous. The professor opened the back of the

SUV, the clunk interrupting my musing.

We unloaded the cooler first, setting it down with a thud on the dried mud in a space overlooking the vista. A beetle, disturbed from his mid-day nap, scampered out from underneath its weight. After a silent apology to him, I took out the folding chairs and rested them against the cooler, resisting the temptation to open one and plop down right then and there in our makeshift kitchen. Next, we turned our attention to the tents. We poked around the grounds searching for flat areas on which to pitch. Finding our spots among the trees, we cleared away pebbles and brush to avoid complaints from our backs during the night. There was nothing like rolling over on a pinecone to ruin a night's sleep. As I leveled my area and smoothed out the dirt, I found it ironic that the very nature to which we long to escape suddenly becomes filth when brought to floors indoors upon returning home.

Professor Singh's army stint clearly had not escaped him. Within minutes, his vintage, two-person tent was assembled, rainfly and all. Mine took...somewhat longer. I struggled with the four-man tent Jake and I used to share. But a half-hour later, it stood firmly in the ground. I admired my handiwork and let out a long, satisfied sigh as if I'd mounted Everest. Minutes later, my rainfly was up, creating a shaded porch in front of the entrance. I was about to ask the professor if I could use his car adapter to inflate my travel mattress, but I let the joke pass.

We put up a large blue tarp to improve the kitchen area, stringing rope through the grommets and tying it around a stand of four trees, which seemed planted for this very purpose. Our heads barely cleared the top, but it gave us a dry, shaded place to arrange our meals. We hung our animal-attracting food in an empty sleeping bag sack from a high tree, then buzzed about camp taking care of details one by one to make the place home. Setting up the site felt primal. We were in control of our destiny up here, and what we created around us on the outside would dictate how we felt inside. There was power in that. An independence that is hard to find in any other endeavor in the modern world. My sole focus was the task at hand, and I didn't notice the time pass.

"I think that we should go and gather firewood, Jim. After all, storms can blow up quickly. If we collect it now, we can leave it under the tarp to keep it dry, just in case."

"Fine by me," I said, pulling on a pair of heavy leather work gloves I had in my gear.

We set out down a path to the west to conduct our search, our eyes fixed on the ground, piling sticks and branches into our arms. The methodical bend-and-stand meditation of wood gathering is a rhythm all its own, and I noticed that my back was not protesting as much as usual.

"Professor? What was it like being in the army?" I had always wanted to know more about that time in his life, beyond the few stories I'd heard in school. After watching him put up his tent with such swift precision, I felt the time was safe to ask.

"Well, it was…interesting." He kept his attention on his task.

"Interesting?"

"I joined during a time of great tension between Hindu and Muslim in India – a conflict that continues today. But I felt that even though there might be great risk to my life, it was my duty to serve my homeland, as it had fostered me in my formative years. Its schools educated me. Its philosophies saved me. When I felt the calling, I answered it."

"Wow! I admire that."

"I wanted peace, Jim. Peace in the country I love. India has seen many struggles because of sacred-land disputes. Rarely was my unit engaged in war against other nations. We were often asked to keep the peace and negotiate among our own people. Often it is more difficult to quell aggression between one's own countrymen than to fight off a foreign adversary. Foreigners can easily be objectified, and labeled 'not I.' However, when one must look a fellow citizen in the face and arrest him, he truly makes 'I' contact."

"So you didn't see any international combat?"

"Very little. Mostly I was stationed where religious conflict was rife. We kept a vigilant eye on our own streets, guarding sacred places. My academic interest in religion crystallized at this time. I also learned powerful lessons about the ego, and humanity's unfortunate propensity to cling to judgments more than each other."

"It must have been hard for you having to see all the fighting between Hindus and Muslims. I mean, how did you work that out in your mind?"

"By constantly reminding myself of what my guru taught me."

"Huh." I piled a few sticks onto my arm and met his gaze. "What was that?"

"We are individuals in our minds only, Jim. In reality, we are all one."

Chapter 19

The Idea of One

Eventually, we had gathered enough wood to build a guesthouse at our campsite. The weather was warm and pleasant, so we didn't immediately start a blaze in the fire pit. Instead, we piled the wood and kindling under the tarp next to the cooler, covering it with a plastic garbage bag. The day, though still young, had been long, and the professor seemed a bit weary and excused himself to rest.

I unzipped my tent and climbed in. Pushing the clutter aside, I rolled out my sleeping bag and opened the air vents. A cool breeze blew through, bringing with it the tantalizing smells of the forest. Mesmerized in a natural cloud of pine and fresh air, I thought about a nap, but instead, reached for my backpack and pulled out the yellowing journals. I leafed through them with great care, like an archivist inspecting ancient documents in a museum basement. I felt privileged to have them in my possession, as if regarding secret knowledge to which the world was not yet privy. I came to a series of entries under the heading, "One Source." Remembering our earlier conversation, I read the entry.

All is an expression of One, equal in how it came to be, even if not equal in form or function. All things exist as a perfect expression of One – the creative force behind all things. In the illusion and story of life, everything fulfills its allotted role. I am not really the 'me' that I, or others, perceive. I am simply a metaphor for creative power, playing the role of 'me.' Your neighbor is playing the role of neighbor, and your colleague the role of colleague. All things discovered, invented, or named in scientific or philosophical pursuits were already in existence as the idea of the one creator. Our perception of things is only a function of naming and definition. Their being-ness is the expression of the One that manifests this world.

The passage was both academically familiar and metaphysically perplexing. I was getting used to this feeling. I knew ideas of unity permeated the world's religious and philosophical traditions, but it was hard to get beyond that to see the concepts as something useful for living. I read the paragraph again, but it was still jumbled in my head. This wisdom was no artifact or dusty teaching of a bygone age. It was living here in front of me. So well-known and so hidden from view.

"I'm not me?" I whispered. "How can that possibly be?"

I felt the urge to rush out of the tent and question Professor Singh, but I guessed he would rather I explore this concept alone. But for all of my confusion, there was something about this idea that seemed real. Endemic. I reached again for the pile of journals, plucking out the empty one and opening it up to the first page where I'd scribbled the previous evening. The yellow page rested patiently, awaiting my green, untrained hand. I pulled a pen from my pack and removed the cap with my teeth. The tip hovered above the paper, making a few false stabs. I wasn't sure what to do next.

I allowed some deep, clean, purifying breaths. Suddenly, I felt alive…intense…as if on a real mission. I decided my approach would be to mull over the passages in the professor's journals and jot down my thoughts on them as entries in my own book, but with confidence – confidence in my interpretation and my ability to be one more voice in a sea of commentaries.

Empowered and brave, I re-approached the professor's text on oneness. Its growing familiarity excited me. Here was another lesson from the silence, manifested in the material world.

As I meditated on the passage, the Hindu idea of *Brahman* floated into my mind. I made a notation in my own journal. Indian philosophers, such as Shankara in the eighth century CE, believed that reality as we perceive it through our senses is not a duality of this and that with an existence all its own. In fact, for Shankara, there was no twoness to be found. All things, including our individual soul, or *Atman*, are just expressions of the supreme essence, or *Brahman*. In other words, our perceived little self is identical to the bigger Self – the ultimate reality. That which we cherish as truly ours in this world really belongs to that which manifests everything. Distinctions between 'me' and 'you' or 'mine' and 'yours' disappear, leaving unity in its wake. Small and grand consciousness are one and the same – millions of voices in a choir of one. All else is an illusion. Suddenly, an idea once only a theoretical curiosity, struck me to my core.

Varieties of this self-and-ultimate concept always led to interesting discussions in my philosophy and religion courses. Are gods in the world right beside us, or are they somewhere distant watching us? Is there a 'me' praying to an 'it' that is other than me, or am I honoring something deep inside me that is lasting and divine? For many, the suggestion that the 'me' and 'it' are one is blasphemous. But who would argue that we are not our parents? After all, it's their genetic material that created us. Yes, we're individuals, but we are created from existing materials. Was this the same idea?

If this idea of unity, or 'not-twoness,' holds sway, there is really no separation between beings. All things that seem like two are merely an expression of one, to the point where all things are linked in their essence. Bound together for eternity. I was intrigued by the unity experiment. It meant uprooting my conditioning, both academic and cultural, and not just seeing a different perspective, but feeling it. Living it. What if this was why my feelings of depression seeped into the stream of my relationships and darkened the waters? If we're all really linked, could others feel that emotion, even when I tried to hide it? What about my anxieties? When I got a feeling of panic out of the blue, was it really me? Maybe I was just picking up on others' energies. On the flip side, did my anxiety make others anxious and drive them away? Did Maya drift to arm's length because I slowly, imperceptibly, nudged her there? Were we all really that connected? Did we all possess the power to attract and repel others?

My breathing quickened as my hand flowed across the page. Frenzied thoughts flew from my fingers and into the journal. Ideas arrived in my awareness faster than I could put them to paper, as rivers of thought cascaded into my mind. What was once academic and technical took on a new life. I was seeing these ancient truths in a new way – ripe berries in fresh crust, baked in time-honored tradition in an antique oven. I loved my conversations with the professor, but this was just as liberating. A personal connection with these ideas blossomed – ideas that didn't require specialized training in philosophy, religion, or spirituality. They existed for all, in any form, and at any time. I turned back to the professor's pages to continue reading. The words seemed different now. Illuminated.

There is unity. One. It can only experience itself by creating an illusion of two. Only by attempting to see by moonlight do we appreciate easy vision in the blazing sun. But remember – your desire to advance as a unity will bring pushback from bold egos in the opposite direction. People say the mystic lives in a personal fantasy. Ah, but the opposite is true. To live a mystical life is nothing more than to recognize the full and complete reality of total unity. Such a life perceives the physical body for what it is – a vehicle for spiritual experience. The person who lives in fantasy is he who convinces himself that the only realities are the fleeting dramas of money, fame, or duality. The unwise is the materialistic jester who laughs at the mystic as they both fade away – the jester further into the solidity of his comedic illusions, and the seeker into the immaterial joy of One. Transcend duality, and not in jest. Do not become blinded by perception. Live your life. Work your job. Walk your path with your

own two feet. But along the way, go in trus
destination of unity. Rely on logic and the five
at your peril.

136

I jotted down more thoughts. A mystical
doesn't mean we ignore relationships and deny ourselves ...
fruits, but that we stay mindful of the connection we have with others.
The jester and the mystic can, if they so choose, both acquire fame
and riches. The flaw is not in being famous or accumulating wealth.
Rather, it is becoming bound to things to such an extent that we
believe there are no connections between people or purposes to life
that transcend them.

My mind drifted to my individual experience on the planet – being
crushed by anxiety and squeezed by a constantly creeping depression.
Struggling with love and relationships. Trying to make my life work
and to be there for my family and my clients when I was hardly there
for myself. But did all of this energy, pain, and worry help anything?
Or was it just burying me deeper in the illusion? I knew my struggles
– and for that matter, the struggles of my family and my clients –
mattered and were real from one point of view. We have responsibilities
to attend to in this life, bodies to protect, and chemicals in our brains
that can get out of balance and may need a boost. But beating
ourselves up over situations…was that necessary? The now-familiar
sense of self-loathing I often carried…was that reality? Or was it just
nonsense I perpetuated because of my beliefs about what I should have
or where I should be by this age? I jotted down some ideas about how
my life was part of a bigger flow, and that my circumstances were only
one aspect of something much bigger. I put down my pen and
continued reading the professor's entry.

The Universe is vast – bigger than anyone can imagine, for the source
imagines and emanates it anew and distant each moment for each soul.
Each being, though ultimately connected, is also a universe unto itself, as
it is for animals and plants – all things. Once we grasp this idea, we
must become explorers…frontiersmen. We must find the wellspring of

rage to explore the universes around us, learning shapes and contours, planets and stars. As we study, we begin to understand how these other universes affect us – how they press in and pull upon our apparent self. Everything we meet on the path is connected to us and is here for our benefit, and it is that idea which must guide us. The placid waters of comfortable love, as well as the fierce tides of unsettled relationships, illustrate for us the wondrous possibilities of expansion and contraction of the space we share with all else. The tattered threads of life's lessons eventually intertwine into one fine strand. As we come to see that all experience, seemingly separate, has a common source, a needle of awareness bearing silver thread pierces the veils that separate one from another. This is the tie of understanding that binds our personal soul to unlimited source. Indeed, we are ourselves in this moment, but we are also the experience of others in every moment.

I was already invigorated, and this entry only heightened the experience. But as I drew my hand to write, I drifted into a mental fog. My hand felt drained, and my mind protested another round of journaling. I needed to clear my head.

I crawled out of my tent as quietly as possible, so as not to disturb the professor. I stretched, arching my back and becoming acutely aware of my spine – its curves and protrusions, and the endemic tensions that so often become a source of complaint. But for a moment, I didn't complain. I just noticed the pain. Acknowledged it. It was there. I was here. I cast my eyes upon a trail, my feet now carrying me down a dirt path to the main road. I was restless. It had been a long day, and I was hoping to catch a great sunset. Ever since I could remember, I loved watching sunsets. I was even convinced that once, long ago, I heard a pop as the sun disappeared below the horizon.

I ventured into the afternoon, determined to be a blank slate and leave the pondering behind. But alas, lonely in my absence, my thoughts joined me. As I felt the wind and became conscious of my footsteps, I thought about the unfolding events of my life. It seemed, in retrospect, that all the experiences I could remember, or at least the ones to which my mind attached significance, happened on some sort of schedule beyond my control. My family life, education, friends, tragedies, and joys all seemed to enhance, and advance, my life, no matter how anxious I was about the future or how consumed I was in sadness. In fact, the only reason I was here now, in this place, walking this path, was because of the winding trail of my past – even events that I considered limitations and failures. I was burning out at work, but that feeling forced me to take vacation and spend precious time with a cherished mentor. My relationship with Maya was gone, but I was starting to see my life in relation to others in a new way because of that. I only had the capacity to reflect on my life because I had occasionally been present for it, in whatever form it took, no matter how I felt about it.

The people in my life had their own unique, distinct experiences, but experiences that intersected with mine in significant ways. I didn't want to move to Arizona and spent months in agony over my parents' decision. But on my first day at my new school, I met Jake. He taught me so much about life and friendship, and then, in an unexpected turn at my lowest point, offered me a key to his cabin. The professor was with me at the cabin because the events of his life unfolded in such a way that he actually wanted to move to Arizona. And, I only met him because of an apparent disappointment. If I'd gotten into my first-choice afternoon class instead of my second choice in the morning, I might never have found my academic passion and advisor. Perfect synchronicities disguised as imperfect chance conspired to put my feet exactly where they were in this moment.

I was struck by the idea that billions of people on the planet were experiencing one great unfolding of life. They had feelings about the unfolding events and experienced the consequences of those feelings, but those were only a layer on top of the moment. Anxieties didn't make the moments happen for us. They simply accompanied us.

These thoughts flashed quickly, as it usually is with realization. But occasionally, I was able to follow one newly formed idea back to its source in an active meditation that revealed the tangled webs of emotion, experience, and commentary that bring us to new levels of awareness. I suddenly understood why so many people misunderstand each other. We often exchange the sweet, tender fruits of ideas, but can't seem to share with one another the experiences that grew them to a given point – the human connection.

I stopped and checked my progress in the forest. The path spread out before me. I had choices. I decided to veer right and wander down a wooded lane.

Chapter 20

Surprises and Snapshots

I had been in this backcountry many times with Jake and his family, but we had never taken the rutted road this far. We usually stuck to the well-groomed cattle tracks, covering the familiar territory that makes for easy return trips to places of cozy memory. I stayed to the outside of the grooves to avoid twisting my ankles in the deep depressions. These roads were not exactly maintained by the highway administration, and the merciless monsoon rains kept them reliably treacherous. The ground crumbled easily when dry and was unpredictable underfoot. I approached an area where this road ended, and another trail began. There were faint tire marks leading into a stand of trees where the courageous had ventured over the years, though most had likely turned back.

I wasn't more than a ten-minute hike from my camp, but the relative inaccessibility gave this place a different feel. Isolation was a scenery all its own. Wildflowers were interspersed with wild grasses and the ancient, exposed stumps where the forest service had cleared sick or dead trees. Wildfire danger was high in the remote areas from lightning strikes in the older growth, sometimes setting it aflame like matchsticks. I sat down in a half lotus on a flat stump and tried, with some difficulty, to meditate, awaiting sunset. After a few unsuccessful minutes of trying to center myself, a fleeting rustle in the trees froze me cold. The last thing I wanted was a confrontation with a wild animal. I'd been awake since five in the morning and wasn't sure how much strength I'd have to fight. I fixed my gaze on the trees, intent on materializing my fate. When the creature revealed itself, it was a dog. I remained as still as the stump beneath me. My breathing halted as I kept my eye on it. My gaze was drawn to its neck where I noticed a green bandana bobbing around.

"Casey?" He bounded towards the sound of his name before darting back into the trees. I leapt from my post and chased after him. I emerged into a clearing where, on an old, weathered log, a man sat in the company of a low campfire – his gray hair wild and unkempt. A vintage Jeep was parked to one side. The orange fire was almost occluded by the red of his flannel shirt. This carnival of color was highly visible from a distance.

"Silas?" He turned in a casual motion as if expecting to hear his name called in the middle of nowhere. A smile crossed his lips.

"Hey, kid. Tire flat again?" Silas hadn't lost his personality in the woods. Although our ages were probably closer than he thought, somehow calling me "kid" seemed to suit his demeanor.

"What are you doing here?" I asked.

"Same as you, I guess. Enjoying the great outdoors!"

"No, I mean…well…right." I realized how silly my question was. His life, like mine, was simply unfolding in the woods. He was camping. That's all. The synchronicity made his presence seem wild and crazy, when really it was just what it was. Whether or not something was drawing us together, in the end, he was just a guy on a log. "How long have you been out here?"

"I donno. What day is today? Probably since that day you and I met by the side of the road."

"Yeah, Silas. I want to thank you again for that. I really appreciate it."

"Not a problem." He stoked the embers with a crooked stick.

He smacked the log with the broad side of a large hand, and I accepted the invitation. The makeshift wooden bench was big enough to seat five large people, and I suspected he moved it to the fire all by himself. This was my first opportunity to really see him – to focus on the man and not the image of rescue. His skin was leathery and dark, suggesting much time in the sun. He sported a rough, gray and black beard, and his clothes held the smoky odor of his fire. His eyes sat weary under a deeply furrowed brow that suggested a life of seriousness, not smiles.

"What brings you up this way, kid?"

"Nothing, really. Just exploring."

"When we first talked at the side of the road, you mentioned a cabin."

"Oh, right." I told him about my meeting with my old mentor and the escapades at the Davis home, including what had been going on with the kitchen plumbing.

"You don't seem very handy," he said.

"What? The plumbing?"

"That. And tires." We laughed. A gritty cough followed his gruff chuckle. I guessed he didn't use it that often.

"Yeah. The people who own the house don't want anyone touching those pipes except the plumber. I don't blame them."

"Well, kid, at least it's an excuse for you to be out in the air."

"That's for sure! It was my friend's idea to camp once everything went to hell at the cabin. What's all that?" The equipment I spied in his Jeep days ago was now assembled. A tripod with a camera sporting a tremendously long lens was standing near his tent.

"That?" he said, turning to look. "That's my…life."

"Your life?"

"Well, yeah, sort of. I'm a photographer. I spent years as a photojournalist, taking pictures and writing freelance stories."

"What kind of stuff did you write about?"

"I started as a news guy in the army near the end of Vietnam, then worked for the last few years editing a small magazine in Phoenix. But before the Phoenix gig I traveled the world – back in the days when you could make a living as a freelancer."

"Where were you published?"

"Oh, too many to name. But all the biggies on the newsstand. When things went online, I contributed images and digital articles to even more outlets."

"Impressive!"

"I guess. But when it's an all-day gig, you kinda get over the excitement. A job is a job, no matter how glamorous it seems." He smirked and poked mindlessly at the fire.

"Well, it sounds great to me."

"At times, it really was. Mags sent me all over. For some reason, when they heard about my military tours, they stuck me with political stories. Mostly in Asia. My time as a war correspondent got me interested in that part of the world. But what I really love is snapping shots of people and nature. Black and white, mostly. I'm pretty much retired, but I travel around to various places and shoot for fun. I still make a few bucks selling photos. I do digital and film. It's great. I love it!"

"Can I see some of your pictures?" I was genuinely interested and wanted to encourage his good mood. Clearly, his passion for photography lit him up inside.

"Sure. Check my tent. There's a box just inside. I was cataloguing earlier. It's not my best work, but I usually carry some proofs with me, just in case."

Casey escorted me in wild circles to the gigantic tent. I guessed Silas had this mansion to house his equipment in case of rain, and I also surmised he probably had it assembled and ready in half the time it took me to get my gear out of the car. Casey led me back to the log where I sat down and took out some pictures.

"Silas, these are great!" The pictures were from the 1960s onward. There were shots of world leaders and nature – a virtual tour of the globe in personalities and natural phenomena.

"Thanks. These are just for casual show, so the matting isn't too hot. They're not professional or anything."

"They're amazing." I picked out a picture of an Indian man waving to a crowd. "Who's this?"

"Rajiv Gandhi. I was assigned to cover nuclear peace talks in 1988. He was assassinated a few years later. This picture, and the story I wrote with it, won a few prizes in the journalism scene."

"Wow! The nature pictures are great, too." I flipped past a natural history of the planet. Yosemite, the Grand Canyon, Victoria Falls, and so many other wonders swept through my fingers in a torrent of beauty. "Silas, these are all in black and white."

"I told you, kid. That's the medium I like best. Makes for a clean shot and nice contrast. Not a lot of distraction."

"Do you ever print in color?"

"I just like this better."

"Well, they're terrific."

"Thanks."

"Listen," I said, taking some more pictures from the box, "why don't you come by my campsite for dinner. Seven-ish? I'm sure the professor wouldn't mind. We're just down the path there, along the road you came in. We're the only group up here. There's no way you can miss us."

"Sounds good, kid."

"Great. And bring Casey."

"Will do. But I'm afraid he doesn't have a thing to wear."

"That's ok." I scratched Casey's neck. "We're casual around here."

Chapter 21

A Reluctant Idol

My feet carried me light and easy from Silas's camp, though my mind was still wading through the thick of our meeting. I laughed thinking about all the movies I'd seen that turned on a chance encounter or seemingly impossible synchronicity. I'd always rolled my eyes at those parts, but now that it had happened to me, there was no one to roll my eyes at by myself.

I reflected once again on my friends who, like Jake, appeared when I needed them most. They were still a large part of my life and had, quite literally, kept me alive. I was bullied mercilessly in middle school, and when I entered high school, I had no idea how I'd survive. But sure enough, people came along who helped me forge a personal identity besides victim. In college, Professor Singh's classes changed how I viewed the world, and under his current guidance, my life and my spirit. These little nuggets of headshaking, impossible possibility probably happen all the time as unity cloaks itself – wandering through the world as an invisible wizard performing hidden magic right in front of us.

I arrived at camp to find the professor stoking a fire in the pit. A steady wind blew ashes around in a devilish play. He didn't hear me until I was a few feet away.

"Did you have a nice walk?" He held a steady gaze on the growing blaze.

"Yeah." I knelt next to him by the pit. "I had the oddest experience."

"Oh?"

I told him what happened, and about my history with Silas and Casey. A broad smile broke across his lips. When I told him about the invitation I'd issued, he was pleased.

"I look forward to meeting them," he said.

We spent the rest of the late afternoon in relative silence, letting the crackling fire speak its wisdom. I considered broaching the subject of the journal entries, but didn't. My own journaling experience, mixed with the conversations of the last few days and the chance meeting with Silas, all crystallized in a silent confidence. I felt a growing trust that the right conversations would have a way of happening, whether I forced them or not.

As night closed in, we prepared a dinner of rice and vegetables. I hadn't asked Silas what he wanted to eat, but I anticipated that a man so well-traveled would like the assortment of foods. I wasn't sure if he was hoping for meat, but judging by his size, I assumed he was. I hoped he wouldn't be too disappointed.

"Jim, I have a treat!" I looked over as Professor Singh was opening our cooler. He pulled out two packages of chicken breasts.

"Where did you get those?" I could hardly mask my relief that an unspoken prayer had been answered so quickly.

"At the store. I knew you would want this, and I am happy to give it to you."

"Thanks!"

I opened the packages, cut away the skins and lingering fat, and tossed it into the flames so the fire could consume it. I sliced the meat into bite-sized pieces and put it into an iron skillet resting on a roasting rack across the pit. Within half an hour, we had chicken, vegetables, and rice simmering away. Memories flooded in of my friends and I whipping up steak and potato bonanzas around these fires, with hot sauce and dripping fat sending flames high into carefree nights of beer, cigars, and stories. Small joys. I'd forgotten how much I relished the informality of outdoor gourmet cooking – an accessible artform with no pretense or expectation. Simply nourishment for its own sake, and an excuse for revelry that's absent from city dining.

The sound of an approaching car drew our attention. Silas pulled his Jeep behind the professor's 4x4, waving as he hopped out. Casey jumped from the passenger side and lumbered over to us, tail wagging.

"Out of camp!" Silas bellowed. Casey retreated, sitting obediently outside our ring of chairs. I imagined dogs retreating from campsites all around Mormon Lake as Silas's voice echoed through the trees.

"Hello!" I took his hand for yet another time that day.

"Hiya, kid."

"Hello, I'm Arjun Singh." The professor extended his hand. "I apologize. My hands are covered in vegetables."

"No problem, Arjun. Mine're covered in dirt. I'm Silas."

"Pleased to meet you, Silas."

Silas looked the professor up and down. "You wouldn't happen to be *the* Arjun Singh, would you?"

"Um…" he stammered, "I'm *an* Arjun Singh. To which one do you refer?"

"I refer to the Arjun Singh who advised the Indian and U.S. governments on Muslim-Hindu relations for almost two decades. The Arjun Singh who attended the 1988 nuclear arms talks with Gandhi. The Arjun Singh who wrote an internationally multi-award-winning piece on religious tolerance. *That* Arjun Singh."

Professor Singh busied himself with pots, pans, and nothing in particular. My jaw slightly closer to the ground, I realized he seemed to enjoy synchronicity when it was my experience, but this was probably a little much for him – tipping the scale from interesting and intriguing toward awkward and embarrassing. Silas had rattled off a list of things about this man well beyond my knowledge.

"Well, yes. I am the vehicle for those things." The professor didn't seem quite sure how to react.

"Wow!" Silas lit up like the moon above. "It's an honor. I heard you were a professor of religion and philosophy, and I started to put the pieces together, but…wow. Anyway Arjun, I was telling your friend here that I used to cover Asian politics, among other things, as a journalist." Silas, probably sensing my bewilderment, looked at me and said, "You couldn't cover Indian politics in the eighties and nineties without hearing this man's name."

"I couldn't take a course at college in the nineties without hearing his name." Silas and I laughed. I glanced over at Professor Singh who was still finding things to busy himself.

"Well," the professor finally said, "I think dinner's almost ready. Shall we?"

I pulled three chairs closer to the fire and set out three tin plates, three tin sporks, and three knives. Silas walked over to his Jeep and grabbed a large sack. He brought it back to the fire and pulled out a case of non-alcoholic beer.

"Something from the cooler for just such an occasion," he said, setting the box down to a chorus of clinking. "Had to give up the real stuff years ago. The cigarettes had to go, too. But I still love the taste." He ripped off the cardboard top and grabbed a bottle. "Arjun?"

Professor Singh eyed it with hesitation. "Well, I usually don't. But it is the end of a long day and I have been known to indulge once in a while. Seeing as there's no alcohol…"

Chapter 22

Random Garbage and the Common Foundation

Silas and I ate all the chicken, with side helpings of rice and vegetables. The professor helped himself to copious amounts of the latter two. He also produced a small bag of rolls and we used them to soak up the curried gravy on our plates. Even without alcohol, the beer was intoxicating, and conversation flowed easily. Even Professor Singh appeared more at ease as the night went on, talking politics with Silas. Silas, intrigued with behind-the-scenes information on Indian political figures, peppered the professor with questions about the life and times of many prominent Asian politicians whose names I did not recognize.

"Jim tells me you take amazing black and white photographs, Silas. I should like to see some."

"Sure thing, Arjun. I put some in the Jeep before I left, just in case anyone asked."

I detected a giddiness in his stride as he retrieved the photos. Clearly exhausted from the day's excitement, Casey had fallen asleep once any chance of wayward food disappeared. Silas produced the picture box, as well as a folder I didn't see before at his camp. He brought them over near the fire, dragging his chair between the professor and me. He supplemented the fire's light with a small flashlight from his vest pocket.

The professor was clearly emotional as he pored over the photos. There were pictures of children in India, living in monumental poverty in the poorest districts of its larger cities. Political discussion is fine, I thought, but it's those who suffer from political sins who touch us most.

"This is Kiran, a child I met in Calcutta on a recent trip." Silas handed the picture to the professor. "He lives in a home for orphans. But I noticed he always had a smile. These other boys in the photograph live there, too. Kiran's like their dad. He teaches them to read. And, he plays a mean game of soccer. I even saw him give his dinner to a malnourished kid who had just arrived that day."

"He is very much enlightened," the professor said. "This boy is wise beyond his years. We could learn from him." He looked over at me, then into the fire. I saw a tear in his eye, or maybe it was an illusion in the light.

We set down the pictures, picked up our beers, and wandered to the edge of the campsite to a wide expanse and an outcropping of long, flat rocks that led down to a cliff. The rocky terrain formed a ledge with a great view of the narrow valley by day and the gaping chasm of the cosmos at night. Each of us relaxed on our own slab.

"It's incredible," I said, staring out at the faint, cottony ribbon of the Milky Way, ever-present, yet invisible in city lights. "And to think, it all emanates from one source. We're a speck of dust in the grand spectrum of consciousness, yet inseparable from it." I spoke without my full attention. I wasn't sure where the words came from. Maybe it was the intense night air mixing with the beer. I felt clear. The professor cast his eyes in my direction. I could just barely make out a raised eyebrow, but he remained silent. Instead, he leaned back and stroked the key between his fingers. I let the words replay in my mind, and a flush crossed my cheeks as I pondered their fanciful, ridiculous ring.

"Ah," Silas said, pulling me back to the place. "That old saw again. A conscious speck of dust in the mind of an intelligent creator. Why does the night sky and beer have that effect on everyone? And this isn't even real beer!"

"What effect?" My words may have been whimsical, but I didn't believe they were false. Although a new initiate to this point of view, I was ready to defend it. "And by the way, I don't think I mentioned an intelligent creator."

"That whole, 'grand creation' thing." Silas tapped his foot against a nearby rock. It made a hollow thud against his boot. "What if we're the most real and most intelligent thing in this whole cosmic ocean, kid? This whole business of God and consciousness…heard a lot about that in my travels, but I'm thinking it's really just chaos. Bang!" Silas clapped his hands. "And just like that it all arrived on the scene."

"Chaos?"

"Yeah."

"I don't know, Silas. It seems like there has to be some kind of order. Just because we can't figure it out with our five senses doesn't mean there isn't something keeping all of this together."

"Hmm…" I couldn't tell if Silas was pondering this idea of mysterious cosmic glue or dismissing it. Perhaps over the years he'd picked this bone clean. After all, this debate had been raging around the globe for so many millennia, it was practically cliché by now.

"So, you're good with chaos, Silas?"

"Random chance works for me, kid."

"Maybe you're right," I muttered.

"There's a lot of pain out there," he continued. "I don't pretend to know what it all means, or what the solution is. But I do know that no one and nothing has come to lend us a hand. The garbage pile keeps growing, and no one, including some god, seems to want to help clean it up."

"Random garbage?" I asked. "That's chipper."

"Well, what would you call it?"

"I don't know. But it's hard to believe people suffer because they made a bad spin on the blind wheel of fortune. Look at your pictures,

Silas. Look at the suffering. It's hard to beli'
like to think our species can pull together to
    "Wait, I'm lost. How would humans cor
single-source creator hypothesis, kid?"
    "Well, it's not so much that it supports it. 1 gu⌐
of hope."
    "Hope?"
    "Sure. Coming together as one humanity is probably more likely
when we think of things as having a common beginning, or a common
foundation. Maybe the opposite of your premise is true, Silas. Maybe
chaos is really the appearance until we begin to pull together and
discover the order. Maybe there's one source giving itself many minds
that seem separate so that it can see how many different experiences
it can have from one starting point. Maybe the appearance of suffering
is part of that. Who knows?"
    "Maybe. But my pictures…" His voice trailed off into the ponderings
of quiet. His boots shuffled on the ridge, sending a scratching echo into
the night.
    "What about them?" I pressed.
    "I focus the camera on those kids, and I see joy and innocence
through their pain. As a journalist, I sometimes found myself at a loss
for words to describe the plight of the people I photographed.
Especially children. It's beyond words. Something that always escaped
my pen. I felt connected to these kids even though we seemed so
different. Their memory followed me home like a tragic souvenir.
That pain burns when you see it."
    "Maybe that's the point, Silas. Things only seem different across
cultures or arbitrary class structures. It's empathy that connects it all
together – that lets us in to see the truth. Maybe the fact that you burn
inside when you see someone else suffer is the sign that it's all
connected somehow."
    "Yeah, kid. Maybe. I've never really thought about it like that. But
why does one child suffer while another thrives? Either God or luck is

152

cold and
is not
me

indifferent. And the former, at least as I've heard it defined, usually prone to indifference. You're the religion guy. You tell what's going on!"

"I don't know, Silas. I guess everyone suffers in their own way, y'know? I was engaged. The whole thing imploded. Not entirely sure why, but I think I'm figuring it out. She probably had a hard time living with my depression and anxiety. Probably didn't like that I thought about suicide. That's on me, but I'm sure it made her suffer. I'm not proud of it."

"I'd imagine that would be pretty rough for her, kid."

"I'm sure it was. But those things are no picnic for me, either. But I get up each day and try again. I still can't say for sure why we suffer and what it all means."

"You think the two of you still have a shot?"

"I donno, Silas. I've thought about it. Then stopped thinking about it. You know the routine." He emitted a light cackle and a sigh. "Maybe we can piece it back together someday. The point is, I never realized how much my suffering made her suffer. I guess I can see it more from her perspective now. When relationships crash and burn, they leave two people with the common experience of pain, even if it looks different to each of them."

"It's true, kid. The children in my photos…and the adults, single folks, couples, engaged people, rich, poor. Everyone has their date with pain in some form or another. But I'll tell ya this, after shaking hands with evil so many times, you get tired of the introduction. Get back to me with your all-one-thing theory when you have the courage to live all the suffering in the world."

The comment sliced through me like a razor. Some of my friends, and even a few therapists, had told me I needed courage to fight my depression and suicidal thoughts, and it always left me feeling victimized and blamed. The assumption that I woke up every morning and just gave in to my struggles like a sacrificial lamb was insulting. I felt the knots in my gut and the acid rising in my throat. But remembering another exercise from Doctor Eastman, I stopped, counted to three in my head, and took a breath. I wandered closer to Silas and joined his gaze into the void of the stars.

"It might take me a few lifetimes to do that, Silas. Can I get back to you on it?"

He laughed. "I'm sorry, kid. I shouldn't have snapped like that. I'm not always a crotchety old man, I swear! Maybe I'm just tired." He tapped my shoulder with a light fist bump.

"It's okay," I said, shoving him with my arm. "I always have room in my life for a few exhausted cynics."

A swirl of wind caught the trees. The gravelly rumble of Professor Singh clearing his throat in the pause caught our full attention.

"Well, Silas, I'll say this." He worked the key gently. "With the way things are in the world right now, the breath in a person's lungs is proof enough of their courage. To awaken each day in a world containing sadness and suffering – and to take the time to examine and explore it as you and Jim have this evening – is akin to living sadness oneself and searching for a solution. Everyone has a measure of pain, and we must not use another's personal struggles to gauge our own. Any experience of sorrow is one we all share."

"Maybe, Arjun." Silas stretched mightily and tilted his neck in hard motions. It cracked in a torrent of bullets and softened on his shoulders. "Maybe."

The conversation ended as gently as it had started. The mood on the ridge cast a pensive glow on our little group of relaxed philosophers. Eventually, Professor Singh and I walked Silas and a very groggy Casey back to the Jeep. It was late, and we were weary after traveling so far through the great arguments of history. Silas agreed to stop by the camp the next day to pick me up on his way to shoot photos. After his headlights disappeared into the night, we put out the fire and headed for bed.

Chapter 23

A Lousy Life Motto

The sun arrived at my tent early the next morning. I rubbed the night from my eyes and squinted at my watch – 5:40 a.m. I flipped onto my back and stared up at the domed ceiling, tracing the seams as they rose in sync, summiting at a lone, silver button. I thought about the Buddhist parasol with its ribs joining at one point. Each track represented one step on the Noble Eightfold Path – Buddha's recipe for wisdom, ethical conduct, and a pure mind.

I grabbed for the professor's journals and reread the sections on oneness. The ideas splattered again across my neatly pressed academic mind, seeping deeper and deeper into my consciousness. They crowded out so many long-held beliefs, I grew restless – yet alive – in their presence. I lay in my sleeping bag and mulled the possibilities of consciousness, unity, and source in a silent reflection. I closed my eyes and practiced breathing. I felt my body sink into the earth. I became acutely aware of pine needles resting under the floor of my tent. The smell of the trees heightened to a crescendo that overwhelmed me. A peculiar sensation arose, as if my physical body was expanding…elevating.

After a while, however, I came down from the lofty heights of quiet introspection and craved earthly dialogue. I wasn't sure what was happening to me. All I knew is something had been unlocked inside me. A caged animal deep within was now free and awake, hungry to explore new lands, stalking conversation. The professor had been so quiet last night that I was hesitant to approach him with questions. I felt he was still waiting for me to figure things out for myself. But how would I know if I had figured anything out unless I talked with someone who already knew? Nevertheless, I delayed my exit, picked up my journal and pen, and tried to capture some thoughts from the previous night and my morning reflection and meditation before they faded.

An hour later, I unzipped my tent and peeked out. I saw the professor on the precipice, twisted in a yoga pose. As I watched, he switched positions, then switched again. One moment he was standing tall, extending his hands toward the sky, and the next, he was balancing on one foot with perfect precision. The sight of this man performing flawless postures people half his age could only dream of, raised his excellent esteem in my eyes. I munched on trail mix and tore off a tiny corner of an energy bar before venturing out to join him. He was now seated in meditation, and I took my place next to him. The air was brisk, yet he sat only in shorts, with nothing else but the key around his neck. I was self-conscious in my sweats, but quickly got over that when I felt the chill creeping from the rocks beneath me.

I assumed the half-lotus and straightened my back, appreciating with new awareness each knot and tight spot in my body. However, they no longer had the power to dissuade me. In fact, they faded rather quickly under my devotion to posture. I shifted and shuffled my position, eventually settling myself into the earth. I reveled in the feeling of soft breath and hard rock – the breeze the only sound as we turned to the inner winds. In…out…in…out. My slow, steady breaths arrived and departed in a quiet, rhythmic, controlled way. For a fleeting instant, I felt that everything was here on the ridge. Everything was contained in this moment. After what seemed like an eternity, and as if exactly on cue, we snapped from meditation and looked at each other. We stood in unison and walked together to the fire pit. The professor lit a match and tossed it into a fresh pyramid of wood and kindling, and I poked it deep into the embers. I worked the pile of logs until flames slithered through them. Within minutes we were heating water for tea. The crisp morning air heightened my appreciation of the fire's warmth.

"So," the professor said, putting on his sweatpants and a t-shirt, "you and Silas really talked last night."

"Yeah." I scooted my chair closer to the fire. "He's an interesting guy."

"But?"

"But what?"

"You tell me, Jim."

"Well, I hate to admit this, but he may be right about me."

"Which part of you?" Professor Singh set a chair down next to me. He blew into his hands, rubbed them together briskly, then held them near the fire.

"The part about courage. I haven't really done all that much in my life. I mean, who am I to speak about common experience and unity? I probably sound like a privileged jerk or something."

"Do you think you sound that way?"

"Well, no. I don't think so. I certainly don't feel that way."

"Then it's settled!"

"Is it, Professor? I'm just learning about the deeper meaning of all this stuff. I'm no expert on it. So I've read some academic books. So I have a few degrees. So I've meditated a few times." I plucked a weed from beside my chair and twirled it in my fingers. "A few journal entries do not a spiritual or philosophical master make."

"That's quite a life motto, Jim."

"Thanks. I worked hard on it."

"But this is also dangerous thinking you have about courage."

"Dangerous?"

"Yes. This type of thinking is what causes good people to do nothing in the world. They hold back much-needed advice or support for friends if they haven't experienced their friend's problem. Or, they may feel that since they haven't grown up poor, they have nothing to offer those in poverty. Occasionally, the roles reverse. Sometimes the needy refuse help from those whom they feel do not understand their situation, or friends shut out their contemporaries because their ego will not tolerate good counsel from one who is not in their skin."

"Pretty sad." I smirked and shook my head. "I don't know, Professor. It's just…it's hard sometimes. We try to do the good thing. The right thing. To help ease suffering. But we talk ourselves out of it. We judge ourselves out of it. We let the opinions of others chase us away from doing what we know to be right and real. Or…I donno…maybe that's just me." I pulled an orange from a sack in front of us and started to peel it. I focused on my fingers as they worked the rind, noticing the bumps and valleys in the bright orange skin. I could feel the professor's eyes upon my task. I tried to keep the rind in one spiraling piece but couldn't do it. Instead, I ended up with an orange-rind jigsaw puzzle and a sticky hand. I tossed the peelings into the fire, watching them expel moisture and curl in on themselves. What was once so bright and vibrant melted into a black, charred mess. "I guess you're probably right, though. If we never took advice or guidance from people with different experiences, there would be no male obstetricians."

"Very true, Jim. Very true. But this ego-based practice of shutting others out because of different circumstances only arises if we believe our identity is separate from others. That's the road you two were on last night, if you recall. If we realize that all people suffer in some way and that we can all have empathy, then that can connect us."

"Right, Professor. I agree."

"And we can help ease that suffering in different ways. There's active giving in the form of charity, there's compassion in the form of a shoulder to cry on or a kind word, and, yes, even meditation."

"Meditation?"

"Yes, Jim. Meditating can calm us down so we can be present for others, or it can shift energies in a way that helps people around the globe. Any of these forms of easing suffering can change the world, and just as we all suffer, we can all help."

"I guess it's all about intention, Professor."

"How so?"

"Maybe this is my social work background talking, but if it's our intention to be useful and to serve, then that's our qualification. It's not whether I've suffered like you have or if I'm depressed, anxious, addicted, young, old, single, or divorced. It's if I understand suffering and want to help."

"An excellent point, Jim. It is not about experiences, then, but intentions."

"So then we should help and accept help because we know our life is connected to everyone else's. We don't all have to fight in wars to work for peace."

"That, Jim, is a much more life-affirming motto than your previous attempt. I think you should use this one going forward in your life."

"I'll bring it up at the next board meeting."

The conversation gave way to a quiet moment. I bit into a sour section of orange that caught me off guard. I was not prepared for that taste after so many sweet pieces. I pulled a seed from my mouth and flicked it into the flames. The lingering silence was my opportunity.

"Professor, I read your...um...the entries on oneness in your journal. I also jotted down some thoughts in my own journal."

"I'm glad."

"Well, I have a few questions. Can I ask you some?"

"Why on earth would you not ask?"

"When I look at Silas's pictures and I hear him talk about them, I feel like he identifies with them...with the images."

"Yes." The professor was now deftly peeling a grapefruit. "I noticed this, too."

"He feels like that, even though he says he's not a very spiritual guy."

"One's devotion to the personal soul is not a measure of his capacity for compassion on a universal scale, Jim. You defended a version of that argument last night."

"No, Professor, I know that. I feel like it's all connected, right? I can feel it somewhere inside of me, and it sounds right when we talk about it. But I guess I'm not sure…how is it that we are all connected? There sure seems to be evil in the world. Does that really negate God or gods? If it does, what connects it?"

"Well, Jim, you say evil exists. But does nothing else exist? We just talked a few minutes ago about helping others and the good acts we can do to change the world and connect it. Humans are capable of such amazing kindness. It's all through history."

"You're right. In the aftermath of 9/11, the world came together. And there are stories of Christians who risked their own lives to hide Jewish people during the Holocaust. Stuff like that."

"This is true, Jim. And sometimes people who don't know anyone in the communities they are helping, help anyway. They clean up trash. Build houses. Send money."

"Right, Professor. So, I guess I want to know why. What is that?"

"Well, as with all who are asked to give an answer to questions like that, all I can give you is my best assessment." He pitched a single, flawless, springy rind into the fire and proceeded to perfectly section apart juicy pieces with his thumbs.

"That's all I can ask, Professor."

"Jim, if you read what was in the journals, then you now have a better understanding of what I am going to say. Indeed, you know it already. But let's investigate." He popped a wedge of fruit into his mouth, and I could see he was savoring the flavor.

"Okay," I said, munching another piece of orange.

"Very well." He moved his chair closer to the fire. The necklace bounced against his t-shirt as he shuffled forward. He set the grapefruit on his lap and again rubbed his hands together methodically before the flames. A few hundred miles south, on the desert floor, it was already over ninety degrees. "Let us begin with an understanding. Much like our discussion concerning time and living in the moment, reflection on oneness is not new. You used this ancient concept in your discussion last night, and I'm sure you've lectured about it historically and academically in your classroom. It has been around for thousands of years. It is again important to remember the idea did not spring anew in the sixties."

"It probably could have." I laughed. "My dad loves to tell stories from his college days back then."

"Oh? Was he interested in these things?"

"Sort of. He spent a lot of time at concerts, idolizing folk singers. I listen to some of his old tapes and records on occasion."

"It was a great sound, Jim."

"It was. Great messages, too. A lot of the songs have a theme of unity or love. These singers had disciples, too, I think. Just like the wandering gurus."

"But don't forget, the first hippies were thousands of years old."

"Folk rock in ancient India." A smile broke over my face. "What a great thought!"

"No doubt you already know from your studies that this oneness proposition has been part of Eastern and Western philosophy for millennia. It's the idea that somehow, events in life are connected, and that either God, or perhaps all of creation, is one. Remember we discussed this in our Asian Traditions class?"

"I do, Professor. But again, it's sometimes hard to see how all that academic stuff has anything to do with practical living."

"How so, Jim?"

"Well, I've given a few lectures on Eastern metaphysics, but for most of my students, and, until recently for me, it was an academic curiosity. Just something to ponder for an hour until we go back to our lives outside the classroom. But now, it's crazy. These ideas are leaping out of the pages of history and coming alive. I know that sounds nuts, but…well…the chance meetings with Silas, or the occasional insights people have that all things come from one place. Or, maybe we finally get that our time on earth is just a temporary thing, and when we die, we don't really end, but just continue as part of some other thing or mystery. How do we know where duality ends, and unity begins? How do we have meaningful dialogue with others who don't even want to consider this kind of stuff? How do we even talk about this? Where do we put it?" I took in a deep breath to let my questions and frustrations settle. Professor Singh was patient for the exhale. "Anyway, concepts are one thing, Professor. My feelings on the matter deep in my gut are one thing. But putting them into practice in the practical world? Explaining how it all fits together? That's something else."

"Jim, your observations reflect the disconnect between the philosophical world and the world of experience. The idea of oneness straddles the line and is complicated."

"I'll say."

"Let's start with this premise: Oneness can mean a variety of things."

"That's a weird sentence, but okay. I'm with you."

"Some say it is God that is one, and our continued existence after death is that we live in separate relationship to that supreme power. We can be near it in some heaven, or far from it in some hell, but we don't merge with it. For these believers, it is possible to speak of emergence of our world, our universe, from a creative source, but ironically, one cannot re-merge with it. For them, speaking of merging with the one power in a mystical way is akin to saying we are God."

"Yeah. Heaven for those folks is being in the presence of God, and not away from God. God's whole as it is, and we just kind of hang out in that glory."

"Right, Jim. For example, in mainstream Judaism, there is a creed from Deuteronomy 6:4 which you may know from your studies. 'Hear, O Israel: the Lord our God, the Lord is One.'"

"That's called the Shema, I think."

"You are correct. One interpretation of the Shema seems to be that the Lord – the masculine, personified God of the Hebrews – is one entity before creation, and now lives in relationship to us, the created. From this way of thinking, there can never be a merge, but only a relationship. Again, it is from God that we emerge, but cannot merge."

"Is there anything wrong with that?" I found myself taking on Silas's role in this conversation.

"No, Jim. There is no 'wrong.' It's just a point of view on our relationship with the source. In most streams of Christianity, Judaism, and Islam – with a few exceptions – this is the prevailing belief. But this is not the only way of looking at the experience of God. This is not the only way people can relate to God. Many monotheistic traditions have mystical sides. As I said, there are exceptions – Kabbalah in Judaism, for example – that guide the faithful to different relationships with this force. The concept of merging with the source is not out of the question for these mystics. It's not better or worse. Just different."

"Yeah. That was the stuff I loved lecturing about in my classes, Professor. We would dive into definitions of the divine. Like the 'Tao' of Taoism." I paused for a moment to get my bearings on this elusive concept. The professor waited for me to return. "My favorite line from Lao Tzu's *Tao Te Ching* is, 'The Tao that can be named is not the eternal Tao.' I love the idea that labeling the thing that emanates all things actually negates the ultimate idea. If you name it, it loses something. A good reminder that language is symbolic."

"Indeed, Jim. Sometimes defining or labeling an idea destroys its deep meaning. If I am in a silent room with another person, sharing a peaceful moment, and I say, 'My goodness, it's quiet in here!' I have shattered the peace. I have named silence, diminishing its essential quality. In many ways, that is the difficulty of speaking of the oneness of divinity. And, I'm guessing, this is what is giving you trouble applying the concept of unity to everyday life. The oneness to which we refer is, in all likelihood, beyond name or title. It doesn't seem to have a place in our day-to-day life because it's hidden right in front of us. Once we talk about this monolithic idea, it dissolves. It can only be identified in relief to duality. You can only know of the one when you emerge from a belief in two."

"It's hard to do. It's hard to see past appearances."

"It is, Jim. It is hard to do. Some will arrive there. Some won't.

Some will want to try. Some won't. And, in the end, who really knows the right point of view?"

"It's funny, Professor. We're two people sitting here trying to discuss this concept of oneness that may not even exist or be anything like we think it is."

"That's right, Jim. Even the mere suggestion that it is one thing is troublesome, as it is quite possibly no 'thing' at all."

"Hmm..." I mulled over the paradox of how 'no thing' could potentially create something. I launched back into my readings in sacred history. "There are so many ways to think about this power, Professor. Like in the East. In Hinduism, some believe the individual self comes from one source – *Brahman* – and that's what brings us all together. I doubt this *Brahman* has any personal identity. It's not named "Frank" and it doesn't have a job or a mailing address, but yet, there is a term being used. *Brahman.* And...oh wow..." my face contorted into a smirk of confusion and realization.

"What, Jim?"

"We're sitting here using definitions that defy definition to illustrate a point about definitions!"

"I think we have another entry in the 'lousy life motto' contest, Jim."

"I don't know, Professor. I think that's our winner."

"Indeed. But let's not give up so quickly. Let's back up a few steps and try for a greater understanding. We've already laid a good foundation, but keep in mind that we are ultimately dealing with an elusive mystery. We can know about these concepts, but it would be impossible to actually know them."

"I'm not sure what I know at this point," I said.

"Excellent! Now we can go higher."

Chapter 24

Behind the "Seens"

Professor Singh pushed his chair further away from the fire. He closed his eyes and took a deep, quiet breath. He opened them slowly and faced me.

"'There is one ruler, the self of all things, who transforms his own form into many forms.' That, Jim, is from the Katha Upanishad."

"Hindu scripture."

"Yes. These words exquisitely capture the core messages of the mystics. There was a time before the Upanishads when the living experience of divine knowledge was reserved for those in positions of power, such as priests. But others wanted to explore. The Upanishads shared mystical ideas with a wider audience."

"Isn't that always the way? The elite race to the top and plant their flag in something awesome, but eventually, the rest of society finds a way to get up the mountain, too. I remember watching TV with my dad as a kid. The news was on. A riot was going on in some country where a dictator had just been overthrown. My dad told me that the push for freedom would always find a way. Spiritual freedom is the same way, I guess."

"Very wise. As far as I can tell, Jim, that idea from the Katha Upanishad is that everyone is at once one, yet on a unique journey through the ages. In other words, there is one spirit, energy, or whatever you may suggest, emanating the world. Therefore, the things that we see, including named gods that we envision with the eye of the mind, and their temples that we build with the hands, are just many expressions of one phenomenon, or one energy – what some have called *Brahman*. This is a powerful idea and we must not ignore it. Under this view, 'one' becomes the largest number, as all is accounted for within it."

A flood of realization smashed against me. This stream of words flowed over me and cooled the hot, delicate skin of my confusion. This new insight into ancient wisdom trickled into the cracks of my consciousness. Here by this fire, the concepts sizzled, seeped, and steamed.

"So, if everything is one emanation of *Brahman*, or a common source, then all things matter."

"They do, Jim."

"All lives are significant."

"Indeed."

"All suffering is a common experience."

"It is."

"Even if it doesn't look the same."

"Correct."

"And all attempts to alleviate suffering spring from the basic human feeling of empathy."

"Yes."

"And we should feel empowered to help and to receive help, because it's all...we're all...whoa!"

"What we do to one, we do to all, Jim. But don't get lost in the all-encompassing emanations of the East!"

"What do you mean?"

"This idea also rings true for the God of the Western world. If there is one God who creates beings with the capacity to love one another, then we have a duty before this creator to love our neighbors as ourselves, as Jesus said, because these neighbors spring forth from the same place of love that we do. The same divinity, if you will. In that way, we honor ourselves."

"How?"

"Well, kindness and charity, when given freely, are not just about loving others, but a way of loving ourselves, regardless of whether we are a unity or a separate creation. When we give like that, we honor what is lasting and loving within us by sharing it with others."

"What's that Bible verse about doing for others no matter what or who they are, Professor? From Matthew, I think."

"Ah. 'Inasmuch as ye have done it unto one of the least of these my brethren, ye have done it unto me.'"

"That's the one. And bonus points for using the translation with the flowery language. 'Brethren' and 'ye' should make a comeback."

"That sentence is flowery, as you say. And, it is one of the great cornerstones of empathy and compassion in all of religion and literature, Jim. So you see, whether we accept the idea of mystical union or instead see ourselves in relationship to one God makes no difference. What is important is that whatever we believe, we must discover something deeper about the way we ought to live and how we ought to treat others."

"But Professor, why doesn't anyone do that? Sometimes I read these threads about religion on social media, and one mentioned a poll that said a large number of people believe in God. But, like Silas said, there is so much evil in the world, it's hard to imagine people actually believe wholeheartedly. But forget religious belief. It seems like so many people are just checked out of kindness, whether or not they believe in any god."

"In the daily doings and stresses of life, it is easy to forget our natural, loving state, Jim."

"Boy, is that true."

"Even if we desire to honor that beautiful unity – spiritual or not, it makes no difference – we find ourselves caught up in the illusion that things are separate and, fundamentally, at odds. If we accept that all things are part of one experience – and we must entertain that idea for this conversation – then this belief of human separation is, as you suggest, odd, indeed. The prevailing winds of economics, politics, and popular culture do not help the situation. They suggest we are separate sailors pursuing distant shores, and not common explorers united in one search."

"It's that way in relationships, too. People have different goals. Different things they want to do."

"This is very true, Jim."

"Maya and I would talk about our dreams, and somehow, the conversation would get around to the crossroads we'd come to. If we did what she wanted, I'd have to give stuff up in my life. If we did what I wanted, then she'd have to make some big changes. Even two people supposedly walking the same path feel like they're on two different roads. It's crazy! So much in life seems to be about boundaries and differences and…two-nesss. Separateness."

"Well, the separations of the modern world are, through the lenses we're using here, far from the truth, Jim. In fact, things are more likely intermingled."

"It's so hard to see. Division seems so real."

"Yes, but if you at least try to see the intermingling, the view changes. You have your life experiences, and at the same time, your storylines are dependent upon all other things and all other people. Your story only makes sense when set in relief to others. Oh sure, you may pursue liberty, autonomy, and individuality. But quite often, all of that is found only in relationship to others' pursuits. But as dependent as we are on each other, news and current events of any age reinforce strict duality or opposition. That is the false seat of worldly power."

"And that's too bad, Professor, because I really believe that we're all in this together. When there's some world calamity or massive scandal, things go downhill. Or recessions come along and leave us with empty stores. No jobs. A crap housing market. It seems we're all dependent on money and economy to the point where when it goes bad for one, we all go bad."

"Yes, Jim, but often, it is we who choose to rely on arbitrary divisions and categories."

"How do you mean?"

"We're the ones who create a separation from others in this world. It is we who decide to put shareholders before customers, we who decide to make risky investments, we who put faith in hypocrisy, we who struggle with lovers and lives and create complications where they don't need to exist. If we choose unity, then we can finally see the bigger picture and appreciate it. Live it. Work to make it better instead of living for ourselves only."

Scenes of Maya smacked me in the face. We would fight and walk off in separate directions to stew instead of coming together to figure it out. Awful bosses I'd worked for enforced policies that made me and my co-workers feel isolated or kept us from providing the best services to customers and clients. Or worse, would try to turn us against each other.

"That makes sense," I said. "Maybe that's the idea behind reincarnation. It's almost like there's one emanation trying to see how long it needs – how many lives – to remember itself…its unity. How many steps it has to take to get on the same path."

"That's an interesting idea, Jim. In that way, the soul is our real experience and the body is its protective shell. The source gives itself a body to see if it can conceive of itself as more than the body."

"Right! Can what's really lasting and eternal see itself through the fog of material stuff? Can it see that all apparent limitations are just a representation of a bigger reality?"

"This is why we meditate and do yoga and breath work, Jim. These tools discipline the body and quiet the mind. From there, more sensitive self-perception is possible. It's not unlike setting a bed with a fluffy pillow and soft blanket so that we may better concentrate on sweet sleep and dreams. We must use the body as a positive tool for transformation, not deny it or denigrate it."

"You know, Professor, it's so funny – I've often thought that humanity was like a team, striving for one goal. It's why I became a social worker. But it's so hard to describe what that one goal is. Is it a thing? Is it a force? We're having this nice chat about it, but what the heck is it?"

"A good question, Jim. Everyone has their own way of pondering the eternal. It's a gift of the mind."

"Yeah. Even if we don't call it by a name, so many of us want to reconnect with it. When I'm in a bad funk or having a panic attack, I call out to something. It's like, if I can connect with something higher, maybe the suffering will end. My clients have that too, I think. Some of them can't really describe the 'something greater' that gives meaning to their recovery or their life. They believe in something, and they want to reconnect with it, but they're not sure how to talk about it. I wish I could help with that. To help make that connection."

"Well, I don't know if there's one image that can solve a riddle as old as infinity, Jim, but for day-to-day discussions of connection I have always found the spider's web to be a very useful way of looking at this – the idea of a single creative force weaving one substance into a variety of patterns. It appeals to and applies to everyone around the globe."

"Unless they're afraid of spiders."

"The web's material springs from the spider. This creative thread is of her making. Each strand of the web she weaves reinforces the others, serving its purpose in the grand design. If you have ever seen a spider's web sparkling in the morning dew, no doubt you noticed the unique patterns in the collective enterprise – whirls, circles, and squares – it seems that it could be repeatedly woven forever, in finer and finer points of detail. There is no end to the shape or patterns to discover. The web is the work of one conscious weaver, with many parts uniting."

"Yeah. I guess if I really think about it, that's how I perceive the universe now – humanity, animals, plants. Even things we don't think are alive. All things are just one expression of something much larger

– the human architect and the inert bricks and mortar. All just one thing."

"Jim, many in the East and West will tell you that life is not about pushing uniqueness to the point of isolation. Rather, the goal is to appreciate the mosaic-like beauty of individual travelers bound for the same destination. Every element is a unique expression of oneness that is only understood for what it is because of the things around it. The grand context. All things are what they appear to be, but they are also something else."

"What do you mean, 'something else'?"

"Well, let's explore some of the great religious traditions again. We've already talked about a *Brahman* that emanates all things. But remember the Tao? It manifests and permeates all things, but is itself beyond direct perception or given name. The Tao is nothing more or less than that from which all things emanate. It is simply the way of things, the way of nature, and is beyond categories. Therefore, the things that appear in the world are what we see, but they are also the power of this indefinable force."

"Okay. So, things are trees, rocks, and fire, but they're also the thing that created them."

"Yes, Jim. Some might say this."

"That makes sense."

"The interconnectedness of all creation is exquisitely conveyed in the idea of Yin and Yang, the famous Chinese symbol of the softly divided circle."

"I love that image, Professor."

"It is quite striking. The circle is not cut down the middle. Rather, the separated halves flow endlessly." He took the stick we'd used to stoke the fire and scratched a circle in the dirt. With a deft hand, he swirled an 's' through the middle and drew two small circles in each side. "On one side is darkness of passive yin, the other side, light of active yang. However, residing quietly within the heart of one, is the other." He tapped each small circle with the stick. "An eye that sees the other for what it is, and appreciates it. Things are yin or yang, but they are also the interplay of yin and yang. Things are what they are, but they are also an act of creative will."

"But in yin and yang things are still separate, Professor, gentle or not. Cold and hot. Sun and moon. Mountains and valleys. I only know there are two sides because there are…well…two sides."

"True. But yin and yang direct our consciousness upward. We spin around in the swirling wheel and fly off into a higher recognition."

"Which is?"

"Oneness, as revealed in the world, appears dual – light and dark. However, all things carry in their hearts the hearts of others. The ideas of light and dark are not sharply divided antagonists, but loving partners, appreciating the other's innate qualities. One isn't better. Meditation upon yin and yang eventually reveals these two sides are not really separate entities, but necessary complements. One could not exist without the other. Day is, in one sense, a creation of night. True rest is a complement to hard work."

"It's a lot like human relationships, I suppose. The hard divisions between people are really just illusions of difference or, I guess, a naïve belief that we're all completely different. But that's probably a myth. What lies under our clothes or skin is…I donno…an energy…a spirit that's the same. Maybe. Who knows? I have to say, it sounds a little crazy. But somehow, I'm on board."

"I know how it sounds, Jim, but if you think about it, it is like you and Maya, if you don't mind a return to the comparison."

"Not at all. I'd like to hear more about that."

"You are not physically her, nor she you, but you kept each other close inside for a time, even in disagreement."

"I've never thought about it that way. Even when we argued, we always came back to a…well…not necessarily a swirling balance like yin and yang, but a peaceful place. Some of the time, at least."

"An excellent word, Jim. Peace in relationships is not found in mere tolerance, but respect and compromise. Do not judge a lover who does the opposite of what you think you would do in a situation or who walks in a different direction. Instead, see a piece of yourself within them. True understanding is non-resistance to another's action or thought. The lesson is as simple as it is elegant."

"I see that. If we're all on the same journey, even the most misunderstood act is an expression of our communal experience."

"Precisely. In that same way, we can reflect again on *tathata*, or suchness – the reality of things beyond the names we ascribe."

"Like the Tao?"

"Certainly. Never forget that all things have an essence beyond description. They just are as they are in this moment, even before we arrive to acknowledge them, name them, or chart their progress. A flower in this moment is not merely the story of a seed that became a seedling that exploded in mature color that will someday wither and die and then return to the earth to cradle and nurture a new seed, continuing the cycle of life and death. In this moment, it is the petals before us, just as they are. A flower is what it is, and it sprung from the universal source."

"Whatever that is."

"This recognition of the unseen source behind the 'seens,' so to speak, is more significant than just seeing something pretty in the moment. It is a reminder that in our daily lives, earnest and honest reflection and awareness must precede all judgment. Once I recognize the essential in you is the same as the essential in me, and we are both in existence now, I realize all judgment of your story is a crooked finger. As I point at you in judgment, my finger points back at me."

"You're right. Sometimes when I have a problem with something someone is doing – like maybe a client is making me mad or I wanted to scream at Maya – and I judge them, I realize I'm accusing them of doing something I do, or that I've done. Or something that, if I really think about it, I could do if the conditions were right. As much as I don't want to admit it, I'm only a decision away from being the person that's enraging me."

"So, why judge?"

"I guess it makes me feel better to point out other people's shortcomings instead of looking in the mirror."

"A very human answer, Jim. That's the plight of us all."

"Yeah. I have some friends from social work school who were really on board with the whole non-judgment thing. They worked with the toughest of the tough. The most challenging folks. Rushed to it the minute they had their diplomas. They couldn't wait to serve. I'm still struggling with it."

"Indeed. But now, we have a more difficult question facing us."

He dropped the key to his chest and made his way to the kitchen area. He opened the ice chest and held up two bottles of water. I nodded a silent thank you. He walked over and handed one to me. Repositioning his chair, he rested his feet on the fire ring and took a long drink.

"So refreshing," he said, admiring the half-empty bottle. "Let us never take for granted the feeling of thirst. It makes quenching possible, and that is a gift."

I took a small swig. "Here's to water," I said, raising my bottle high.

"Alright, Jim. Let us return to the business at hand." He took the key up from his chest again and twirled it slowly. "The difficult question is why be concerned at all with this issue of unity in the face of individual pursuits? Why not just content oneself believing things are separate and isolated?"

"Heh. Yeah. Why look around in the clouds for that one source when we have so much to do around here? In the end, who cares?"

He smiled a toothy grin, shook his head with a laugh, and pointed a finger dead at my chest. "You do."

"I do? Actually, since we reconnected, I do care. But why do I care, exactly?"

"Awareness, Jim."

"Awareness."

"If one contemplates a common foundation for the experiences on this planet, it creates a staggering awareness." He raised his hand and slowly extended his index finger to the sky. "We are *one*. We are, in our essences, beyond name and description. We look different, drive different cars, and work different jobs, but we have one common source."

"We've established that, Professor. But again, why does it matter?"

"Purpose! That awareness makes our purpose clear."

"And that is?"

"In this moment, if we are aware that we are part of something much bigger, then we hold the shining silver key to ultimate growth and realization!"

He held the key around his neck at length. A shiver flowed up from the base of my spine and raced around the top of my head. After so many years of watching him twirl that silver key, I finally saw it for the first time.

"So, our purpose is really this moment, then?"

"Jim, I submit that our purpose is recognizing in each moment, no matter what we're doing, that we are being given the opportunity to evolve our souls. Or, if you prefer, grow as the powerful humans we are. Right here. Right now. I propose the possibility that we have all come here as unique expressions of one energy, field, or whatever you would call it, and that our goal is to remember this. As you suggested earlier, Jim, the source gives itself limits to see if it can transcend them. Our journal entries are written, and words are limits, that is true, but think of the information as a metaphor for something available to all, regardless of education or experience. Contemplation creates words. Words create awareness. Awareness opens our eyes to a powerful truth. And, as I said before, this is why you should care about awareness. Because of a powerful truth."

"Which is?"

"That life is unfolding for everyone in this moment. And what we do with this moment – no matter what we do – is for the purpose of realizing our connection to others and to source, however you define it.

We connect. We grow. We're free."

Waves of fire rose and fell in the pit. I took in a breath and felt the power of air rush into my nose and fill my lungs. The sound of a plane in the sky. The feel of my clothes against my skin. My pulse. It was all here. All happening at once in this moment – happening while people I couldn't see or hear were also participating in sight, breath, sound, feeling, and pulsation.

"So, have we arrived, Professor? Have we become one?"

"That's for you to decide. But I will say this: A person cannot remove a drop of water from the ocean and call it something other than water. The drop's essence is that of its source. Water is water, whether from the sky, the Atlantic, or the kitchen tap. It may be salty, clear, or sweet, but it is what it is at its core. So diverse is water in purpose, but so unified in essence. Water is water whether spinning the miller's wheel, quenching my thirst, or nourishing the earth." He tipped his bottle towards me, pouring a few drops upon a wildflower. "The purpose of water in any moment is to uphold its watery essence."

I kicked away the wet dirt to expose the dry ground beneath. "The truth is buried right at our feet. It's so hard to see. These ideas sound so simple, but they're overwhelming."

"Well, the work is never done, Jim. The accumulation of life's knowledge is nothing more than discovering eternal wisdom as revealed in the world."

"It just sucks when we're the victims of injustice or feel like we've hit a pocket of bad karma. If we could only see the whole ocean instead of one drop, we might treat each other better. Maybe we wouldn't hate others for what they do to us, but learn to kinda love them."

"Yes, Jim. All of that bad karma we run into – what some would call evil, greed, and injustice – they keep our focus on fear and personal ego, making tolerance and forgiveness so difficult."

"Forgiveness. Somehow it always ends up there, doesn't it?"

"Indeed. Forgiveness is a key to unlocking the power of this new perception."

Chapter 25

A Brief Entry of Insight

Diamond sunlight sparkled through the trees. Dancing shadows ringed the dying fire as the embers smoldered. Lunch was the rest of an energy bar and trail mix. Professor Singh and I retired to our tents. I lay on my back on my sleeping bag, and spread my right hand over my chest, feeling my heart's slow, rhythmic meditation vibrating through the stillness of my fingers. I imagined the world's population with its hands on its pulsating hearts. My mind drifted to thoughts of a universal energy emanating from all of these beats. Hearts beating as one. The One beating as one. One. One. One.

I turned onto my stomach, again aware of my body and all the perceived imperfections on the ground through the tent floor. Out of nowhere, a stream of words entered my head like a tickertape. I grabbed for my journal and pen and began to write.

Individual, city, state, country, globe, and universe are united by a field that has existence as sure as it has content. We are surrounded and permeated by an energy, constantly creative. Our very life is the evidence. The source is like breath – we cannot see it, but it is there, sustaining us. When we breathe on a mirror, we see the condensation – the residue of breath. The world, in this very sense, is the creator's residue. The world we see is proof of the presence's ever-living breath. We are one. We are surrounded by an energy that contains all knowledge. There are no secrets. Plans are laid bare before us, free for perusal. In the common fabric of our existence is the ability to acknowledge our unity and access information. We must learn from and respect the streams of intuitive information. It flows equally for all, for it is all things.

I reread the words. They weren't anything new, but they felt new. They carried old insight, but they struck me here...now. As the professor had said, it was a drop of water from a larger source. I wanted to run and show him, but I decided to keep the experience to myself. I wanted to savor this moment. Though I didn't fully understand the entry's origin, I was sure I wanted to experience it again.

Chapter 26

Catching the Perfect Moment

I awoke from an unplanned nap to the sound of feet crunching in the dirt and pine needles outside.

"Anyone here?" A gruff voice broke the sleepy mood.

"Silas?" I poked my head out of my tent. Casey's wet tongue greeted me. "Yeech!"

"Watch it, kid. You'll offend him!"

"What's up?"

"Heading off for an afternoon shoot, remember?" Silas motioned toward his Jeep, stuffed with gear. A tripod was sticking up in the back with a duffel bag packed in next to it. "Don't tell me you're hung over on non-alcoholic beer, kid."

"I'm not," I said. "Just snoozing."

"So, are you joining me or not?" He grunted and kicked a pinecone towards my tent.

"Sure." I scrambled to get my shoes on.

"You'd better bring a jacket, too."

"Will do, Mom."

Silas walked back to his Jeep and shifted some things around to make room for me. I grabbed my journal and a pen as an afterthought.

The professor's head emerged from his tent. "Do you want to come with us?" I asked, falling victim, once again, to my habit of extending invitations that did not originate with me.

"No, Jim. You go. I have some reading I'd like to do. You two enjoy, and I'll start dinner for us all later."

"Thanks," I said.

"How are you, Arjun?" Silas returned to the campsite and greeted the professor with a smile. Casey ambled over to Professor Singh's tent for a head scratch.

"Fine, Silas. Going to capture nature?"

"Yeah. There's a nice vista and some exquisite stands of trees nearby. I want to be there when the sun is at the right angle. It's all about shadows, you know."

"Well, no shadow without light."

"Right, Arjun." Silas stepped back and regarded him for a moment. "See you later. I have some beans and cookies to offer the kitchen gods tonight."

"An embarrassment of riches," the professor said. "I'll see you three later."

I waved back at the professor, now emerging fully from his tent and stretching. I jumped into the passenger seat next to Silas and caught a faint whiff of dirty laundry, sweat, and dog breath that might have been called 'Rugged Loner.'

"Argh!" Casey jumped over my lap into the back seat.

"Sorry, kid. Dog's got a mind of his own. Doesn't seem to have much regard for where he steps. Kinda like his master!" Silas grinned.

"I'd like to have children someday, Silas. It would be unfortunate if that dream came to an end because of a 100-pound dog."

"Don't let him hear you. He's sensitive about his weight…and it's only 80 pounds."

We roared out of camp in a cloud of dust and headed back down the rutted path toward Silas's camp. As we passed it, I saw his bright blue tent with the school-bus-yellow rainfly. A trace of smoke curled up from the fire ring, remnants of the cool morning. The temperature was pleasant now, and the wind through the Jeep was exhilarating. After ten minutes, we stopped at a fork in the road. Silas exited and

Casey leapt after him, thankfully via the driver's side. Silas looked around, checking a map against a lurching, weathered wooden signpost that read *Road 5216.*

"Well?" I asked, jumping out and watching the dust settle around my shoes. "Are we there yet?"

Silas traced lines on the map with his fingers. He looked comically perplexed.

"I hate maps, kid. I'm used to navigating by chance. I once found my way through the Philippines on a motorcycle with nothing more than a sleeping bag and some luck. Remind me to tell you that story sometime. Anyway, according to this map, we're close. I think it's over this ridge."

"What's over the ridge?"

"A vista." He squinted at the map and let out a grunt. "Looks like the mountains come to a halt, so it has to be there. The other way takes us back towards the campsite."

"I thought you said you'd been here before."

"I have, but it was a while back, kid. Gimme a break. I brought my…er…a friend here, and I wanted to photograph it then, but the light wasn't right. I've always wanted to see that view again, but all I have is this damn cattle-road map."

"Nothing else sticks out in your mind about the place?"

"Nope. I remember it was near Road 5216. That's about it. It all looks different than I remember. Mind's not as sharp as it used to be."

We piled back in the Jeep and veered off sharply to the right. Silas turned the wheel with such determination, I had to brace my knees under the dashboard to keep from tumbling out. After a few minutes, he slammed on the brakes, almost sending Casey and me spiraling through the windshield.

"We're here!" he yelled.

A large stand of aspen trees rose up in front of us, as if an overzealous arborist had been through the place with a bag of seeds and a personal mission. Beyond them, a cliff dropped off into the valley.

We all jumped out. Casey and I were drawn like magnets into the trees. I picked up a rather large stick and tossed it. Casey, ever mindful of mindless tasks, was off and running. Tail wagging, he grabbed the stick and brought it back to me at his leisurely lumber.

I pulled the slobbery mess from his eager mouth and hurled it a few more times before turning to check on Silas. He was rummaging around in a large pack stuffed to the gills and held together with bungee cords and carabiners. I had no doubt it had seen many continents. Without looking inside, I knew it would be filled with lenses and other camera whatnots, probably mixed with stale food, scraps of paper, and more than one pair of dirty socks. He picked up the pack and a load of equipment, including a tripod with a camera perched on top. He groaned under the weight of it all, straining to lift it. I imagined him trying to haul it all up a mountain in some distant country to catch a sunrise.

Casey darted back to Silas's side and the three of us wandered out to the overhang. My camp was nice, but this was amazing. Instead of many rocks jutting out, we stood atop a small stone peninsula, barely wide enough for two people to stand. This part of the canyon wall jutted out further than the others, so the view on the flanks was totally unobstructed. Silas set his camera gear down with the gentleness of a nurse handling a newborn. He caught his breath and looked at me.

"Okay," he huffed through a labored exhale.

"Okay, what?"

"Okay, now we wait."

"Wait? Why wait? Shoot away, Silas. The view is spectacular."

"You don't know much about photography, do you, kid?"

"Well, no. I usually just use the camera on my phone." I pulled my phone from my pocket and showed it to him. "I have enough trouble figuring this out."

"That's great, kid. Really professional rig you got there." He rolled his eyes, then shifted his demeanor. A serious mood crossed his face as he prepared to lecture me on the finer points of his craft. "Look out there. You see those clouds?"

"Yes."

"Well, if we're lucky, they'll build, shift, and then reflect colored light as the sun drops. The sky is soon going to look totally different than it does now. I want to see rays shooting through those clouds. After that, I can square off against the trees. With stuff like this, you may only get a few perfect minutes. Minutes, kid…or even seconds. I need dark and bright. Contrast. I need the light to be just right so the colors will burst."

"I thought you said you only shoot black and white."

"Well, mainly I do. But you still have to be sensitive to color and light. Shades, kid. When the light hits things in a certain way, it creates shadows. Gives you a different perspective. The camera has to be able to pick up the contrasts of light and dark that make the scenery stand out. The picture's gotta pop. If I turned around and shot the grove right now, it would just be a stand of washed out, flat trees. But if I'm patient, the light will create a great effect. The trees will cast long shadows…invade each other's space. The picture will reflect the contrast – light tree, black shadow. Timing, kid. Plain and simple. Like I said, photography is the art of managing minutes. The things we see through the camera are the things we see, but if we do it right, they can also be something else entirely."

"That sounds familiar," I mumbled.

"Huh?" He was alternating between tinkering with a knob on the camera and squinting toward the horizon.

"Oh, nothing. I was just saying that makes sense."

"It's like lenses." Silas was now poking around deep in the recesses of his pack, pulling out wads of crap and camera gear. A piece of old tissue blew around the ledge in a swirl and tumbled into the canyon. Silas didn't flinch, his concentration honed to a piercing point. "I can use various filters over them to make it all stand out even more. Each filter allows and disallows various colors. Helps the shot emerge so that—"

"But Silas," I interrupted, risking another show of complete photographic ignorance, "I'm no expert on this, but aren't you taking a snapshot of the scene? You were a journalist. A reporter of facts. You took snapshots of world news in words with, I assume, a goal of accuracy. Don't you want to represent what you're seeing?"

"Yes and no. I mean, I can't recreate the moment as it is, kid. Nothing can do that. The camera isn't my eye and my eye isn't the camera." He tapped his temple with a rough knuckle. "The brains in our noggins are way more advanced than a camera in terms of taking in the whole scene. I'm only getting a slice of the life out there, if you will." He swept his hand across the vista. "The revelation of the scene to my mind via my eyes is a one-time deal. The camera can't see it like I can. Can't feel it like I can. All I can do is compromise with the elements to create an image. The true picture is only in my mind. I'm just representing it with the camera."

"Are you representing or misrepresenting?"

"I've never thought about it like that before." He paused from screwing on a filter to look at me. His brow furrowed in deep grooves. He raised a graying eyebrow, then shook off the thought, blew on the filter, and continued fitting it. "It's an art form to me. I mean, the women Picasso painted didn't have faces like a jigsaw puzzle, but that's how he painted them. It was his vision of their form. His representation of them."

"True, but isn't your photography different? You said you like to take pictures because sometimes you identify with the scene…like the Indian children in your photos. You don't pose them in any way. What you saw in Kiran is what you want to try to show to me in a photo. In my opinion, that's what makes them so special, right?

"Right."

"You told me at the campfire that poses would ruin the image. They'd make it artificial. Is the landscape any different? I'm not saying it's not art. I'm just wondering if maybe…" I could tell Silas had tuned out. I left the thought unfinished and decided to watch his active camera meditation – shifting knobs, adjusting settings, and wiping infinitesimally small particles of dust from lenses and filters. He maintained a deliberate silence. I cleared my throat and coughed.

"Pipe down, kid," he snapped. "I'm trying to focus here."

"Alright. Cool."

I wandered away from the ledge and slapped my thigh to get a napping Casey's attention. He sat upright and regarded me before looking at Silas and yawning. I wandered deep into the stand of trees and sat on a decaying log, picking at the rotting bark and watching a confused ant crawl haphazardly at my feet in the chaos of my presence. I tried to guide him back on course with a dried leaf, but I only made his situation worse. Casey, finally weary of his master's inattention, plodded into the shaded grove and rested his head on my lap. I scratched his ears and listened to his labored breathing. He was one of those dogs that tire out even in restful times. Together, we watched Silas fiddle with his camera and tripod. The preparation was exhausting to watch and mind boggling to comprehend. He took one lens after another out of his backpack, testing each one with painstaking precision. There was a great deal of control in his routine, to capture a nature so unpredictable and beyond control.

Watching the sun filter through the shimmering leaves, I thought about the beings that have had a fascination with that fiery ball in the sky. I remembered reading about baboons barking at the sunset, or the ancient Greeks who believed Apollo drove his chariot across the sky, the sun his precious cargo. But then I spared a thought for poor, brave Icarus who soared too close to the orange flames that melted the wax on his wings, sending him plummeting to the sea. I took out my journal and recorded these musings, Casey now asleep at my feet. When I pulled attention from my pen, I noticed Silas had turned his camera on the grove of trees. He was, no doubt, hoping to create that one perfect moment in an infinite series of already perfect moments. Once he started dismantling the incredibly involved camera apparatus, I walked over to him.

"Hey, kid, go over to the Jeep. There's a cooler in there. Two bananas and two bottles of water should do it. Oh, and something for the dog. I think there's a rawhide bone buried in there under all my crap. Good luck."

I dug around and found everything. This was no mean feat, as the Jeep was totally crammed with stuff. It was his mobile office, closet, kitchen, and who knows what else. As I was putting the lid back on the cooler, a box slid from a pile, dumping out pictures. I looked over and saw Silas's head buried in his backpack. I leafed through them until I came to one with no date or title. It was a color photo of a striking woman with flaming red hair. Her porcelain skin was covered in freckles. She was leaning up against a tree, a floppy straw hat shading half her face. She flashed a seductively wry grin at the camera, mocking the look of a woman who didn't want to be photographed. My mother, grandmother, and Maya always gave me the real look of annoyance when I wanted to take their picture at get-togethers, but something about this picture told me this woman wanted this moment remembered somewhere. Recorded for a long time. I had no doubt who was behind this particular shot.

I returned to the cliff with the snacks and bone in tow. Silas was in total focus mode, checking out some of the recent images on his camera's digital screen. Sitting with one leg stretched before him and the other tucked in, he looked like a child focusing on a game of marbles.

"Some of these should be great!" he exclaimed. "The vista shots are too washed out, but the trees came out nice. The sun just didn't want to cooperate early on. Oh, well. We get what we get out here, and we make the most of it." He looked up at me with a smile and grabbed for the snack. "Thanks, kid."

Casey snatched the rawhide bone from my hand and hauled it to the ledge to mangle it. Silas tore the peel off his banana with abandon and took a big bite, chewing while reviewing shots. He reached for his bottle and tapped it on the ground. Casey dropped his bone and lumbered back to us. Silas poured some water into a cupped hand. Casey drank it in earnest.

When the dog had gone back to his bone, I blurted out, "So, Silas, do you have a woman in your life?" He shifted his legs beneath him.

"Why do you ask?"

"No reason." I placed my focus on the banana, peeling it with total attention. I took a bite and savored the sweet, creamy fruit as it sloshed around on my tongue. Silas pitched the rest of his fruit to Casey, who eagerly accepted it. I swallowed with intention before continuing. "It's just, when I was in the Jeep, I saw a picture…I mean, it fell out of a box. It was a woman with red hair."

Silas stared over the cliff, with a look suggesting he'd rather be hurling me down the ravine than talking to me.

"You're a nosy son-of-a-gun, you know that, kid?"

"I'm sorry, I just thought—"

"That's your problem, kid. You think too much."

"Look, just forget—"

"Kayleigh."

"Huh?"

"Her name is Kayleigh. Kay, for short. She's my…well, was my…" I had cast him into rough rapids with no oars. "She's my wife."

"What?" After years of social work counseling training, I knew better than to let disclosures get the better of me. I'd had clients reveal all kinds of wild things to me over the years and had always maintained a sense of outer neutrality. But all my work boundaries fell away on this cliff as I could barely contain my shock. "You're married?"

"Sometimes."

"Sometimes? What does that mean?"

"Well, Kay and I have had a rough go of it. We're just too much alike. And too different."

"Where is she now?"

"Phoenix. We're separated."

Silas chucked his banana peel into the trees. Casey jumped from his rawhide to chase it. He sniffed it hopefully, eventually turning his attention to a log he found more entertaining. Silas watched him pee on it and sniff it, then he shook his head, and laughed.

"Kay. The only woman I know who would get someone a German Shepherd and give it an Irish name. Green bandana's hers." His hard expression softened into dreaminess. "She took it out of her hair the day we adopted Casey and tied it around his neck. He could fit in my palm then." Silas huffed. "But now Casey's palms are almost the same size as mine. Anyway, Kay said it gave him Irish flair, like he was our son. My dark features with her attitude and green bandana. He growls at me when I try to take it off to wash it. I've stretched it and sewn new sections onto it over the years. I guess it's grown up with him."

I smiled at the delicate disclosures that seemed so automatic. But reverie crumbled before reality, and Silas emerged from memory, defending himself in an unspoken battle I didn't intend to start.

"Kid, when you're on the road as much as I am, you lose your perspective. You get caught up in yourself. That isn't a good way to make a marriage work."

I launched into thoughts of Maya. Silas had just pinpointed one of our major problems. Maya and I had a terrible habit of accusing each other of not making the other a priority. We got so wrapped up in our own individual politics we forgot to maintain good foreign relations.

"How did you and Kay meet?"

"I met her in my college days. I'd been a solo act for a long time…been in Vietnam. Had seen things. Did things. Kay came along and was like a salve. Cooled my hot spots, kid. Plain and simple."

"So, what happened?"

"Hot spots flare. We dated on and off for a while. I traveled with my camera. She got tired of waiting for me and married another guy. I was married, too, but to my work."

"Couldn't you have taken her with you to the places you went? Made her more a part of that? More a part of your life?"

Silas set his camera on the ground with care. He stood to his full height, stretching. A solitary bone cracked somewhere in that large body, betraying a hard and lonely life. He walked to the edge of the cliff, picked up a stone, and cast it over the side. The sight brought on thoughts of the ancient scapegoat, where, in times past, communities put their sins on the heads of goats and then sacrificed them or sent them off into the wilderness. I imagined Silas putting his emotion into that stone before chucking it, hoping the valley would swallow up the pain.

"I guess I could have done that, kid." He turned to face me. "But I rebelled against us. I thought my freedom was more important than Kay. God, that's so cliché, isn't it?"

"Yeah. But I didn't want to be rude and point it out."

"Funny, kid. Funny. Guys tell themselves that stupid freedom story, and it always has the same stupid ending. All Kay wanted was to help me. To support my work. I guess I didn't want that. I don't know why. Just a feeling."

"Well, you said it, Silas. Freedom."

"Yeah, but…I don't know. Maybe it's more than that. Or less. Kay asked to come with me. Begged me." He sighed.

"If I've learned anything from my work, Silas, it's that humans do wild things, but somehow, it's always something they thought was best at the time, even if the consequences stink. People take drugs to feel better but end up losing their family. People commit dumb crimes to get a little more money, but then go to jail, leaving their partners broke and alone in the world with kids and bills. Or, we get depressed and lost in our emotions—" My throat closed off, choking on the sentiment and the reality. "And we push people away."

"It's true, kid. We feel threatened when others want to be a big part of our lives, and I guess we hold 'em at arm's length because we want to protect our freedom. Sounds good when we're doing it, I guess. We think we're becoming free when we run, but really, we're imprisoning ourselves in isolation."

"The power of the ego," I whispered.

"What?"

"Nothing. Just something the professor taught me. Lessons about pride and the difficulty of appreciation."

"Yeah, well, when Kay's marriage fell apart, we got back together. I was working in the U.S. again as a magazine editor. We got married."

"What happened?"

"An intern named Allison."

"Ah."

"It was just some drinks and a kiss. It was stupid, but it was enough. Anyway, I blew it again. Kay said she forgave me, and made me swear never to do it again, and I kept the promise, but I'm not sure she believes me. Anyway, we've been drifting apart for a while."

"I'm sorry."

"You got nothing to be sorry about, kid. It's alright. My choices, my consequences."

"Well, still..."

"Anyway, I came on this trip to give us both some breathing room. Kay deserves it, at least. That's why I came to Mormon Lake. We've had some great outings here. I guess I just wanted to visit a happier time. A better place."

"It really is all about timing, Silas. Catching the perfect moment."

"You said it." He looked dead into my eyes. "Learn from my mistakes, kid. Whatever is next for you in the relationship department, learn from my screw ups. And tell your clients out there in the world not to be idiots about this stuff, either.

"I might say it differently, Silas, but I appreciate that."

"You seem like a good person. Don't let nonsense mess it up. You have my complete and total permission to use me as your exhibit A if you do relationship counseling or any of that crap. I don't have plans to donate my body to science, but I can sure as hell donate my mistakes to a counselor. And believe me, Kay would agree one hundred percent. I really hurt her, and if she knew our story could help prevent that pain in someone else, well…let's just say that's Kay in a nutshell. Giving until it hurts, then giving more."

Silas let out a laugh with an air of discomfort behind it. But even through his pain, I caught a hint of brighter emotion. I wanted to continue, but decided to let him end the conversation on his own terms. Processing life events was a strong part of my social work counseling practice, and I knew better than to mess with even the slightest hint of an elevated mood. I simply finished with an affirming, "I hear that, Silas."

"Well, it's getting dark." He tucked the rest of his equipment neatly away into the depths of the pack. "We should probably get back to camp. Arjun said he'd be making dinner, and I want to make my contribution before he finishes cooking. We're already pretty late."

We drove back in silence, letting the wind scream through the Jeep while the rocks and ruts shouted underneath. The return trip seemed smoother in the encroaching dark when the bumps were harder to anticipate, and we couldn't stiffen to brace against them. In the fading light, they melted into the mud and simply slid by. Silas stopped in his camp to grab a can of black beans and a bag of chocolate chip cookies. We arrived as Professor Singh was finishing up with dinner preparations. He waved to us from his chair as he stirred a pot near the fire.

"Did you have fun?" he asked, standing up and wiping his hands on his shirt.

"Yeah," I said. "It was great!"

"I'll tell you Arjun, the light wasn't perfect today, but it helped me out at times."

"It has a way of doing that," the professor said.

Silas handed over the can of beans. Professor Singh turned a slow can opener around the top and emptied them into a pot on the cooking grate. Soon, they simmered away. Silas put a bowl of kibble down for Casey while the professor dished out piping hot portions of rice, beans, and vegetables, and we spent the evening talking photography. Silas explained the artistry of knobs and buttons, and by the time he left, I felt confident that I was still as confused as before.

Chapter 27

Forgive, and Lay Down the Load

After the professor and I cleaned up, we sat quietly, watching tongues of flame lick the night air. We were bundled up against a cool wind blowing through camp. Although I was quite content to sit in the quiet, my mind was restless, wandering here and there and taking me down roads I hadn't visited in a while. The day's events with Silas had an effect on me, and I couldn't get his struggles with Kay out of my head. I turned the pages of their relationship story over and over in my head, looking for an answer. An excuse. A theory as to why Silas and Kay, and people in the world in general, had such a hard time with relationships. Why did they work? Why did they fall apart?

Fingers of depression flicked at me. I reflected on my own failures with Maya, convincing myself that all the bad things about our time together were my fault. I pictured her somewhere hating me and blaming me for the negativity in her life. A lump in my throat turned to a tear straining to leave my eyes, but I battled the demon back and took a deep, jumpy breath.

Minutes passed before a shot of anxiety ripped through my gut. A feeling of loneliness overcame me and stole my breath. I breathed in hard through my mouth. Professor Singh glanced my way, and I pretended to shudder against the evening chill to cover. I thought about Maya and where we would be now if she were still around. Would we be planning our wedding? Talking about having kids?

Thinking about moving near the beach like she'd always dreamed? Lonely feelings turned to near panic. I had my pills with me, but I hadn't had to take one in a few days. I decided to try to control the feeling right here by the fire. I focused on the flames and took my mind in another direction, taking a tip from my own social work bag. I again focused on the strengths I'd found since our breakup. I had taken a vacation and reconnected with Professor Singh. Our meeting had me thinking in new ways about old concepts, and I had actually managed to string a few days of calm together under his watchful eye – something I hadn't done in years.

The volleying of negative and positive in my head was overwhelming, and I decided I needed to process. I had to break the silence of the night to calm myself down. I wanted to work through the struggle of relationships to know if pain or hope waited on the other side. Silas told me to learn from his mistakes and to use his story, and now, I needed it.

"Silas is married, Professor."

"Oh?"

"Or, separated now. I don't know all the details. I found a picture of his wife in his Jeep. Her name is Kay."

"That's very interesting, Jim. I would not have guessed that."

"Me neither. They're separated. I guess he…well…I'm not sure. There was an incident with another woman."

"Infidelity is difficult to overcome."

"Yeah. But I think Silas and Kay still really love each other."

The professor raised an eyebrow. "What makes you say this?"

"Well, he was really open about the whole thing. Really beats himself up about it. Their story is wild. They met, parted ways, she married, then divorced. Then she and Silas got married, and I guess there was more trouble. They're separated, but…I donno…together. There has to be something there, still. It just seems like a shame to throw a journey like that away. That's too long a trek to make in vain."

"Has she forgiven him?"

"Don't know, Professor. He said she did, but...what a sad story."

"Forgiveness is difficult, Jim. It takes a lot of strength to let go of anger and resentment. It requires tremendous courage to let someone into our trust again."

Silas seemed so quiet and solitary – so much a part of the lonely woods and isolation of the roving photographer's life. It was hard to imagine he had a life back home. It was difficult to see him in a marriage, trying to make it work in between mishaps and deadlines. I decided not to pursue the issue with the professor any further.

Back in the tent, my mind wandered despite my desperate attempts to keep it still. I was calmer now, but my brain was active. I thought about forgiveness and how difficult it was to achieve. My imagination took me back to situations with Maya, and I lingered dangerously close to emotions I didn't want to feel again. When we had the occasional argument or disagreement, it sometimes escalated into a battle of wills. It seemed like we got into matches to see who could hold a grudge longer. And now, to add to all that, I wondered about forgiveness. Could she forgive me for being depressed? Could she forgive me for being so anxious that some days death was preferable to life? Were those things that even needed forgiveness? Could I forgive her for wanting more than I could give her? What about forgiving ourselves for being human? Why do people insist on punishing themselves for their limitations?

I lay back on my pillow and tried to let these musings pass. I felt the mechanics of my breathing, hearing it mix with sounds in the woods. I was awestruck by its operation. I calmed the torrent of thoughts and closed my eyes, staring deep into the vast void behind my eyelids. I was overcome by a feeling that everything I needed to know was right here in the darkness. A light of inspiration trembled through my being. I sat bolt upright, fumbled for my flashlight, grabbed a pen and my journal, and scribbled madly:

That we carry burdens makes us human. That we realize we don't have to makes us divine. All struggles can end immediately. When we let go of struggles, we become free to roll again with the flow of life. But we don't always do that. We pack a trunk with all the clothing of our past and carry it with us through the years — unpacking it again and again, dressing in old wounds and hurts, forgetting they are mere clothing, and believing they are our very essence. We cling to them as if banishing them would end our existence. But then we reach that breaking point. Our arms grow weary and our backs ache under the strain of our burdens, and we have a flash. A sudden realization that we can lay the trunk down and that we need carry it all no longer. It has built a little muscle, yes, and we have benefited by the presence of the lessons, but now we can lay it all down. Once a situation outlives its usefulness, the weight is extraneous. We don't have to take it up again. Pain to which we cling never becomes inert. It merely stops our inertia. Our humanity attaches to the heavy guilt and pain of the past, but our spirit realizes it is not necessary to haul this around anymore. Our spiritual self urges us to forgive. We must use this powerful tool of forgiveness to realize our true Self — the one that carries no burden. We soon recognize it is the spiritual nudity in which we were born, and not the clothing in the trunk we convinced ourselves we needed, that is essential. People carry a heavy load. Spirit forgives, and travels light.

I put down my pen and turned off my flashlight. After a few more minutes staring into the void, I disappeared into sleep.

Chapter 28

A Prayer to Remember

I saw a light go on last night." Professor Singh stoked up the fire and scrambled the last of our eggs in a pan. I was attempting to eat a banana around a very brown spot. It was clear we needed more provisions if we wanted to continue this somewhat rugged existence.

"I wrote something, Professor. Or, I guess…something was written."

"Oh?"

"Yeah. Something about what we'd talked about…about forgiveness. An insight came up through the silence last night after we talked."

"I'm glad it did. I knew it would."

"Well, I was doing some breathing exercises and it just sort of showed up."

"The breath?"

"No…well, yes…that, and the words."

There was a pause. "Is this something you'd like to share with me, Jim? I should like to hear it."

Doubt overshadowed my enthusiasm. As exciting as the insights were, once public, they were open to additional scrutiny. What if they couldn't stand up to it?

"Uh…okay," I said. I went back to my tent and grabbed my journal. I walked back out to the fire and read the entry as he divided the eggs between two plates. When I finished reading, he stared at me for a moment, then turned his attention to his meal. I plunged my fork into my breakfast.

"What do you think it means?" he finally asked, putting silence out of its misery. The consequence for a humble flow of insight is the open floodgates of difficult questions.

"Well, I'm not quite sure. There are a lot of ideas mashed in there – forgiveness and whatnot – and it's hard to get a sense of what the lesson is."

"Scrambled?" He smiled.

"Like our eggs."

"Indeed."

"Yeah, but the words feel strangely familiar, Professor."

"One often has to go backward to see the way forward, Jim. This is just how it is. If that's too daunting, however, then think about our previous discussions as steps up to a station platform. Relax, find your footing, and ascend. After that, simply board the train of thought and ride easy out of the station."

"Okay," I said, struggling to link all these cars together. I took a few more bites of breakfast and reflected on where we'd been together. "I guess if we assume we're all one, or that we come from one source, then we have to acknowledge on some level that we all have similar urges to act in the world. And we have to acknowledge that we'll be acted upon in certain ways."

"Yes. This is true. Even though we all take different paths, we will all experience urges and take action, and we will all be the target of others' urges and actions."

"Right. And when we do things in the world, it's like we're performing. We're all actors in a play…the universal source dressed up in costume and playing out a drama."

"A time-tested metaphor, Jim. Shakespeare himself told us the world is a stage."

"So, the dramas of life are our human nature. They're those temporary things we do that fill us with emotion and feeling. We act, we feel, we react. We're acted upon, we feel, we react. It's a cycle.

We're all doing stuff and we're all having stuff done to us, right? It's just scenes in a play, like we said."

"So, what's the problem, Jim?"

"Well, instead of just seeing events as passing scenes, we hold on to things – we hold on to hurt, emotion, and guilt. All the costumes. All the scripts. All the sets. Like it's all on tape and we're hitting the rewind button over and over again to see parts of the performance. The show goes on, but we never really get into it because we keep living in what's just happened – how it looked and sounded." I felt a fire rising in me – a frustration with my own situation that cast a wide blanket on my life as I had always lived it. "I guess it's like a Buddhist might say."

"Which is, Jim?"

"Well, we cling to our deeds and wounds like they are ourselves, or our identity. We carry around the burden of things we've done, or that others have done to us, and we weigh ourselves down. We cling and cling. To expectations. To hurt. To unhealthy ideas and relationships. We cling and carry."

"This may be the case. There's lots to cling to."

"But that only gets us part of the way there, I suppose."

"How so, Jim?"

"Well, the journal entry seems to say that we're all, at our core, creatures of spirit, but that our human ego, or the center of our human consciousness, strives to make us think that we are our wounds and hurts as well, and that for some reason, it's good to hold on to all of this."

"Yes." He traced a hard roll in a smooth line across his plate to retrieve a piece of egg. "And?"

"Um…" I was stuck. I stared at his plate. I stared at mine. I searched the sky for the answer, then wrinkled my face in confusion.

"Go with that resistance, Jim. Think through it. The train rolls on even though you think the tracks are blocked. Go on."

"Okay, Professor. So, wait. If we think in terms of our ego and our hurt and our baggage and our bodies, then how do we live in the other realization of spirit...or energy...or whatever? What good is an answer if I don't even know the questions exist?"

"Wait, Jim. We must deal with the first part first. That would be the logical starting point."

"Logic?" I laughed. "Professor, no offense, but logic seems to have little to do with crazy journal entries that materialize out of thin air."

"Well, go along with it, Jim."

"Hey, why not? I never did pay attention in logic class, anyways."

"Let's look at the world as it appears to us, then we can set about seeing it as it could be." He picked up the key around his neck and twirled it between his fingers.

"Okay."

"Jim, what do you think of perception?"

"Perception?"

"Yes. If I ask you to look at the scene in front of us, what will you tell me?"

"Professor, didn't we go through this days ago?" I had the growing feeling that we were caught in a metaphysical revolving door.

"Humor me."

"Well, I suppose I'd say that there are beautiful trees and wildflowers. I see the beauty of nature."

"What if you have allergies?"

"I do. I'm allergic to milk. Technically, I guess it's more of an intolerance to lactose."

"Really, Jim? I had no idea. When did you—? Wait, let's stay on track. What I'm talking about are allergies to nature."

"Oh. Then I suppose I'd tell you that what I see around me is a potential disaster in the making. I could sneeze from the pollen or die from a bee sting."

"Yes. Possibly. So, what are we to say about the scene before us?"

"Hmm." I sat back in my chair and worked the question through in my mind. "Are you saying it changes because of the person?"

"Not exactly, Jim. I'm saying that it stays the same but changes according to whom you ask. Take your father, for instance. I met him at your college graduation, and he was so nice. But I met him in his capacity as father. But really, is he a father, a doctor, a boss, a friend, or a husband?"

"I guess it depends who you ask."

"Yes. Now, what if I told you your father's existence is deeper than peoples' perceptions? If he lost any of those identities, would he be less than who he really is? Things become things to us only when they are labeled, remember? Before that, things are what they are, or they are only ideas."

"Okay. That makes some sense. So, getting back to my milk issue..." Professor Singh flashed a wry smile. "Go along with it, Professor!" He rolled his eyes. "I look at a cheesecake and see misery if I don't take a lactase pill before I eat it. It's a risk. Whereas another person might see a way to immediately indulge with no risk of gas or bloating. But either way we see it, it's just a cheesecake. It's people who give cheesecake a description and judgment other than what it is. In fact, even calling it cheesecake is dubious! It's really a bunch of separate ingredients mixed together that form something new that some baker gave a label to."

"That is very much the same, Jim. Your milk struggles were on track after all."

"Alright, Professor. So, what does this tell us about being forgiving and forgiving ourselves? How does any of this help us? Should I forgive the cheesecake for my stomach cramps?"

"Not exactly, but that would be a good start."

"So, are you saying that when I get hurt by someone else, I'm *choosing* to see it as a wrong? The way we choose to see an allergen instead of a pretty flower?"

"In a sense, Jim. In a sense."

"But that's terrible!" The professor erupted in laughter. I joined in and then jumped onboard the train again. "That means that people can do whatever they want. If someone steals money from me, and I get angry, they can say, 'Hey, you're only seeing it as wrong. To me, stealing is right. Now I can go buy a new computer.' Or...I donno...whatever else people who steal go and buy with the money. Or worse, they can just take my computer!"

A look of calm washed over Professor Singh's face, couched in a slight smile. He dropped the key to his chest, put his hands out, and gently pushed them toward the ground, trying to ease my near-frenzied flow of thoughts with the universal sign for "calm down!" Then, he took the key up again.

"Jim, the world isn't necessarily a relativistic place where anything goes and what feels good is what we should do."

"It sure seems that way." I huffed.

"Yes, but that kind of egoism only brings on an ethics of despair. Moral anarchy. What we're dealing with here is a subtler idea."

"I didn't think we could get subtler."

"It's a step removed from pure right and wrong, good and bad, Jim. It's the idea that our essential identity transcends these apparent wrongs. Theft is wrong, but we still exist in spite of it."

"Huh?"

"Jim, if you are on the freeway, and you get cut off by another driver, what happens?"

"I get angry."

"At what?"

"At the other driver."

"Why?"

"He cut me off! You know. You drive."

"And when he has you in his rearview mirror and is on his way to wherever he's going, how does all of that anger help you?"

"I guess it makes me feel good to get upset."

"That's the ego, Jim. Go deeper. How does it really feel?"

"Well..." I put myself squarely behind the wheel of my car and imagined being on the receiving end of a bad driver. A shot of adrenaline went through my gut, and I felt a dull ache. "I guess not so good. I get irritable and angry…I think terrible thoughts. I guess if I'm really honest, I feel bad for the terrible things I say and do, even in the privacy of my car."

"Indeed. Regret follows quickly on the heels of anger."

"Yeah. My character changes. A good day can get kinda crappy after that."

"The day hasn't changed, Jim. It's your perception that changed. What you witnessed was a person involved in one life, in one car, moving ahead of you one space. He simply occupies that space and moves on his way. However, through the lenses and filters of the ego, it is an affront to your own space and personhood. Dare I say, manhood? This is where road rage happens. If you ask the offending driver what happened, he'll develop a story through his lenses, and tell you that you were making him mad by driving slowly. Your story, on the other hand, will involve tales of an unjust, reckless speeder encroaching unnecessarily on your right to drive the speed limit. But really, that's all commentary. What really happened is one person passed another person. A bit too closely, perhaps, but you can still arrive at your destination peacefully, and be thankful you are safe. Or you can let this unfortunate highway encounter ruin your mood and turn an otherwise basic day into something acidic. How you see it is your choice."

"My choice? But how? I mean, there's another person doing something wrong, isn't there?"

"Jim, I am not asking you to be happy with all of this. I am not asking you to condone humanity's more troubling actions done in the name of the ego. You don't have to follow the driver to his destination and present him with a cake, balloons, and a thank-you card. What we can all do, however, is widen the view and see the concept at a broader level."

"How?"

"It is like in your entry on forgiveness. We carry burdens, and that makes us human. We need not carry them, and that makes us divine.

The point is simple. With all the loads we carry in the course of our lives, why add more? It's really an amazing fact that many wrongs in the world have no material substance, yet they are the heaviest of weights. People will fight you on this idea. But in the end, it's all about choices. Choices to forgive and lay it all down."

"Choices aren't so cut and dry in the heat of the moment, Professor." I copped a defensive tone, spurred on by the guilt of all the middle fingers I'd shot at others on the freeway over the years. I wanted them to be justified. I didn't want to forgive. "When someone does something to me, it's hard not to get angry or carry a grudge."

"I want to caution you here, Jim."

"Uh oh. What did I do now?"

"Nothing, yet. But you are in danger of carrying the idea of forgiveness too far."

"Too far? Is that possible?"

"I mean placing forgiveness on a pedestal. Going too far into the idyllic."

"What do you mean?"

"Don't think deep forgiveness means the family of a murder victim should immediately tell the murderer 'all is forgiven' and have them over to their house for coffee. That's not realistic, except in a few extreme cases."

"Okay, okay. I get it. So how do we tone it down?"

"Let's begin with this idea: Forgiveness starts with the self, not the other person. People in life will wrong us. Or, to say this more honestly, people will sometimes act in ways that contradict our ego's expectations and desires, and then we will take on a mantle of anger and resentment towards them, hurting ourselves in the process."

"Ouch. Too much honesty, Professor!"

"Jim, I have no control over how someone treats me. What I do have control over is how I react. You have heard that before, I am sure."

"I think it was on a bumper sticker on that car that cut me off before. But actually, I use that phrase a lot when I'm working with clients. We do a lot of work around the basics of forgiveness at work, and I know it really can be powerful. It's just, we've never gone this deep."

"Well, any start is a good start. Understand that real forgiveness requires the twin virtues of discipline and responsibility. Those start with me, right? Therefore, I must be disciplined to control my raging emotions and take responsibility for my reactions. I can either lash out at someone, punishing him, and myself, for acting contrary to my expectations, or I can dig deeper and try to see things from the perspective of one who lets go of passing hurts and forgives them."

"But anger is so much easier!"

The professor let out a lyrical chuckle that lightened my protest. "I'm not saying there's no anger, Jim. I'm not saying there isn't bitterness. I'm saying those things have a price. Boiling blood makes poor tea. It is your own peace that evaporates in that heat."

"I guess so. When I stop to think about it, that's where a lot of my clients get stuck. Where I get stuck. We either let things get the best of us and fly off the handle, or else we fail to take responsibility for what we've done, and we carry that crap around with us forever and push people away."

"Right. It all starts with the person behind this wheel right here, Jim. Not the other driver."

"I guess so, Professor."

"Do you remember my story from childhood? About the drink I stole from the vendor?"

"Yes."

"Well, I went back to him a few days later, of my own accord, and apologized again for what I had done."

"That was brave."

"But necessary, Jim."

"How'd he react?"

"He was very understanding. He invited me to sit and have a drink with his family. His treat."

"That's cool."

"It was. We spoke about our lives, and I learned so much about him that day. He had inherited the cart and his particular street corner from his father, and it was enough to support his family. He wanted to send his daughter to university. When I heard him speak so passionately about his work and his future, I realized that my actions, my stealing, affected much more than I could imagine in the heat of my crime. His anger was powerful. Not because I stole some liquid, but because I was stealing his livelihood. His family's hopes and dreams."

"That's intense, Professor. It really puts small things we do to others in a new light."

"But he forgave me. And when he saw me later, instead of holding a grudge and chasing me away with a stick, he invited me in. He turned my transgression into an opportunity. His willingness to shift his perspective was instructive. He taught me how quickly healing can happen when we take it upon ourselves to release others' misdeeds. He chose to shift his perception of an injustice, making it something positive. It was a choice that changed life for both of us."

"Okay, but it isn't always that easy, Professor. The guy you stole from received a blessing from the holy man, remember? Your guru. Maybe that helped in some way. But what about the rest of us? What about those whose lives get crushed under the weight of old hurts and bruises?"

I was thinking specifically of wounds inflicted in relationships. I had my share of unresolved issues.

He leaned back in his chair, closed his eyes, and took in a long breath. He had been alternatively twirling the key and letting it drop, and he again picked it up and worked it through his fingers. I could tell he was considering my question in earnest.

"Forgiveness, Jim, at its most fundamental level, asks us all to let go of anger and resentment, opening up to the possibility that I can release myself and another from the clutches of my own limited perception. I must practice, remind myself each day to forgive, and remember that I and the people who harm me are not so different. Once that is accomplished, I am free to lighten my load and send us both on our way."

"I guess. After all, Jesus said 'Let he who is without sin cast the first stone.' That applies here, right?"

"Yes, Jim. This is a wise teaching. If we all reflected before blowing up at another person or deciding to carry a grudge, we would see that we have all done things we are sorry about, and that nobody's perfect."

"A lot less stones cast around, huh?"

"Exactly. How many stories are there of siblings who have not spoken for years, or children who cannot bring themselves to forgive a parent for one deed or another? 'I hate them,' they might say. Or, you might hear, 'How can I forgive someone I can't stand to be around?'"

"We all have that person somewhere in our life."

"That's right, Jim. But forgiveness doesn't ask us to like another person. It asks us to love ourselves enough to lay the burden down. Forgiveness only seeks to bring harmony back from discord. Let us be honest, though. As you said, sometimes carrying grudges feels good. It is just another reminder of the 'I am right, and you are wrong' mentality. That's a hard barrier to cross."

"Yeah. When I think that way, I guess it's me not wanting to take responsibility for getting angry. It sometimes feels good to make another person the source of my disappointments and regrets. There's a guilty pleasure there when they feel bad."

"An unfortunate truth. A truth that destroys relationships."

"I'm sure it had a hand in destroying mine," I said. "But why do we like that feeling so much? It seems so awful to like hurting others by not forgiving them. What's that about?"

"The ego again."

"Of course."

"Carrying resentment is an easy way to feel powerful. It's the very definition of equality."

"How so?"

"Well, think about it. We can all can carry grudges. Large ones, small ones. No matter if we are young or old, tall or short, weak or strong, we all have this ability to carry a grudge, no matter the size. And when we do, it's because we don't want to give another person the benefit of our good graces by forgiving them. We make them seek out our benevolence instead of granting the gift willingly. But who really suffers? In bed at night, fuming over what some so-and-so did to me, accomplishes little except contribute to a sleepless night."

"I'll second that." I thought about all the sleepless nights after an argument with Maya, and how the ensuing days were agony until we made up again. I hated it. Even if I didn't originate the problem, I participated in it and kept the pain alive.

"Carrying around wrongs from the past is like the scab you can't stop picking, Jim. The jarring pain is strangely satisfying. In some ways, it reminds us we're alive."

"Like the pinprick?"

"Not exactly. The pinprick has a benefit – focus and awakening. But in a non-forgiveness pattern, the pain I'm referring to doesn't have any benefit, because the moment it creates is only filled with negativity. And, it cuts two ways. You hurt yourself with your inability to let go of an old wound, and you punish the target of your anger by putting up an obstacle over which they can never climb – an obstacle that traps you as much as it blocks them. Carrying a grudge is a way of erecting barriers and hiding from healing emotions."

◆ ◆ ◆

The ideas crystallized. Images of me and Maya arguing and slamming doors crept into my consciousness. I felt the pain of all the wrongs we never righted, and all the loose ends of disagreements lost to time.

"I guess we feel like if we punish a person for not living up to our expectations, it justifies our ego. We try to make them responsible for our disappointment."

"That is at the root of it, Jim."

"Pretty sad." I cast a frown at the ground and sighed. I looked up at his smiling face and brightened my own. "I can feel our revolving door turning again, Professor."

"And so it is, Jim. But there is hope. Throughout modern history, prominent leaders have shown the way to forgiveness in the most difficult circumstances. Forgiveness is an effective catalyst for social change. Look at the struggles of the exiled Dalai Lama, or the powerful forgiveness of Dr. Martin Luther King, Jr. or Gandhi. They all used a message of love, tied in with forgiveness, to spark entire movements in the face of harsh, even violent, opposition. They moved mountains by simply moving out of the way."

"That's an interesting way of looking at it, Professor. And you're right, I guess. Love is key."

"Love truly is at the heart of the forgiving nature. It is the wind upon which the wings of forgiveness soar. But the love I speak of must also be a love of oneself, or it will be impossible to love another enough to forgive them."

He let the key drop and took up a stick to push embers around in the fire pit. They were losing patience and power as the morning wore on. As he got comfortable again, he took up the key and twirled it. He stared off into the trees, a dreamy look on his face.

"Professor?"

"Yes?"

"What about Silas and Kay?"

"What about them?"

"Well, why is he out here without her? Why is he going through life without her? She says she's forgiven him, but he's still not sure. I'd give anything to have a woman in my life who was that forgiving and loving. My anxiety…my depression…it's crushing. If someone was willing to stick it out with me…" I held my emotion back and pushed the rest of my thought out. "If she's forgiven him, why can't he bring himself to believe her? Why can't…this sounds so corny…why can't he believe in her love?"

"I'm not sure it's belief in her forgiveness that's missing, Jim."

"Then what is it?"

"The street vendor forgave me those many long years ago, but I must say, it took me many years more to forgive myself."

"Why?"

"Well, when I thought about what I had done to him on that scorching and awful day, it was emotionally crippling. The enlightened person lives with the calming foresight that all things, in hindsight, will benefit him and the world. Meanwhile, the rest of us grapple with regret. I didn't want to face my deed. Sometimes I would take a different route to school to avoid him, even though he was pleasant to me. Even friendly. Even though I had a standing invitation at his home. Many times, the ones we hurt forgive us, but we can't get over the deed ourselves. That is very precarious territory. My victim may sweep my deed from their mind, but I cannot ignore a persistent problem in the household of my own head. There is no room where I can stash it that I do not dwell. Choosing to forgive others takes a strong will, indeed. But to forgive oneself? Such a task! Mahatma Gandhi, may he rest in peace, once said that a weak person cannot forgive…that forgiveness is for the strong. Truer words were never spoken, especially when applied to oneself."

"Are you saying the problem is with Silas? Is he not strong?"

"I don't know. I am not living in his conscience, or consciousness. But quite often, long after we make peace with others, we fail to make peace with ourselves. You met Silas on one particular leg of his trip of personal reflection. Or perhaps he's just hiding. Maybe he is out here in the silence trying to find a room in his mind where Kay and his misdeeds towards her do not dwell. He is here with Casey, thinking and mulling."

"Hey, at least he has a companion."

"Dogs are good listeners for the ego, Jim, because they cannot offer suggestions, counter-arguments, or sage advice. Silas likely knows where Kay stands. Now he must find his own balance. His own strength. He must stand on his own."

"I have a feeling Kay is a saint."

He laughed. "Perhaps. Perhaps. Many strong men balance on the stronger shoulders of a supportive partner."

"Why don't we forgive ourselves, Professor? I think I have a better understanding of why we don't forgive others, but why do we carry around the burden of guilt and self-hatred after another person releases us from all of that?"

"Good question. And difficult."

"Karmic payback for those many years in your classes."

"You always did ask the challenging ones." He pointed the key at me, squeezed between his thumb and index finger. "One would be inclined to think that once the wronged person forgives, the wrongdoer would gratefully release the burden from himself, but this often does not happen."

I thought about Maya. For all of our difficulties, there were times when she really did release me from the wrongs I did. I was often too critical and too harsh with her, because I was mad at myself. But there were times when I truly believed she loved me, nonetheless. "Jim," she'd say, "don't worry about it. I know you're sorry. It's okay." I knew there were times she really meant it. Yet, I still felt tinges of guilt. I would actually feel guilty for being myself...for expressing my nature. Why couldn't I get over it? Sometimes I even found myself pushing her away because I couldn't accept her release.

"Jim," he continued, "in the end, it comes down to us and our expectations of others and ourselves. Our ego wants to be in charge. It wants perfection. It expects things to be the way it wants them to be. Maybe we torture ourselves because the bad feelings keep us tied to our vices and limited thinking. Maybe this is what the ego wants, so it keeps our deeds on display long after others have put them away."

I mustered an "I suppose," and remained in my thoughts.

"Are you still feeling lost?"

"Yeah. I mean, I get what you're saying, but it's just so much to sort through, y'know? There isn't one part of my life, one part of my mental health, that isn't being impacted by all of this stuff. It's a little overwhelming."

He turned to face me. I felt all the love and support he could muster coming at me, willing me to get it. To understand. To find a way to put all of this information to use in a way that could help me heal and move on.

"Listen to me, Jim. The best summary of all of this business of forgiveness is that as we proceed through the years, we must have love and respect for humanity. In that way, we see others as ourselves. Indeed, love, in the best of worlds, would be a constant in our lives. If we looked at others as just manifestations of the same energy that manifests and motivates us, we might see that what angers us about them is something we might grow to love. Or else, it is something with which we can empathize. We could call this new principle a 'respect for the discipline of energetic diversity.'"

"Catchy, Professor."

"If we resolve to love people despite how their words or actions act against our expectations, we might live more peacefully. We are all just trying to make our way in this world as spirits or energy encased in flesh. And we all fall short. This is the understanding that will allow forgiveness of others for the things they do. Then, when we also release ourselves from the prison of anger and hate, everything becomes lighter."

"Isn't there a Jain prayer like that, Professor? Something from your class readings, I think. Or maybe I'm making it up."

"You're not making it up, Jim. And thank you for paying attention that day. I believe it goes, 'I forgive all living beings. May all living beings forgive me. I am friend to all beings. My hostility is non-existent.' This is a prayer truly worth remembering."

With that, the professor dropped the key to his chest and excused himself to the kitchen area. I returned to my tent to eat the last remnants of a stale energy bar and scribble in my journal. I tried to be open to the silence, but my mind was distracted by thoughts of Maya, Silas, Kay, and forgiveness. I spent some time writing about those topics, including my personal foibles. It was frustrating, yet illuminating.

The Jain prayer sparked memories of old religious studies lectures, and I jotted down a few notes on Mahavira, the enlightened being who laid Jain foundations over 2500 years ago. Much like his contemporary, the Buddha, Mahavira gave up a life of luxury and wealth to pursue self-investigation. He became an ascetic, practicing renunciation and meditation. Some even say he gave up wearing clothes in his zeal to release attachments. I also reflected on *ahimsa*, the principle of non-harm and the obligation to show kindness to all living creatures. *Ahimsa* is a cornerstone of the Jain worldview, and has been so influential for many others. Some believe Mahavira swept where he walked and sat, in order to remove any creatures upon which he might step or sit. Today, Jain monks and nuns will emulate this practice to reduce the number of life forms killed by their activity, thus reducing the amount of bad karma they might accrue from an act of killing. Water is strained to weed out microbes, and some faithful do not bathe. Where preventable, no animal life is taken, and the life of vegetation is taken sparingly.

Ahimsa coupled nicely with the professor's notion of forgiveness. Gandhi was influenced by these principles, and they guided his non-violent protests against the British occupation of India.

I finally decided to use that as the inspiration for a brief journal entry:

Nothing is given or received without effort, including forgiveness. It can be difficult to find the love to accomplish forgiveness, but it can be so rewarding. Our reactions to the perceived misdeeds of others will cause us some discomfort as our life lessons unfold, but we must understand there is a time to lay that down and progress. We will get to our ultimate destinations one day. However, we alone determine the ease or difficulty of our progress.

Chapter 29

The Hero's Journey of Less Than a Mile

The previous evening was quiet, and there was no visit from Silas and Casey. I had trouble getting to sleep, and even more trouble getting moving this morning. My mind wandered and wandered corridor after corridor. I visited places long past – places in my head I'd forgotten even existed. It was an interesting, and very uncomfortable, journey. The sound of the professor's tent unzipping, and the clinking of keys, caught my attention.

I looked out as he was unlocking his car. "Where are you going?"

"I'm heading back into Mormon Lake to get supplies and food. Take your time this morning."

"Let me give you some money, Professor. Hold on."

"Please, Jim. There is no need for that. When I return, we can explore around here a bit more."

"Thanks," I said. "That would be great!"

I emerged from my tent with my wallet and tried a bolder attempt to offer him money, but he politely declined again, and closed the door. He rolled down the window and said, "Perhaps we can head to the cabin later to check on the plumbing. If it is repaired, we can wash up and do laundry, then return to camp for a few more days."

"I'm game," I said.

After the car rumbled out of sight, I got moving. The air was fresh and crisp, and I was impatient for more adventures in the woods. I grabbed a rotting piece of fruit from the bag in the tree and turned on my phone. If luck was on my side, I might get cell service. I wandered down toward Silas's camp, thinking the open field might provide an opportunity. It did, but I had to stand very still in one spot and hold the phone at just the right angle. One weak bar flitted in an out of view at the top of my phone. I seized the moment and called my parents to make sure Dad was okay.

"I'm fine," he said, in his chipper and nonchalant way. "Don't worry about me."

We chatted about sports and doctor's visits. In a lull, Mom took the phone. She asked how I was, and I repeated the report I'd given Dad five minutes earlier. Then, she said the two words I never expected to hear again: "Maya called."

"She did?" I tried to keep my tone even and calm, even though a burn of anxiety coursed through my gut. "Why? I mean...what did she want?"

"I'm not sure, Jim. She said she's been trying to get ahold of you for a few days. She didn't give a lot of details."

From the background, Dad shouted, "She said she's left you a few messages. Didn't you get them?"

"I haven't turned my phone on in a few days," I said. "And nothing showed up just now."

"Well," Mom said, never missing an opportunity to hurl barbs at modern technology, "those cell phones. You'll probably get the message two weeks from now. But you should give her a ring."

"I tried that, Mom. It didn't work out so well."

"I meant on the phone," she snapped. "Just see what she wants."

I said goodbye after listening to my mother's twin mantras of "be safe" and "keep eating," and decided to call up my messages. Sure enough, I had two. One was from Jake, "just checking up," and the other was from Maya. Usually, her voice bubbled through the phone, but this time, it was a more subdued tone. "Jim," she said, "I've been doing some thinking, and...well...maybe we should talk about some things. I've been traveling and trying to make sense of stuff. I'm coming back into town and would like to get together. Please call and let me know." She ended the message with the dates of her trip, which coincided with the last few days of my vacation, and a muted "Love ya."

I stood alone in the clearing, my body on fire. I felt sick. I felt elated. I felt a mix of emotions and hormones creating a cocktail of dread and joy. In skillful movements of muscle memory, I scrolled to her name in my contact list and let my thumb hover over the number. The signal indicator on the phone held strong. One bar. One chance. After a few false stabs at the screen, I locked the phone and stood like a statue in the clearing. Dallying in my delusions, the familiar soundtracks began to play.

"Maya," I said aloud, to no one in particular. "I can't believe it." I turned my face to the blue skies. To the sun. To any deity that would listen. "Any chance I could get a sign here?" Nothing came. Nothing stirred. I filled the pit in my gut with arguments and justifications for every course of action.

I felt like how I imagined Silas was feeling. I was getting used to being on my own schedule and having my freedom. Or maybe I'd just found a safe place to hide. Would Maya and I even recognize each other anymore beyond physical appearances? Things were different now. If she wanted to get back together, would she be patient as I worked through all of this old stuff in a new way? As these questions rolled on, they became more and more distasteful. I could hear how unfair they sounded, and I didn't like myself for asking them. I connected the dots between my ego, my burning questions, my ongoing battles with depression and anxiety, and the life I wanted so badly to live.

Everything spun out of control as I teetered toward a stump. I dropped my weight into the rotting wood and imagined myself rooted to the earth as puffy clouds rolled free and easy above the trees. My fears and desires sounded ridiculous to my inner ear. Was I so special? Was I so different than anyone else? Did I deserve more space than others? More peace? Wasn't life about the search for love and making it work?

My fragmented concentration crystallized around a furious barking in the woods. The smoke in my mind cleared away and I tipped my head to the familiar sound. "Casey?" I wandered down the road toward Silas's camp and entered to find Casey bounding around at the rear of the Jeep. "Silas?" I yelled. No answer. I picked up a half-eaten rawhide bone and tried to tempt Casey with it to calm him down. No luck. This wasn't his playful frolic. As I inched closer, I saw the foam dribbling from his mouth. "What's wrong, boy?" I asked. But then, the answer was clear. My eyes caught a glimpse of a dusty boot on the ground behind the Jeep. I ran to it, tripping over the camp log and stumbling on rocks and pinecones. My heart pounded. Silas lay motionless, his expressionless face staring up at me.

"Silas?" I tapped his cheeks – gently at first, but then with a criminal force of desperation. "Silas!" I couldn't hold back the panic rising within me. Serenity was nowhere to be found in my mind or body. I didn't know what to do. But then, out of sheer will from a place I didn't understand, I engaged my calmer side. I knew my scattered thoughts and pleadings wouldn't rouse him. I took in a mighty breath, focused my entire being on Silas and the task at hand, and placed a hand on his neck. A weak pulse tapped at my fingertips. He was alive.

"Thank God," I said to Casey. "He's still with us, boy." I weighed my options. I could return to the field to hunt down the faint cell signal to call the paramedics. But even if I reached them after who knows how long, which was no guarantee, we were still in the middle of nowhere. I thought about getting the professor, figuring his army training would probably be useful here, but I didn't want to leave Silas alone for that length of time. I had no idea how long he'd been like this, and it would take me too long by foot or car to bring the professor back here from the store, if he was even there.

Suddenly, a thought popped into the gap between those choices. I remembered the fire station on the road leading into Mormon Lake.

I had played bingo there with my friends years ago. The small station was so quaint, so much a part of the town's charm, I completely forgot it had another function besides hosting social events and potlucks. It was close by, and it was my best option. I dug through Silas's pockets and found his keys, wallet, and cell phone – shoving them into my pockets. With newfound strength, I hauled all of his weight to the Jeep. It was an impossible task that somehow took care of itself. I tossed out coolers and random bags full of clothes and heaved him inside so that he was lying down, face up.

"Casey!" I yelled. "Come!"

He jumped in and we were off like a shot, tires raising dust and spraying chunks of dirt as we screeched out of camp. The Jeep bounded over the rutted road like a rabbit. I remembered how I'd seen Silas wince in pain and struggle with his camera equipment. I wondered if I was responsible for this current state of affairs by not mentioning anything to Professor Singh or to Silas. Had I been ignoring an impending heart attack? With my dad's condition, maybe I should have known better. Was it all my fault? I felt like an idiot.

"This is just like the side of the highway," I said to Casey, whose face was as intense as mine. "I let him down again. Damn it!" I pounded my hands against the wheel. "Damn it! Damn it!"

I forced my mind to banish those thoughts so I could focus on the trail. Adrenaline pumping furiously, I tore into the parking lot of the fire station less than a mile from the campsite, skidding to a halt on the loose gravel. I was at the door before the dust settled, pounding for help. An elderly woman opened the door wide. An unfinished game of solitaire and a half-empty glass of iced tea waited patiently on the desk behind her.

"Yes? May I help you?"

"Ma'am." I gasped for breath and tried to streamline my thoughts. "I have a man in the back of this Jeep. I'm not sure what happened. I don't know if it was a heart attack. Help me!" She hurried out to the parking lot with me at a pace that did not match her frail appearance and placed her hand on his neck as I had done.

"Hold on, son. I'll make a call." She disappeared into the fire station, emerging a minute later with a bottle of water. She cracked the cap off and shoved it to my face. "Drink," she ordered.

"No thank you, Ma'am. I—"

"You need to stay focused and hydrated, and this is how you can do it right now."

Her tone carried unexpected seasons of authority. I took a swig and poured some into my hand for Casey who was now in the back with Silas, standing over him. After two of the longest minutes in history, a green forestry truck pulled up, and a ranger got out, his hat bobbing up and down against his neck as he approached.

"Is he still breathing?" the man asked.

"Y-yes," I said, releasing the catch in my throat.

The woman took my hand in hers. "The ambulance is on its way. In the meantime, put this blanket over him to keep him warm. Don't move him again." She sized up Silas's large body, then looked me up and down. "To be honest, son, I don't know how you moved him the first time. Heroic stuff. You're a blessing to him, and it may have just saved his life."

Before I could answer, the sound of another car pulling into the lot caught our attention. It screeched to a halt in the gravel, and Liv and Mo hopped out.

"Mom!" Liv said to the woman. Then she turned her attention to the ranger. "Hiya, Billy."

"Liv." The ranger tipped his hat.

"What's all the commotion?" Liv asked. Her eyes caught mine. "Jim. Mo and I were just headed to Flagstaff. Are you alright?"

"My friend," I said, pointing to Silas. "I don't know what's wrong. But he's alive."

Liv looked at Silas and frowned. "I'm sorry, Jim. But you're in good hands here."

Mo came up on my side and tugged at my shirt. He'd been clutching

Beary since exiting the car. But now, he held Beary out at arm's length and shoved him into my hand.

"You better take it," Liv said. "It's the best way I know to keep calm."

I took Beary and thanked Mo. I told the group how I'd found Silas and hauled him into the Jeep. "I don't know how long he's been out," I said.

"Well, you did the right thing," the ranger said. He was with Silas, monitoring his pulse and breath. His attention to Silas calmed my nerves. "He's still breathing, and that's all we can ask for right now."

After an eternity, the ambulance came speeding down the road. Two paramedics rushed over to the Jeep. Casey was visibly agitated, but jumped out and came to my side, allowing everyone to do their jobs. Mo pet Casey's ear, and Casey stayed near him. We maneuvered Silas's limp body from the back seat and onto a stretcher. As one of the medics hooked Silas up to a monitor, the other jumped in the driver's side, slammed the door, and pulled out a clipboard.

"Name?" she asked.

"My name's Jim," I said.

"No. Him."

"Oh," I said. "Er…right…Silas. I don't know his last name." The paramedic raised an eyebrow as I rooted around in my pockets for Silas's wallet. I pulled out his driver's license. I'm sure they were wondering why the hell I was driving around an unconscious man whose full identity I didn't know.

"Hansford," I said. "Silas Hansford."

"Okay," she said, flipping on the siren. "May I have that, please?" I handed her the license and she clipped it to the board. "Thanks."

"Wait!" I yelled over the blaring noise. "Where are you taking him?"

"Flagstaff Memorial," the medic yelled out the window as they sped off.

Within moments, the wailing siren faded into an eerie silence, leaving only the doubt behind. Casey barked a few hopeless yelps, then turned in frustrated circles on the gravel. Mo went to him and pet him on the head to calm him down.

I turned to the assembly. "Thank you all," I said. "I really appreciate your help."

"It was my pleasure," the woman from the firehouse said. "You, Jim, are quite something. How you got him up and got him here...it's one for the ages. By the way, my name's Rose. We never got introduced in the frenzy."

"Hi, Rose. You were amazing, too. And thank you...is it Billy?" I took the ranger's hand and shook it.

"No need to thank me," he said. "It's my duty."

"Thank you for keeping me calm when I pulled up, Rose. Sometimes, I...well...I need help with that."

"That's my job, young man," Rose said. "We all need help sometimes." She ruffled Mo's hair. "I learned to help others from the best."

I got down on a knee and handed Beary back to Mo. "And thank you, Mo...and Beary! I really needed your extra support."

Mo smiled, then slid in behind Liv and buried his face in her shirt. He giggled and waved Beary around in the air, making Beary swipe at the crystal dangling from her neck.

"I'm glad there was help," Liv said. She took my hand in both of hers and held it tight. "I know he'll be fine."

"How do you know that?" I asked.

"Just a feeling. Come on, Mo!" Liv and Mo got back in the car. Liv rolled her window down. "Jim," she said, "I think Arjun is at the general store."

"Thank you," I said.

Liv and Mo pulled out of the parking lot and turned towards Flagstaff. I thanked Rose and Billy again, and gave them my cell number in case they needed a contact. I hopped back into the Jeep with Casey and headed straight for the general store. Professor Singh's

SUV was parked outside. I burst through the door, leaving Casey pacing in the front seats. I found the professor inside, engaging Hiram in conversation about fishing spots in the area.

"Jim!"

"Professor!" I felt as if I hadn't seen him for days.

He looked past me to the Jeep parked outside. "Are you here with Silas?"

"No. He's sick. I mean, I think he had a heart attack."

"What?"

"I found him at his campsite."

"Where is he now?"

"I got him to the fire station, and they called the paramedics. They're heading to Flagstaff Memorial with him."

"He's in good hands, son," Hiram said. "There's good people there."

With an apology, Professor Singh handed his grocery basket filled to the brim with meats and produce to Hiram. "Go see your friend," Hiram said. "I'll keep these until you get back." We thanked Hiram and left the store.

"Jim," the professor said, "before we go to check on Silas, we need to take Casey to the cabin. He cannot come with us, and we must not leave him without feeding him."

His rational demeanor conquered my nervous energy. It felt good to have a plan right now. We drove back to the cabin and fed Casey from the bag of food Silas kept in his Jeep. Luckily, I didn't toss it out with all the other things at the site. Then we walked him in the woods to tire him out before leaving him in the kitchen with a rawhide bone, a large bowl of water, and some extra kibble. A note was taped to the sink:

> *Mrs. Davis, we came and fixed the plumbing. All is well. Will be added to your account. Regards to Mr. Davis and Jake. -Sammy*

"Professor, I don't want to leave Silas's Jeep here. It's full of his things and I don't want to take them all in the house right now. Plus,

I don't know if he'll need any of it. I think the stuff at the campsite will be fine, and I have his wallet and phone, but I have a hunch all his important things are still in the Jeep here. I think he had a cargo cover over it at one point."

"I agree, Jim. Follow me. I know where the hospital is. Once we're there, we can search for the cover and bring him what he needs."

We headed for the main road and cruised into the Flagstaff city limits. I followed as the professor expertly navigated the streets to the hospital.

Chapter 30

Make the Call

"Hansford," I said to the nurse at the emergency room desk. "Silas Hansford."

"Yes," she said, squinting at her computer screen. "He came in a little while ago. He hasn't been assigned a room."

"Is he alright?" the professor asked.

"I can't say, sir. Please have a seat and we will inform you when he has been assigned a room. Then I will check with the attending physician to see if Mr. Hansford can accept visitors."

We gave our names and thanked her, then found seats as far from the waiting room television as possible. I looked around, taking in the typical scene. In an unpredictable world, an emergency room is one place that will always look like we expect. The chairs were filled with exhausted-looking people with grim faces. A man winced in pain, nursing a hand wrapped in a bloody towel. A woman sat with her arm around him, whispering in his ear and drying her eyes with a tissue. Another woman sat with a lethargic and flushed little girl who appeared to have a fever. The woman had a coloring book on her lap and urged the girl to color in it with the blue crayon the child clutched in her weary little hand.

The TV was broadcasting a talk show about Hollywood and the lives of the stars. It centered mostly on divorce and child custody. My mind drifted back to Silas and Kay. Their drama was every bit as troubling as these stars' problems, but no one paid attention. I pulled

Silas's cell phone from my pocket and turned it on. Thankfully, it didn't ask for a passcode. I scrolled through his address book and found "Kay cell."

"Professor?" He was perusing a wrinkly nature magazine. The pages were crusty and crinkly in his grasp, and I admired his courage for touching it.

"Yes?" he said, not looking up from an article on rafting in the Grand Canyon. He ran the key and beads through his fingers. I suddenly realized that, although he had been doing this on and off for the last few days, the action wasn't as predictable as it had once been.

"Do you think it would be inappropriate for me to call Kay? If they're married, she's his main support. I didn't tell the paramedics about her. I have his cell phone and just found her number."

"Use your best judgment, Jim. You spoke to him about Kay. I did not. Trust your instincts."

I went outside to the parking lot and dialed the number. A woman's voice answered in a cheery, "Hello?" Clearly, she was expecting Silas's gruff voice on the other end.

"Hello, is this Kay?"

"It is. Who is this?"

"You don't know me. My name is Jim. I'm a friend of Silas."

"How can I help you?" Her voice was sweet and kind, with no hint I'd disturbed her.

"Uh…well…I found him." It occurred to me I should have rehearsed this part of the phone call before dialing the number. I felt like a fool sharing important information in this way. As a social worker, I sometimes had to deliver difficult news to clients, families, and courts, but this hit too close to home.

"Found him where?"

"On the ground. At a campsite."

"Oh my God! What happened?"

"I'm not sure. I think it was a heart attack."

"Where are you?" I could hear commotion on the other end of the phone, and I pictured Kay searching frantically for a purse and keys.

"I'm at Flagstaff Memorial. I can't see him yet, but I'm hoping to soon. I'm sorry I don't have more information. I just know he is here, and he was alive when I found him."

"Good lord. I'll be there as soon as I can."

I returned to the waiting room, beating myself up over the seemingly insensitive way I'd broken the news to Kay. Maybe Maya was right about a few things. Maybe I did need some softening up.

"Well?" The professor was now reading an old golf magazine with a giant red stain on it that I hoped was juice.

"She's on her way up from Phoenix," I said. "She sounds like she really does care about him. Like a good friend."

"I'm sure she is."

"I could just tell from the tone of her voice that she really loves him. You know? It's funny. Unlike the people on these annoying talk shows," I gestured towards the television, "all Silas and Kay really have is each other. She's probably his biggest fan, and vice versa."

"When we have a love – a true love that is respectful and caring – there is quite a small, yet devoted, audience of two."

"Yeah," I said, hunching over and regarding my hands as they twirled Silas's cell phone. "Professor?"

"Hmm?" He was studying an article on getting the most accuracy out of a putter.

"I've been doing some thinking."

"Again?" He looked at me and smiled. I looked back down at my hands.

"My parents told me Maya called. She wants to see me."

I watched out of the corner of my eye as he set the magazine down. I could feel his eyes squarely upon me.

"How nice. When?"

"Soon. She's coming back to Phoenix near the end of my vacation. I don't know what to do. I'm afraid to see her. What if she doesn't...I mean...what if we get together and...oh man."

"Jim, what's really troubling you?"

"I don't know. Watching Silas's life and thinking about my own…I just feel like…" I put my elbows on my knees and ran my hands through my hair. Eventually, I gave in and locked eyes with the professor. "I've learned so much since I've been up here. All these conversations you and I have had. All the thinking. My life was so noisy before, and now…well, now I'm much more interested in the messages from the silence. They really have changed me."

"I'm glad to hear that, Jim. What does it have to do with Maya?"

"I'm…well…" I thought about what recent days had meant to me and could mean for both me and Maya – together and apart. "Well, she and I didn't really understand each other before. I can't imagine what that would be like now. It ended so badly."

"Are you sure she wants to get back together?" he asked.

"Well, no."

"Do you know anything about her visit?"

"No. She just said she's been doing some thinking."

"How would you feel about reconciliation, Jim?"

"I guess I'm not sure. How much love does it take to really see things through? What if we get back together and just stumble around again? What if I get suicidal again? What if I can't change and be who she wants me to be? Look at Kay and Silas. They have what seems to be this fated…thing…and he still struggled with it. We found him up in the woods by himself, for God's sake. What if I want to run away someday? What if…I don't know…I sound like an idiot. Is it selfish to talk about this while Silas—"

"Jim, hold on a second."

"Professor, I love Maya, but—"

"Jim!" He interrupted my rant with a bit more force. "Take a breath. Let's tackle this the way we've come to know these last few days."

"Calmly."

"That's right. Let's talk it out calmly and see where it takes us, okay? These magazines are old, and the TV is bad. We cannot do anything for Silas but remain positive, so let's retreat back to the sweet refuge of conversation to keep our minds on something productive. It's not selfish in any way. It's helping us to stay centered."

"Okay. Thank you. I'd appreciate it."

"The issue before us is relationships and love, correct?"

"Yes."

"Good. A happier topic in this dark waiting room. Love, as we commonly think about it, is not quite enough to make a relationship work. True love is more than loving a person." He looked wistfully at the key as it moved through his fingers.

"But I thought—"

"Jim, you have to be in love with the relationship as well."

"In love with the relationship? What do you mean?"

"What do you love about Maya?"

"Professor, we've already discussed this. I really don't see how—"

"Let's revisit it."

"Okay, okay. Well," I said, lingering on the word, "part of it has to do with her nature. Her gentleness. She has a hard side, I know, but when her gentleness comes out, it's really nice to feel."

"This is good. What else?"

"She really seems to love me. I think she has deep feelings, but maybe I confuse her. Is that a thing? Maybe I confuse her, or she doesn't understand me."

"You are that complex?"

I couldn't tell if he was being sarcastic or not, so I chose to think not. I probably chose wrong.

"No. At least I don't think I am. I mean, I did almost step in front of a bus to kill myself. I do lose myself in anxiety to the point where I panic and explode. Maybe that's not so complex. I donno. I guess we really don't know how uncomplicated we are until someone comes along and shows us simplicity."

"This is true. Did you ever get upset with her?"

"Sure! We went through this over dinner on our first night together," I said with alarmingly bold frustration.

"Jim." His voice held enough patience for both of us. "We all need to take a good look at ourselves. And sometimes, we have to take two looks."

"I'm sorry. Yes. I did get upset. A lot. Sometimes very upset. But my grandparents bickered all the time. Isn't that part of being in love?"

"Perhaps it is, Jim, but your grandparents were married and in a long-term commitment. How did you feel after you and Maya had a disagreement?"

"Well, we had some amazing ones."

"I am sure. But how did you feel afterward?" he pressed. "Before you answer, I know you are going to tell me we've already discussed this. But have faith."

I smirked. He'd read my mind again. I acquiesced. "How did I feel? Misunderstood. Angry. Afraid. Pushed. Bullied. All the usual feelings."

"Did you feel grateful?"

"I'm not sure that made the list, Professor."

"Well, add it at the top."

"Really?"

"Really. Did you feel grateful for the chance to honestly investigate yourself? A chance that can only come from disagreeing with one who loves you?"

"Um…" I contorted my face against the truth. "I guess I've never really thought about it. It's strange. No matter what disagreements we had, we carried on. Even when it seemed irreparable, we found a way to get it together and move ahead in life. Sometimes to a better place. Sometimes to a breakup. But life continued. I guess our disagreements also became something for me to use as experience these last few days as I've learned more and more about life and expectations and stuff like that. Is that what you mean by honest investigation?"

"It could be, Jim."

"I suppose that is something to be thankful for."

"Jim, there is a silent energy in relationships."

"I know. But in the relationships I've had, I always seem to be just a little outta sync with it."

"Well, that's the interesting thing, is it not? You will never be totally in sync with someone in a relationship. Not if you are looking honestly at it."

"I'm confused. Isn't that what we're looking for? If I can use another cornball metaphor, isn't being in sync the perfect sun around which we want our relationship planets to revolve? Isn't that what a soulmate is about? Aren't they supposed to be the person who is in sync with our energy?"

He chuckled. "The soulmate concept is indeed valuable, Jim. It reminds us that we are maybe to find someone who is here for us, perhaps for a *special* purpose." The emphasis was ominous. He was visibly considering his next words carefully as the key twirled and twirled. "But this is not where it stops. We don't always marry our soulmate." He paused to let that sink in.

"Aw. That's kinda depressing."

"We may marry them, Jim. We may. Indeed, we may have more than one soulmate, but this is not the point. The point is that even if the two of you are really soulmates, you are still two different people. Two changing beings interfacing with evolving energy patterns of the universe in different ways. No matter how hard you try, you will be unable to see things completely from Maya's point of view, nor she from yours. You two will never look at one thing the same way."

"Boy, is that true."

"It's an enduring truth, Jim. Individual egos collide, creating calamities of perception unique to you. Remember our discussion of cheesecake, and how to one person it can look delicious, but to another it could mean a painful night in the restroom? If you'll forgive the inelegant and crass comparison, being soulmates doesn't change that. Even if you accept a common foundation of spirit or a common beginning for all things on this planet, as we've said, you still have to appreciate individual perception. Once we commit to love another person, we are committing to differences…to the different ways you both arrived at the love you're living now."

"Yeah. I guess so." I slumped deeper into my chair and chewed on my lip.

"Jim, this is not the end of the story. This realization is the beginning of a new kind of experience."

"A new kind of experience?" I let out a chuckle. "With all due respect, if what you say is true, then we can't really ever find the great love of the ages."

"So?"

"So? Well, we can't ever really feel complete with someone, Professor. Not if true understanding is impossible. Not if we never see things the same way."

"Forget the myths of the ages," he said, a gentle sternness of reality polishing my tarnished idealism. "Don't go to the storybooks or the movie theater for your truths or roadmaps. Let's get past that and look at this in a new and different way. Think about love." He gestured toward the talk show on the television and then to the man with the bloody hand and his comforting companion. "Think of love as something detached from your previous training on the subject."

"Alright. I'll try. But no promises. You made us read a lot of mythology in class, and some of those love stories really stuck!"

"Love, Jim – true love – is not only possible, but inevitable, once we allow ourselves to truly be ourselves with another. Love becomes the treasure for which we never need dig. It is there waiting patiently on top of the soil, perpetually brilliant. A precious relationship is not about seeing all things the same way as our partner sees them. It is not about being totally 'in sync,' as you say, all the time. It is about loving another passionately and presently even when things feel amiss. The sooner you realize this, the sooner you will stop expecting perfection, which is simply that ego-based illusion that someone will know us totally."

"I'm guilty of that." I sat up straight in my chair and crossed my arms tight over my chest. "I sometimes wish I could find someone who would just respond to me in ways I expect."

"Does that feel right?"

"No." I laughed and shook my head. "It even sounds narcissistic and ridiculous when I say it."

"Only a little, Jim." We shared a laugh.

"Yeah. But patience isn't really my strong point in relationships. I sometimes expect perfection in others, and myself, and I get really frustrated. It's exhausting. But in my defense, I think we all have been in a place where we ask the heavens to deliver us someone who just kinda gets us and goes with us."

"That's probably true, Jim."

"Who knows? Maybe I'm too much that way. Maybe there's no room for a true connection in my life."

"Perfection is not coequal with connection, Jim. Don't confuse the two."

"Alright, but then what are we looking for?"

"Balance." He held the key in his fingers on a horizontal plane to the floor. "A balance not born of a perfect connection, but born of acceptance and being accepted." He paused to rub the key before sending it through his fingers again. "Love, as we usually think about it, is difficult that way. Often, when we date and fall in love with a person, we are not romancing them, but romancing our perception of them. That approach is very far from center, and it throws things off balance. Later, when the masks come off and we don't see the person we believed to be wooing, we may find we can't deal with who, or what, they really are. Maybe they're way to the other side of our expectations. What we need is to meet in the middle ground."

"Which is?"

"We love a person knowing full well that our perception and their reality may, in fact, be two different things. So, we all meet in the middle, ready to give and take as new realizations and revelations unfold in the relationship. We find our place in the center and do our best to maintain a balance of perception and reality."

"Very romantic." I rolled my eyes.

"The romantic concept of love many run to is nothing more than a mirage of perception, Jim – an oasis tantalizingly appearing then cruelly evaporating in the heat of blind passion. Perception can be very damaging when it gets out of control."

"But how can we get past perception? What are we talking about here?" The man with the bloodied hand snapped his head toward my voice, which I realized was growing too loud for the waiting room. I lowered it and consciously centered myself. The professor waited patiently for me. "Isn't perception worth something in love?"

"It is. But it isn't the whole picture. Truly lasting relationships tolerate changing perceptions against a backdrop of constant love – a backdrop that in this analysis never changes even when our costumes do."

"So, we accept, no matter what?"

"Well, romantics would like that to be true, but in this world, that's a hard standard to live up to."

"That's a hard standard in any world, Professor. I'm sure aliens on other planets probably struggle with that."

"I'm sure that's true, Jim. We can't always love another person enough to accept them without reservation all the time. We don't always want to see our partners as they are. Sometimes we're quite comfortable in our perceptions. And sometimes, staying in a relationship or accepting a person as they are can be unhealthy. Not every romantic encounter can end in lasting partnership, nor should it."

"I guess I don't have that love backdrop thing down yet. I've loved many women but have had many break-ups. Too many reservations, I guess."

"Indeed. We sometimes argue or disagree with those we love. And sometimes it doesn't work out. And the most serious discord is born of utter non-acceptance of another's reality as measured against our perceptions or expectations of them. If we do argue, though, and we make up again, it is because we can accept this particular person. Because we choose to access the unchanging love that lets us shift perception, yet continue on with the same lover at the masquerade. But sometimes we just do not like the costume changes. That is fine, Jim. That is fair. We are not perfect, and not every relationship is meant to be."

"I can see that. Maya and I were so unsettled at times. I guess we don't really know who we'd be if we just accepted each other. We never really talked about it. Who knows? Maybe I could learn to see things from another perspective if I was willing to loosen up and learn to shift a little. To give a little. To drop my perceptions and try to understand her reality."

"I think so, Jim. Remember: You are not falling in love with your idea of the other. That would make lasting love impossible. What you need is love even when the ideas change. This is the type of love that's constant as we grow older. I think you see the distinction. Perception-based love changes with styles. It's a fad. True love can wear old and new clothing equally."

"I think I understand," I said. "But let me see."

"Test the gods, Jim."

"Perception alone is not enough to access true love."

"Correct."

"But if there is a potential for lasting love, perception can be enough to prevent love from shining through if we get all caught up in it and miss the reality."

"I think you're on the road, Jim."

"Ha! Listen to us. To a romantic, we probably sound crazy. Of course, some of what they say sounds crazy, so maybe it works out."

"Well, the romantics may be onto something special at the distant end of the road. Romance is a blessing, and true love and harmony between two people is quite wonderful. But it's only half the story."

"How so?"

"Well, love is a powerful backdrop for sure. But for a marriage or other love-based relationship to evolve to its highest expression, two people must acknowledge the power of ego and perception against that loving backdrop. Once this happens, we become more aware and can better accept the other for who they are – a unique expression of flesh and blood interacting with the energy of the universe."

"That's grand."

"Love is nothing if not grand, Jim. Maya, for example, is constantly expanding out into wider fields of unique experience, just like you. Sometimes disagreement between egos helps us to appreciate the love that urges us onward in the relationship and supports us as we each explore and fall madly and deeply. That's quite romantic. Where the romantic stumbles, however, is in their disdain for that discord."

"So, we should disagree, but like it? Is that the rule to keep love alive?"

"No." He laughed. "No, Jim. This is not a game of soccer. There are no rules. There is no 'should.' You cannot follow a set of rules that says, 'today is the day to disagree' or 'this is the moment to remember the backdrop of love.' You are not competing to see who can smile more in the face of adversity or score highest on the acceptance scale."

"But Professor, sometimes it does feel like a competition. If we don't compete, or try to persuade the other to be where we are or want what we want, then what will we do? How will we ever get our points of view across? How can we ever be peaceful? If I just accept and accept, and change with perception, relying only on that love stuff in the background, then how can I ever feel justified having needs of my own? I'll always feel like a selfish jerk! On the flip side, if Maya keeps accepting everything about me, how will I ever keep my ego in check? It seems like a vicious circle of giving in or being a narcissist. What do we do?"

"You will dance."

"We'll what, now?"

"You'll dance."

"That's the last thing I want to do, to be honest. If you'd ever seen me dance, it's the last thing you'd want, too."

"Come on, Jim. I'm sure you and Maya danced."

"It was scary, Professor. Like nightmarish."

"I take it you stepped on each other's toes?"

"I'd say that summed us up at parties."

"But this did not end your dance, did it? You didn't split to find other partners, right?"

"No. I guess we laughed about it."

"Indeed. You laughed with grade school awkwardness. You took more care with the next step. You adjusted. There has been pain, yes, but also a smile and a lesson."

"What if we never get in step? What then?"

"Well, that's when you have to trust the music. When you go to a dance, the music changes, yes?"

"It'd be pretty boring otherwise."

"So, one moment you might be waltzing, and the next minute jitter-bugging. Or maybe you two just sit and listen to the band."

"Sometimes when things get rough, it's nice just to hear the music."

"Let's shift our metaphors and focus on the music, then. Jim, if you'll forgive an old ego, I'll take us out of the modern party scene and look to the classics."

"I'm good with that. Anything to get away from dancing."

"Fine. The episodes where we learn about each other – whether or not we feel 'in sync,' to use your term again – are like notes and other marks in a song. A great love is more than the sum of its parts. It is a symphony composed of individual notes, pauses, and rhythms that form movements, creating a masterpiece. You were in choir if I recall, yes?"

"Sure. I sang a lot of big stuff by the great composers."

"Do you remember the feeling of the big finish? The audience stands and cheers with the big finale of a great piece of music. It moves everyone." He gestured, key in hand, as if conducting a great work to the finale.

"That was the best. Sometimes I would get a bit emotional myself."

"Indeed. It stirs you to the core. You love it. But what is it that you love?"

"I don't understand."

"Let me rephrase. It is not B-flat or A-minor that you fall in love with in a musical masterpiece. No one falls in love with a forte mark or half rest."

"Some people might."

"Did you?"

"No."

"So, what is it, Jim? What is it about a great piece of music that inflames the passions?"

"I'm not sure, Professor. Hmm…" I thought about some of the great pieces of music I'd sung. And then I thought about the classic rock I loved – the songs that got me tapping the steering wheel. The simple tunes that helped me stay calm when stress overwhelmed me or tamed my obsessive thoughts. He was right – something did inflame the passions. Something did connect inside me when I heard certain songs. But I couldn't quite wrap my head around it.

"Jim," he said, breaking the chain of tunes that had pulled my mind from the conversation, "it's the totality of the song. It's the notes. The lyrics. The pauses. The silences. Fall in love with it all! Don't just be in love with your partner. Fall in love with the relationship. When you are angry or confused about an issue that arises between you, and you're not sure how to react, just go with it. Sing along. Change the tempo. This relationship is your masterpiece. Your magnum opus. It is the laughter, tears, eye contact, misunderstandings, coming together. Each movement is part of something bigger. Come to appreciate and accept each unique expression of the whole. If you can love each other despite dissonance, rather than on the condition of erasing it from the score, you have made beautiful music even in times of discord. You will always have a beautiful, lasting theme in the background, even when the lyrics or some other part of the piece changes. You will have achieved a…"

I sat upright and waited for the big finale. He rubbed the key intensely. "A what, Professor?"

"You will have achieved a relationship enlightenment."

I sat back on my chair and relaxed into the gentle truth. "Professor?"

"Yes?"

"The other day you said something like, 'the enlightened have the foresight to know that all will be well in hindsight,' or something like that."

"I remember."

"Well, I'm worried I'll never be able to discover that, especially in love. Music's a fine metaphor for relationships, but what if I never hear it? That scares me."

He cast his eyes down and took a deep breath. His demeanor revealed the approach of wisdom purchased at the high price of personal experience.

"We are all of us scared, Jim." He looked back up at me, staring intensely into my eyes. "That you can admit it advances you further than you know."

We separated into our own gazes. I tuned in to the TV and watched a few minutes of polished talking heads discussing absolutely nothing of substance. I took in the sights and sounds of the room, and traced shapes with my finger on the chair cushion next to me. The professor sat still, arms crossed, tugging silently at the key.

"I never thought I'd receive relationship counseling in a hospital waiting room," I said. "I guess ever since you showed me the journals, I thought I'd get this kind of information from the silence – but here we are talking about music. What a road, huh?"

He smiled. "Well, this knowledge is indeed contained in the silence, Jim. It is in the still and vibrant wisdom of the ages. The audible silence is there for you when you seek it in earnest. You have access to vast amounts of information and guidance. Journaling and meditation are the powerful means to a peaceful and balanced end. And truly, you can write volumes. But that only takes you half of the way. In the end, you must put it all into practice. Eventually, you must move from the still mind and inert journal pages to the bustling story and rollicking music of your life. On the path of growth, information alone is just information. Committed action based on this information creates practical wisdom."

We looked up as a nurse walked into the waiting room, hopeful that she had some information on Silas. We watched as she approached the man with the bloody hand and escorted him and his companion through the doors to the treatment area. His partner held his good hand in hers as he trudged slowly to the back where, no doubt, many stitches awaited. I wondered how many times they had faced a crisis together and what other stories their relationship could tell.

"Man," I said, breaking the silence. "If I were in that guy's position, I'd want someone with me to hold my hand. I'll find it someday. She's out there, somewhere." In a flash, in my mind's eye, I saw my mom and dad waiting for information about Dad's heart. Next, I was sitting in the car with a tearful and concerned Kay as she drove to Flagstaff with a single purpose. I knew what I had to do.

"Go, Jim," he said. "Make the call now."

I stood up, this time with my own phone in hand, and went outside.

Chapter 31

You Owe Me Another

My phone beeped. The battery was low. Maya and I had been on for a while, and finally, we had to say goodbye. I walked over to Silas's Jeep and dug the cargo cover out from under mountains of stuff. In all the hustling and conversation, I'd forgotten about it until now. I said a silent prayer of gratitude that all of his belongings were still in place. I struggled to get the cover on, but eventually, after half an hour of fumbling with the contraption, swearing, and using a little more phone battery to search the internet for help, it snapped into place. I wandered back into the waiting room. The professor was gone, so I approached the triage nurse.

"Excuse me," I said, clearing my throat.

"Can I help you?"

"Yeah. I was just wondering about Silas. Silas Hansford?"

"Room 444. He's awake. You can see him."

"Thanks."

I walked the long, cold corridor to the main hospital and found the elevators. When the doors opened, I held them for a man mincing out with a portable IV bag, then stepped in. Floated in. I felt light and optimistic as I pushed number four. When I got to the room, I found Silas and the professor, talking quietly.

"I don't know," I heard Silas say. "Everything just went black." They both looked up when I walked in.

"Jim!" The professor smiled. "I was just telling Silas that we have taken care of Casey. It was his first question."

"Hey, kid." Silas's gray hair was matted to his head, and his eyes looked more tired than usual. Otherwise, he seemed in good spirits.

"Hiya, Silas. How are you feeling?"

"Like I have a heart problem. I feel like I was run over by my Jeep, not lying down behind it." We all laughed.

I filled in the details of the story, and he listened patiently, a faint smile never leaving his lips. I put his wallet, keys, and cell phone down on a table next to the bed.

"Thanks, kid. I owe ya."

"Yeah. Uh...I may need to cash that in." My lightness from moments before evaporated into a vague feeling of dread.

"What do you mean?" he asked.

"Well..." I wasn't sure how to proceed. "I called someone."

"Who?"

"Kay."

The silence would have been deafening, except for the faint beeping of a medical device somewhere out in the hall.

"I see," he said. "How long ago?"

I couldn't tell if he was truly calm or just masking a boiling cauldron.

"A few hours now. I found her number on your cell. I wasn't sure how things...I mean...I didn't know...remember your heart, Silas!"

"It's okay, kid. I guess a cardiac issue is a good way to break the ice with her again. She wouldn't hurt a guy in a hospital bed, right?"

"Silas, I—"

"Listen, kid, I love her. I do. Kay and me? Well, we just need to figure out where we are. I guess I can't keep avoiding it. Maybe this thing that happened to me is meant to make some order out of the chaos. Maybe it was...well...I've been kinda stressed lately...keeping crap bottled up. He shook his head and smirked. "At some point, it doesn't do any good to run away from your problems to find yourself.

All you find is a new place to be alone with yourself and your problems."

"I hear that," I said. I glanced at the professor who tipped his head to me, knowingly.

"I just hope she..." Silas stopped. An awkward pause followed, as if he was about to cry. When one is around a person not accustomed to showing emotion, a tear can be uncomfortable. Fortunately, at that moment, there was a knock on the door.

"Mind if I join you boys?"

Kay strolled into the room – a striking vision of surprising calm. Her tiny frame carried great confidence as she strode to the bedside. She was her picture, except her flaming red hair was pulled back in a braid that extended halfway down her back. She looked like she'd been crying, but I couldn't tell if her red cheeks flushed from emotion or simply bore a bit of makeup in anticipation of this unexpected and hurried reunion. Her green eyes were as bright as her freckles, and she had a youthful air about her that lit up the room. She seemed relieved to see her husband alive. After brief introductions, the professor and I got up to leave.

"Don't go on my account," she said. "You're welcome to stay. I'm gonna be with this bozo for a while." Kay was genuine, and I found her invitation authentic and refreshing.

"We appreciate that, Kay," the professor said, "but we really should tend to Casey. We'll care for him for a few days until you can come and get him. Your Jeep is parked on the west side of the building. We'll take down the campsite."

"Oh, and you owe me another one for putting on that cover, Silas. That's enough to give anyone heart problems."

"We'll be by in a few days," Kay said. "Thank you both." She hugged Professor Singh and he smiled an awkward smile. Then she gave me a hug and a peck on the cheek before returning to Silas's side, taking his hand in their relationship purgatory and holding tight.

"Hey, Jim." I turned around to look at Silas who seemed enveloped in peace. "Thanks for saving my life."

Chapter 32

Dancing on the Head of a Pin

By the time the professor and I got back to our campsite, it was dark. We packed up our gear in the glow of headlights, took the food down from the tree, and stuffed our tents back into their bags. We then went to Silas's camp and retrieved his belongings. There wasn't much, as most of it was already in his Jeep. When we got back to the cabin, Casey had his legs crossed. He bolted outside with me running after, bounding indoors a minute later, much relieved. I gave him a bowl of dog food and a pat behind the ear. The general store had closed, so the professor fixed our last bit of rice. We found some sorry looking vegetables and did our best to revive them.

"It's a far cry from our first meal here." I smiled and apologized as I put a plate down in front of Professor Singh.

"Don't worry, Jim. With a little curry and enough salt, we won't really taste them anyway!"

We saved the sagging fruit for the morning.

"Sorry, Casey," I said, as he looked at me and licked his chops. "If you eat this curry, you'll be sleeping outside for sure." He resigned himself to sniffing around in his own bowl for non-existent crumbs. I scratched him behind both ears as a consolation, quite sure he was not consoled.

"I got ahold of Maya," I said, spooning rice onto the professor's plate.

"Oh, that's right! I forgot to ask you about that on our return trip. I'm sorry, Jim."

"It's fine, Professor. I wanted to ponder the conversation with her before you and I talked about it."

"What did she say?"

"Well, we talked."

"Yes?"

"And we decided it was best to go our separate ways. It's over. Officially."

Professor Singh set his fork down on his plate with a clink and wiped his mouth. I lazily built a mountain of rice, then smashed it back down.

"How do you feel about that, Jim?"

"Good. I mean, I don't feel great in my body, but I think it's the right decision for both of us. I think we both know what's true for us now, and...well...I don't think our relationship fits into that anymore." Professor Singh remained quiet, holding space for me to trudge through my feelings – guilt, shame, regret, and the assortment of highs and lows that sweep through when the winds of true endings blow. I looked into his eyes. "I thought about the dance, Professor. The symphony. And in the end, I just...well, I just..."

"Couldn't hear the music, Jim."

After dinner, we retired to the living room. Professor Singh rocked in an old rocking chair and I was on the couch with Casey, who had his head in my lap. He seemed lonely without Silas. Yet, somehow, I got the feeling he knew Silas was fine.

"Professor?" His chair creaked quietly. He was lost in his thoughts, staring out into the trees and the night. I knew he was giving me space with my thoughts. "Is everything alright?"

"Oh, yes...yes." I left him to his gazing and scratched Casey under his green bandana. His fur was softer under there. I did not expect the professor to continue, but I was glad when he did. His voice was soothing. "Just memories, Jim. Friendly ghosts in the closet." He flicked at the key and beads around his neck.

"Memories of what?"

"My wife."

I wasn't sure if he meant to say that out loud. Since her death, in our brief conversations over the years, he hadn't spoken of her much. Professor Singh was a man of great eloquence and wisdom, but he kept a selective silence around his personal life, and I always deferred to his timing when it came to revelations about where he'd been or where he was going on the highways of life. I pictured Mrs. Singh from my college memories. She welcomed his students into her home with such warmth and grace. In the few times I'd seen Professor Singh and his wife together, I had never sensed any tension nor heard one ill word spoken between them.

"I'm sorry, Professor. I guess I didn't think about how the situation at the hospital might affect you."

"Oh, I'm fine, Jim. Really. Things happen in life, including death. That is why we are here...to truly live. That is why life is worth living. But seeing Silas and Kay and how relieved they looked to be back in each other's company...it really brought home the power of love, patience, and forgiveness."

"I know. It's interesting. All the things we've been discussing lately...there they were. All..." I paused, feeling a tinge of elation.

"All what, Jim?"

"Dancing on the head of a pin. The pinprick of the moment."

"Yes, my friend. Yes. That is how it felt when my departed wife and I realized the practical power of all these wonderful concepts. When they all became real."

"What? When was that?"

"Oh, long before your time, Jim. Long before we married."

"What happened?"

"She finally forgave me for stealing a drink from her father's cart."

Chapter 33

Actions and Allowings

Alone in my room with Casey's head again on my lap, I thought about my life and the lives of others. The professor's revelation about his wife reverberated in my mind. I took out my journal and traced lines on a blank page, all radiating from a central point. Those lines joined at other points, radiating off again in the company of other lines, creating a joyful journey of junctions leading off into infinite possibilities. I thought about the choices we make and wondered again about fate. I reflected on how all of us – me, the professor, Silas, Kay, Maya, my parents, and, indeed, all of humanity – were working through our issues in a common sea of energy, but with individual perceptions. Yet, we were often able to reach similar conclusions. Similar goals. Love was so much more intense and real when set in relief to life's choices – when set in the context of the actions and allowings that bring about truly authentic experience.

"Love and relationships aren't what replace other things," I said to Casey. "They're what make them special."

I started to write.

> Our infinite choices are fated, but the choice is free will. If we fall and find no arms waiting to catch us, at least we can say we had the courage to fall. At least we made the choice. Choosing a new outlook on life can be affirming. Invigorating. Tuning into the audible silence can help us tap into the universal pipeline of information through meditation and

journaling, as one might draw water into a jug from a desert well. We can drink mightily of the knowledge contained therein and then put it to good use in our interactions with others, if we so choose, as it gives us strength to carry on in our way. I must learn what I can about the art of forgiveness and then choose to forgive myself and others. I must know patience as a virtue and time as an illusion, but then choose to be patient enough to accept another's timing in my life. I can puzzle privately over deepest love, but then must reach out to another in a loving way. It is all about choices. I know I will reach my fated destination one way or another. The gift of living is that I choose how to get there.

Casey adjusted himself to get comfortable, making me less comfortable. I decided the thought had come to an end, anyway. After turning off the bedside light, I rolled over and tried to sleep. Casey eventually humored me and moved to the floor.

Chapter 34

A Splash of Color

Days passed, and things returned to normal. Excitement mercifully gave way to familiar routine, and thanks to Hiram, the freshly stocked refrigerator provided a new lease on life. My sleep patterns were changing, and I found myself waking up earlier and earlier feeling more and more refreshed. Even energized. I craved activity now. Professor Singh and I took long, brisk walks in the forest with Casey. These treks provided opportunities for powerful conversation, and I could now walk – and talk – as far as any of my companions wanted to go without any shortness of breath or discomfort. On one excursion into town, I played tag with Mo for almost a half hour and felt like I did when I was his age.

At other times, the professor and I would sit, sometimes for hours, and watch Casey bound around in a field. We'd witness the wind blow the trees, and I marveled at their emerald vibrancy. I examined blades of grass for insects and smiled when a bee or fly buzzed my ear. On more than one occasion, Professor Singh remarked that my eyes held a clarity he'd never seen in me before.

Taking another piece of advice from the professor, I found myself saying mantras through the day. I would sometimes stop an activity and give thanks to whatever was listening that I could be present for the task. I brought friends past and present to my mind, including Maya, and held good thoughts for them. Repetition of this practice brought me such joy, that I found myself laughing sometimes for no apparent reason.

We called Silas regularly to check on his status. "No surgery!" he beamed. "Although I have to take it easy. But we'll always have non-alcoholic beer, right?"

One morning, on my way out the door, Casey was lethargic and reluctant to leave the house. He was usually at the door ahead of me, eager for a walk in the forest. The professor and I examined him, and decided he just needed a morning off.

"I'll stay back with him today, Jim. Go and enjoy. Take some time for yourself."

"I will," I said, eager to greet another morning in the pines.

I wandered into the woods alone, hopping nimbly among the ruts and rocks, to think about all the things that had happened since I'd arrived. It seemed like such a short time, and yet, I'd learned so much. I stopped often along the path to sniff the vanilla trees and take in the beauty of tiny blooms. Right on time, I thought, as I knelt down to cradle a soft flower in my hands. I pulled up a stump where the professor and I had shared light citrus and heavy conversation. I sat in silence, purposefully clearing my mind and taking in the peace. The natural surroundings played gracious host, and I decided to overstay my welcome.

The walk home was more like a dreamy drift. I emerged from the woods and opened the front door, expecting Casey's wet tongue. But the only one in the parlor was the professor, sitting on the sofa.

"Jim."

"Hi, Professor. Where's Casey?"

"Silas and Kay came to get him."

"They did? Why didn't you tell me?"

"I did not know they were going to arrive today," he said with a chuckle. "They called from the highway just after you left. Somehow,

Casey knew. They said they wanted to get back to Phoenix before afternoon. It's a good thing I remained behind. I think they're going to be alright, Jim."

"I wanted to see them." I was disappointed that fate did not allow me a chance to say goodbye.

"I feel confident you'll see them again, Jim." I sat down on the sofa and traced my finger through the loopy design in the fabric. "Silas left this for you."

He handed me a large envelope. I opened it and a letter with a business card attached slid out. They were clipped to two pieces of cardboard.

> *Dear Jim,*
>
> *Words cannot express my thanks for all you've done. Please keep in touch and enjoy the enclosed.*
>
> *-Silas (and Casey!)*

I pulled the cardboard pieces apart and a photograph dropped into my lap. It was a picture of me, sitting on a log, with Casey at my feet. I was gazing off into the distance.

"Look, Professor." I showed him the picture and he smiled. "He took it the day we were at the overlook. I went off by myself to think, and he must have snapped it. Kay probably had it processed in Flagstaff."

"Interesting. Do you notice something else about it?"

"Color. It's in color!"

I stared at the picture and my odd expression in it. I mentioned this to the professor who said, "I'm guessing he caught the perfect moment, Jim. But only you would know what you were thinking."

In all honesty, I didn't remember those past thoughts. But I smiled now at the man who was responsible for so much in my present outlook.

Chapter 35

A Death of a Different Kind

The next morning, footsteps in the hall drew my attention. I took a moment to find the light through the window in my room, center myself, and to greet the day. I exited to find Professor Singh's suitcase in the hall.

"Professor?" He was in his room, gathering odds and ends into a cloth bag.

"Good morning, Jim. Did I wake you?"

"No," I lied. "I've been up. Where are you going?"

"I am heading back to Sedona today. I am going to give this wonderful cabin back to your capable hands. Well, you and Sammy."

"But, Professor, I still have some vacation days left. You don't have to rush off!"

"I appreciate that, but I should return to Sedona. And, I think you could benefit from some time in the silence to process all that we have learned. All that we have seen. All that we have done. Would you agree?"

"I guess," I muttered. "I should probably mull over some things. Believe it or not, I'm actually looking forward to what's next. Whatever that is."

"And this time, you'll enter what's next much wiser. Jim, if you would, please take my case downstairs. I will be down in a moment and we can have our breakfast."

I braced myself to lift the heavy case, but to my surprise, I took it up with little effort. I brought it down to the parlor, the creaky stairs protesting under my feet. I found the last of our bananas and oatmeal on the counter and prepared a light breakfast.

"Smells good." He sat down at the table, light and fresh.

"You know you really don't have to go," I said, taking on a tone that was much too paternal for my station. "Maybe another night? We can always leave tomorrow. I'll follow you out of town. Maybe we can have lunch again in Sedona." I placed a piping hot bowl in front of him. He moved his head over the dish. Closing his eyes, he drew in steam through his nose.

"Thank you, Jim. I know I don't have to go. I'm choosing to go. It's my bridge night, anyway. I am sure my regular partner has missed me."

I smiled and shook my head as I cut chunks of very brown banana with smooth, methodical strokes. After breakfast, we sat in meditation together one last time. As the day wore on, we knew this part of our journey together was ending. The professor looked up to the clock on the wall and nodded toward his things.

"Jim, if you would, please?" I grabbed his case from next to the door and brought it out to the car. He went back in to retrieve the rest of his belongings. "I will drive you into town if you'd like to get a few more provisions for the last few days here."

"I appreciate that. But maybe I'll follow your lead, Professor."

"What do you mean?"

"Well, I have a few days left before heading back to work, and I have to say, I'm actually excited to go back. I miss my clients! I don't know. Maybe I should get settled back into my life…to try it on and see how it fits with everything I know now." I patted my stomach. "I may need to try on some new clothes, too. These seem a little big on me now. What do you think?"

"Thinking, Jim. Thinking."

"Alright, professor. Enough!"

We shared a laugh as he packed the rest of his things into the car.

He closed the rear hatch and came back to where I stood.

"Jim." He gazed into me with an ocean of calm behind his eyes. "If you really want to know what I think, then here it is: You must take the road that best suits you in this moment. There is no old life. There is no new life. There is only this life." He tapped my chest over my heart with his palm. "The life inside you. The living, breathing succession of heartbeats."

"Only the pinprick of this moment, Professor."

"Yes. One moment placed on the head of a pin and set to dancing. If you feel free right now, in front of this cabin, under these trees, then this is your pinprick moment. Don't plan around it. Don't try to capture it. Be in it. Let the next one arise spontaneously and, again, be present with it."

In a split second, my old patterns raced in. I suddenly had a head full of questions. So many thoughts. So much I wanted to say. A faint feeling of nerves crept up, but then, something happened. I simply looked at the anxiety in the light of my inner eye as it arose. I watched it. Just watched it. No fight. No analysis. Just a serene gaze into the inner world. Before I knew it, the feeling simply melted into memory. I was calm.

"Professor, I just want to say—" He stepped close. Ten feet tall if he was an inch.

"Close your eyes, Jim."

I did as I was told. I felt a slight pressure between my eyes as he pushed a finger on the point between my eyebrows. A tingling sensation emerged at the base of my spine and flowed upward through my body in a rush of chills. It swept over my head and back down to my tailbone, completing the circuit. In my mind's eye, I saw life as a paradox – an empty space filled with possibility and energy. I knew, now, that my history was truly past. Unique experiences only for me. And I knew that my future, whatever it would be, was not set in stone. The true gift was the moment. This moment. All things were possible from here. From this spot. From this ground. Overwhelming gratitude flooded into the space where, only moments before, anxiety had swelled. Where once it was loud, there was now only silence. I could feel the illusions of my life evaporating...dying...being replaced with the vast chasm of possibility and freedom.

I didn't notice when the pressure on my forehead ceased, but the sound of his car starting up brought me back. He waved at me through the window. I waved back.

"Goodbye, Professor," I whispered. "Thank you for everything."

Heading back into the cabin, I bent down to pick up a pinecone at my feet. As I reached for it, I noticed a key dangling from my neck, dancing a chain of beads.

Chapter 36

Hope...

I sat in silence at the kitchen table, twirling the key through my fingers. My appetite had roared back, so I found an energy bar and ate it quietly, concentrating on each bite. Then, I cleaned everything in the cabin from top to bottom. I didn't just move through the motions. I paid full attention to the tasks. I did a load of laundry and folded the sheets with total focus. I scrubbed out the toilets and listened to the sound of the bristles against the porcelain. I cleaned the kitchen and watched the mop as it traveled around on the floor. I packed my clothes with care, making sure each piece fit comfortably in my suitcase.

As I was doing one last check upstairs, I heard a faint knock at the door. Hoping Professor Singh had returned, I bolted down the stairs and pulled the door open. It banged into my luggage sitting in front of the doorstop. I was shocked to see Liv and Mo standing there.

"Hi, Jim." Liv smiled. "Are we bothering you?"

"No! Of course not. It's good to see you. What brings you out here?"

"The beautiful weather," she said. "And Mo's boredom. We went for a walk and…well…apparently, Beary had to see you."

"Well, hello to all of you. Do you want to come in? I don't have anything to offer you except some comfy chairs and a few glasses of water."

"We have to get back," she said. "But I just wanted to know how your friend is doing."

"Silas? He's doing fine."

"That's so good to hear," she said. "Are you here alone? Did Arjun leave?"

"He did. A few hours ago."

"Oh. Okay. I'm sorry I missed him."

"Listen, Liv. I really wanted to thank Rose again for all of her help the other day. She really is something."

"She is, isn't she? Mom's done nothing but talk about you. She was really impressed with the way you handled yourself at the fire station."

"Oh, I can't take all the credit. I did have Beary there to keep me calm." Mo beamed. "But please, Liv, thank her for me again."

"Well…" Liv took up the crystal around her neck and worked it through her fingers. "That's the other reason I stopped by. I was wondering…I mean, we were all wondering—"

"Mommy," Mo said, "I'll ask." He looked me straight in the eyes. "Do you want to come over later and have dinner with us?"

Liv let the crystal drop against her chest. She smiled down at Mo, then to me, brushing a strand of blonde hair behind her ear and tucking it under the headscarf. I looked down at my suitcase hidden behind the door and rubbed the key around my neck. I didn't need to think about my answer.

"I'd love that. Just tell me what I can bring, and I'll stop by to see Hiram on my way."

Author's Note

This book began as a series of personal journal entries – hundreds of journal entries – reflecting on life, love, and the eternal questions. Immersed in a world of teachers and teachings that were overwhelming and energizing in themselves, I needed to sort it all out in my mind. The human machine of thought is an electric maze, alive with ideas and noise, and quiet reflection can bring a little refreshing calm and direction. I usually emerged from my journaling sessions with a much different vision than when I went in. That is to say, the world always looked a little different when I snapped from the page and refocused my eyes on the world above the journal. Perhaps that's because something small – very small – had shifted, helping me to see the details of the world in a new way. When we write out what we *think* we see, and apply a new filter (or, clean or remove old filters), we cannot help but shift. Move. See the world anew.

If you want to tap into the power of audible silence, I don't suggest starting with a one-way ticket to some distant land or an expensive retreat. Start with a simple notebook, a pen, and a clear mind open to possibility. Your writing implement and the paper you'll scribble on need not be ornate or special in any way. They only need to be available to dutifully record what's already special in your mind and poised to receive your question and to record your answer. I urge you to do this with no filter. No editing. After a few cleansing breaths, dive in, and take the pace of your hand as your guide and trust that the information that flows is the information you need.

Just in case you're wondering, there is no belief requirement to tap into the power of silence. You do not need to be religious or spiritual in any way to harness the amazing power of peaceful reflection. There is no secret club. There are no prerequisites for journal entry, and no fanfare. It all happens very quietly. I still remember opening my very first journal and staring at the lined page. Blank. Waiting. I recalled some old advice to not think too much before beginning, so I heeded that and just started writing. That one earnest motion of the first letter started a whirlwind of words that lasted for years and was a constant companion through the trials and victories of my life in motion.

The journey of self-discovery is scary and exhilarating, passive and powerful. It is a constant negotiation between taking bold action and knowing when to be still and take it all in. *An Audible Silence* is a reflection not only of my own personal journey, but the journey we all take to find out who we are and what this life, and beyond, is all about. If anyone ever tells you there is a correct answer to the questions of the ages, keep moving. If anyone assures you they have captured a truth to which others do not have access, let that truth go. In my years as a social worker, teacher, and writer, I've encountered so many people on this search, doing it in their own, unique way, and I've been so inspired to be a part of others' journeys, as well as my own. And I've learned this: Though there may be one wellspring of truth, we all taste it differently. Though truth may have a texture, we all feel it differently. Though truth may have a form, we all perceive it differently. If truth blooms like a flower, the scent will not be roses for all. And, although there may be a ring of truth, what resonates to our inner ear will be unique.

The purpose of this book is not to end your search, but to encourage you to begin your own. Cherish the mentors in your life, and their wisdom. If you do not have a mentor on the journey, stay open, and one may just come when you least expect it. But always remember: There is no more powerful guidance than what already lies within. That is the true key to unlocking your own truth.

Reading Group Guide

1. Jim almost stepped in front of that bus, pushed to the brink of frustration and despair. Consider your own life. Where are your lines? What do you do when you feel pushed to the brink? How do you step back and get yourself centered again?

2. Professor Singh was Jim's college instructor. Often, we remember the teachers and mentors who took some extra time to help us or who gave us a great piece of advice that changed the course of our life. Who have been the mentors that have had the biggest impact on you? What piece of their wisdom do you remember most?

3. Professor Singh and Jim both found wisdom in the audible silence…that still, quiet place inside where their truth was found. What has shaped your vision of life? Where did you discover the greatest truths in your life?

4. Maya and Jim parted ways after their fragile relationship broke. Are there examples you know of where two people split apart, but then rebuild a love or friendship from the shattered pieces? In your opinion, if one partner has a profound shift in worldview, how does that affect a relationship moving forward?

5. What do you think about the idea of unity? Do you believe the world's religions gaze at the same horizon, or do you believe there are fundamental differences when it comes to the ultimate question of god(s)? Is it possible for different religions to build bridges of true understanding across divides?

6. Think about your expectations in life – the things you like or don't like, or the ways you expect people to be and act. Do you think that letting go of expectations could lessen the stresses and anxieties in your life?

7. Silas and Kay had a difficult road of isolation and broken trust. But there seemed to be an element of forgiveness there. Do you embrace forgiveness in your own life? Have you ever forgiven someone even when it seemed difficult or impossible?

8. The pinprick of the moment is a powerful metaphor for living here and now. Has there been a time in your life when you've felt totally present in a situation? Maybe it was a crisis or celebration of some sort. How did you know you were present? What did it feel like?

9. Mindfulness is about being here, now, free of judgment in the moment. Do you practice mindfulness? Maybe it's washing dishes and being aware of the warm water and the feel of the soap, or maybe it's being totally engrossed in an art or home project. How do you practice being here?

10. Meditation is a practice anyone can do, but it does require discipline. Have you tried meditation? If you do it as a regular practice, why? If you don't, have you tried it and struggled with it? Think of a time during the day you could practice (for example, after just waking up or just before going to sleep) and see if you can commit to it for a certain amount of time each day.

Acknowledgments

Books are never written alone, especially books about personal growth. My partner in all things, Melissa, spent many hours helping me bring this book to life. She also steered me through rewrites I never dreamed possible. I am eternally grateful for her patience and skill (especially her patience). I'd also like to thank my daughter for graciously giving up time with me so I could edit and polish this book. To my main editor of many, many drafts, thank you for the honest feedback and long nights hunched in front of small screens. It all got me down the stretch. I would also like to thank my early readers for your support. It meant a lot to me, and I am grateful.

And to all my mentors and teachers over many years: Without your patient guidance, deep insights, beautiful music, and willing conversations, there would have been no light for Jim, or for me. And for that, there will never be a sufficient amount of old, yellowing journals in which to write "thank you" enough.

Made in the USA
Monee, IL
11 January 2022

88140528R00156